ALBANIAN FOLKTALES AND LEGENDS

Selected and translated from the Albanian

by

Robert Elsie

Centre for Albanian Studies, London

Publisher's Cataloging-in-Publication data

Elsie, Robert, 1950-
    Albanian folktales and legends / selected and translated from the
Albanian by Robert Elsie.
    189 p. cm.
    ISBN 978-1507631300
    Series : Albanian studies.
    Includes bibliographical references.

1. Folklore --Albania. 2. Tales --Albania. 3. Legends --Albania. I. Title. II.
Series.

GR251 .A4 2015
398.2/094965 --dc23

Albanian Studies, Vol. 2
ISBN 978-1507631300

Cover photo: Shoshi Tribesman in Theth (photo: Shan Pici, 1938)

Table of Contents

Albanian Legends

Introduction

Folktales are still very much alive in the mountains of Albania, a land of haunted history. They are recited in the evenings after a day's work or out in the fields, are learned by heart and pass, as if immortal, from one generation to the next. Whose imagination could not be captured by the cunning of the Scurfhead, by the demands of the Earthly Beauty, by the heroic feats of Muja and Halil or by the appearance of a fiery Kulshedra in the forest?

The fundamental theme of Albanian folktales, as no doubt of folktales everywhere, is the struggle between good and evil, a reflection of social values as we perceive them. The cautious reader may rest assured from the start that in the fantastic world of Albanian folk literature the good always win out.

Oral literature is known to preserve many archaic elements. Albanian folktales reveal not only a number of oriental features from the centuries when Albania formed an integral part of the Ottoman Empire but indeed also the occasional trace of the ancient world of Greco-Roman mythology. Pashas and dervishes abound in an otherwise eminently European context. The evident patriarchal structure in the tales and the passive, secondary roles attributed to female characters reflect Albania's traditionally Muslim society. In the first half of the twentieth century, about 70% of the Albanian population was Muslim, 20% Orthodox and 10% Catholic.

Yet despite their oriental background and the remoteness of Albanian culture, one of the last in Europe to withstand the onslaught of our high-tech monoculture, many of the tales will have a surprisingly familiar ring to the Western reader.

Albanian folktales were first recorded in the middle of the nineteenth century by European scholars such as Johann Georg von Hahn (1854), the Austrian consul in Janina (Ioannina), Karl H. Reinhold (1855) and Giuseppe Pitrè (1875). The next generation of scholars to take an interest in the collection of Albanian folktales were primarily philologists, among them well-known Indo-European linguists concerned with recording and analysing a hitherto little known European language: Auguste Dozon (1879, 1881), Jan Jarnik (1883), Gustav Meyer (1884, 1888), Holger Pedersen (1895), Gustav Weigand (1913) and August Leskien (1915).

The nationalist movement in Albania in the second half of the nineteenth century, the so-called Rilindja period, gave rise to native collections of folklore material such as the 'Albanian Bee' *(Albanikê melissa / Bêlietta sskiypêtare)* by Thimi Mitko (1878), the 'Albanian Spelling Book' (*Albanikon alfavêtarion / Avabatar arbëror*) by the Greco-Albanian Anastas Kullurioti (1882) and the 'Waves of the Sea' (*Valët e Detit*) by Spiro Dine (1908). In the last thirty years, much field work has been done by the Institute of Folk Culture in Tirana and by the Albanological Institute in Prishtina, which have published numerous collections of folktales and legends. Unfortunately, very little of this substantial material has been translated into other languages.

The only substantial collections of Albanian folktales to have appeared in English up to the present, as far as I am aware, are *Tricks of Women and Other Albanian Tales* by Paul Fenimore Cooper (New York 1928), which was translated from the collections of Dozon and Pedersen, and *Albanian Wonder Tales* by Post Wheeler (London 1936). The present volume of Albanian tales endeavours to be as faithful as possible in style and content to the original Albanian texts which were recorded from word of mouth in a relatively unelaborate code.

Included in this collection are not only folktales but prose versions of some of the best-known Albanian legends (based on historical or mythological events and figures). The adventures of Muja and Halil and their band of mountain warriors are still told and indeed sung in epic verse in the northern Albanian mountains, and the exploits of the great Scanderbeg, the Albanian national hero who freed large parts of the country from Turkish rule in the fifteenth century, are recounted everywhere Albanians gather, as if events five centuries old had taken place yesterday.

It remains for me to thank the many people who have assisted me in this project, among whom the late Qemal Haxhihasani of the Institute of Folk Culture (Tirana), staff members of the Institute of Linguistics and Literature (Tirana) and of the Albanological Institute

(Prishtina), as well as Barbara Schultz (Ottawa) for her kind revision of the manuscript.

Robert Elsie
Berlin, Germany
January 2015

1. The Boy and the Earthly Beauty

Once upon a time there was a very rich man who had a wife and a son. When he was about to die, he gave his son some advice, the most important part of which was never to go to the village where the Earthly Beauty lived. The boy grew up and lived happy and content, not knowing in which village where the Earthly Beauty lived. But in the end, he was overcome by a great desire to visit her, although both his father and his mother had forbidden him to do so. One day, taking a big sack of gold coins with him, he set out to find the village where the Earthly Beauty lived.

On his way, he rested for a while at the house of an old woman who told him right away that the Earthly Beauty lived in the village and that many a young man had come and squandered his fortune just to catch a glimpse of her finger or her hand. When the boy heard this, he too burned with desire to see at least her hand, no matter what it cost him. After asking the old woman to show him the way, he set off for the maiden's palace and asked to see the Earthly Beauty. Since he was quick to show the gold coins he had brought with him, the servants informed the maiden and she gave orders that he be let in. They put the boy in a corner of the room where he could catch just a glimpse of her finger. Then, taking away his gold coins, they threw him out, for the Earthly Beauty never showed herself completely to her admirers; the first time they just got to see her fingers, the second time her hand, and the third time her arm. When the boy got back to the old woman's house, he was so overwhelmed and excited by what he had seen at the maiden's palace that he could not wait to return. He resolved to go back home and fetch more money. He told the old woman what he had experienced and she encouraged him because she, too, was receiving gifts from him. The next day the boy got home, his heart full of desire for the Earthly Beauty. The moment he entered the house, he began looking for money so that he could return to the maiden as quickly as possible. When the poor mother saw that her son had squandered all of his money and been made a fool of by the maiden, she was saddened at first, and then angered. She tried to persuade him to change his mind, but it was all in vain. The boy was not to be swayed. In short, he took even more money than he had taken the first time, and set off once again.

When he got back to the Earthly Beauty, her servants cheated him a second time by showing him the maiden's hand, taking his money and throwing him out again. In a short time, the boy had wasted his whole fortune on the Earthly Beauty without getting any closer to her. Very soon, although he had once been quite rich, he was as poor as a church mouse.

But he refused to give up, and so returned home to search through his father's bedroom and cellar to try to find something of value to take to the maiden. To his surprise, he found a cap that made him invisible the moment he put it on. His mother could no longer see him, although she could hear his voice. He was delighted with the cap, for he believed that with its help he could win over the Earthly Beauty. So without hesitation, he took the cap and set off for the maiden's village. When he arrived at the palace of the Earthly Beauty, he put the cap on and, being invisible, was able to get right into the maiden's bedroom without being seen by her servants. Now he could see the maiden in all her beauty and stared at her in awe all night long until daybreak. Then he spoke to her. She could hear his voice, but could not see him. After the two had talked for some time, he told the Earthly Beauty who he was and, trusting in her love, revealed to her the secret of his cap. She snatched it from him, called her servants and ordered them to chase the boy away.

When the boy realized he had been deceived again, he was very sad indeed, because he had now given up all hope. In his misfortune, he returned home. But he could think of nothing but the maiden, because his heart was so full of desire for her. Again he went into his father's bedroom and poked around looking for something else to take to the Earthly Beauty. Suddenly, he noticed a jug. Picking it up, he had a look at it, turned it around in his hands, and polished it a bit because it was very dusty. Immediately, a band of warriors appeared and addressed him, "What is your command, oh master? We are ready to serve you."

At this, the boy reflected for a moment and said to himself, "Now I'm sure to win over the Earthly Beauty." His heart began to rejoice, his eyes brightened and he set off once again to win the object of his desire.

On his way there, he spent the night at the house of the old woman again and sent her to the palace with a message for the Earthly Beauty that she should receive him. But hardly had the old woman begun to speak when the maiden summoned her servants and had the old woman tossed out. Much distressed, the old woman returned home and told the boy of the ill treatment she had suffered at the palace. He nevertheless persuaded her to go back a second time and tell the maiden that if she did not receive him courteously, things would look bad for her. Because of the boy's urging and the gifts he had always given her, the old woman went back, though she knew very well that the Earthly Beauty would not listen to her. When the maiden saw the old woman coming, she became so furious that she ordered her servants to beat her and throw her out. And the old woman, wailing in sorrow, had to flee from the fists and clubs of the servants.

When the old woman returned and told the boy what had happened, he realized that courtesy would not get him any farther. He took his jug and rubbed it. The warriors immediately appeared and said to him, "What is your command, oh master? We are ready to serve you." The boy dispatched them, all dressed in fine garments, to the palace of the Earthly Beauty to exercise until he called them back. Then he sent the old woman to the maiden once more to tell her that if she did not receive him voluntarily, he would come by force with the warriors she could see in front of her palace. When the maiden heard this and saw the warriors, she became frightened and immediately ordered that the boy be received with full honours. When the boy arrived, the palace dignitaries received him with such kind words that he was quite flattered. After a while he said to the maiden, "Since you have caused me such suffering, I am now going to send you to Tinglimaimun." But the Earthly Beauty knew how to wrap him around her finger and he forgave her. Now that they had made peace with one another, the boy believed that she loved him and revealed to her the fact that all his power came from the jug. When he was not looking, the maiden took the jug from him and rubbed it, and immediately the warriors appeared and demanded, "What is your command, madam? What can we do for you?" The boy jumped up and shouted, "You're my warriors, not hers!" But the warriors replied, "The jug is in the maiden's hands." She then spoke to them, saying,

"Seize the youth and take him off to Tinglimaimun." And they seized him and took him away.

Having arrived in this distant foreign land with no food and no friends, the boy wandered about in the wilderness looking for something to eat. Finally, he found a bunch of red grapes, and hungry as he was, he began to eat them. But to his horror and amazement, for every grape he ate, a horn grew out of his face. The boy was most distressed by his misfortune. However, because he was still hungry, he wandered around in search of something else to eat. At last, he found some white grapes. After he had eaten the first grape, a horn fell off. Indeed for every grape he ate, one of the horns fell off. Realizing that for every red grape a horn grew on his face, and for every white grape one fell off, the boy was very happy because he remembered the Earthly Beauty and realized he could take advantage of this lucky coincidence. With the red grapes, he would make horns grow on the maiden's face, and then with the white grapes he would heal her again. This way, she would be his.

He quickly filled two baskets with grapes, one with red and the other with white, and set off swiftly to return to the land of the Earthly Beauty. After travelling for a long, long time, he came to an ocean where he had to wait for a ship. Sometime later he spotted a ship on the horizon, and as he had no handkerchief, he took off his trousers and waved them in the wind as a sign for the ship to come and pick him up. The ship approached, took the poor boy in rags on board and brought him back to his own country. He planned to sell the red grapes as soon as he arrived and at last his feet brought him right to the palace of the Earthly Beauty. There were no other grapes for sale as the season was over, so the boy's grapes attracted the attention of the people in the palace. When the Earthly Beauty caught sight of the grapes, she decided she had to have them, and ordered her maid to fetch them for her. The unfortunate maid could not resist eating a grape herself and immediately a horn grew out of her face. She did not know where it had come from and hid in shame in her room. When the maiden demanded her grapes, the maid asked another servant to take them to her. The Earthly Beauty seized the grapes and ate them all with great pleasure. Immediately, her face was covered with horns. She was so horrified at this that she almost lost her mind. A few days later, since the horns would not go away, she sent for her physicians. She received the physicians on the condition that they would be beheaded if they did not heal her. The physicians went to treat the maid first, because they both had the same illness.

The boy knew now that his day had come and that he would be called on to heal the maiden. He wanted to make the Earthly Beauty more desperate than ever, so went away for a few days to prolong her illness and increase her grief. Then he adorned himself with fine garments, went to the palace of the Earthly Beauty where he announced that he was a physician, and promised to heal her. They warned him that he would be beheaded if he was not successful, and to this he agreed. He entered the palace and was sent first to the maid. He had brought the white grapes with him, but had squeezed them into a paste so that no one could see what they were. He began by asking the maid what she had and had not done and about her illness. "Be careful," he said, "if you don't tell me the truth, you will not be cured." The maid told him everything and about the grapes she had eaten. He then gave her the medicine made of white grapes he had with him, and the horn fell off. The maid was cured.

When the Earthly Beauty heard this, she summoned the physician right away and could hardly wait to see him. He entered her chamber and again began by asking questions, as he had done with the maid, saying that he would only cure her if she told him the whole truth. She told him of all her deeds, and when she talked about the gold coins which she had repeatedly taken from the boy, he said to her, "Give me the money." She also showed him the cap which she had stolen from the boy, but pretended to have forgotten the jug. The physician said to her, "There is something you have not told me yet." Finally she brought out the jug which, like the cap and money, she had taken from the boy. Thereupon, he gave her the medicine and she was immediately cured. When the boy rubbed the jug, the warriors appeared and asked, "What are your wishes, my lord? You are our master." The boy then turned to the Earthly Beauty, saying, "Now I have you in my power. I am the one you caused to suffer. You sent me to Tinglimaimun, but now it is my turn. I am going to marry you and take you home with me." He commanded the warriors to seize her and take her back to his village, together with her palace and everything she owned. When the mother saw her son with the Earthly Beauty, the palace and all the treasures, she was overjoyed. And so they all lived together happily ever after.

2.   The Scurfhead

Once upon a time there was a king who had three sons. He also had a beautiful garden with a quince tree in it which bore only three quinces a year. Every time the tree bore fruit, a dragon came by and gobbled them up. The king desperately wanted to eat one of the quinces because they were so beautiful, but the dragon got them every time.

The eldest son decided to guard the quinces and went to his father to ask him for a net, a rattle and three candles to light his way in the dark. The father gave him what he asked for and the youth went into the garden and chose a place in the tall tree to wait for the dragon. The dragon arrived at midnight as usual and, seeing the light, guessed that a trap had been set for it. It therefore let out a frightening roar, threw itself with all its might against the tree, plucked a quince and was off in a flash. The youth was so frightened that he could not even move. The next morning he returned downcast and pale with fear to his father and told him what had happened. The father was very disappointed that his son had proved to be such a coward.

The second son then said, "This time I will go and guard the quinces!" At first the father did not want to let him go, for the second son was also a coward just like the eldest, but eventually he gave in. The second brother took a net, a rattle and light with him and set off for the garden to guard the quinces. That night, the very same thing happened. The dragon arrived, stole the second quince and disappeared, and the second son, having failed to put up any defence at all, was obliged to return to his father in shame.

The third son was a scurfhead. He was delighted at the failure of his brothers and went to his father saying that he too would go into the garden to guard the last quince. He gathered together everything he needed to guard the last quince, entered the garden and hid behind a tree. When the dragon arrived, the youth bravely lunged forth, struck the beast and wounded it so badly that it took flight. When the two older brothers saw how courageous the scurfhead had been they hung their heads in shame. They were jealous because they themselves had failed to fight the dragon. Nevertheless, when they heard their brother shouting and the dragon roaring, they ran to help him and the three of them pursued the dragon with fury until it disappeared into a hole in the ground. Standing in front of the hole, they talked to decide which of them would enter. The two older brothers were too afraid. Only the undaunted scurfhead was still willing to pursue the dragon. He tied two ropes around his waist, a black one and a white one, to be lowered into the cave, and they agreed on a signal. If he tugged on the white rope, everything was all right, but if he tugged on the black one, it meant he was in danger and they were to pull him up immediately to save his life.

And so the scurfhead entered the cave, looking for traces of the dragon. He wandered around for some time until he saw a small slab of iron on the floor, covering a hole. With all his might, he lifted the slab and descended three steps. At the bottom of the steps, he found a tiny house and knocked at the door. A fair maiden came out, one of the three Earthly Beauties. She welcomed him and asked him what he wanted. The scurfhead replied that he had come to slay the dragon which frightened everyone. The maiden replied, "The dragon is very strong indeed. If you want to slay it, you will first have to find out if you are strong enough to do so, otherwise you will be killed yourself. Anyone who does slay the monster will become known as the saviour of our country and I will take him for my husband." As a sign of their betrothal, she gave him a spindle which could make gold. He threw it onto the floor and a golden apple appeared.

He then continued on his way, came across another house, and knocked at the door. The maiden who answered was even fairer and more attractive than the first. She too said that she would marry the man who slew the dragon. As a sign of their betrothal she gave him a bowl. When he placed the bowl on the floor, another golden apple appeared. He accompanied the maiden to a third house and knocked at the door. There, too, a maiden answered who was more beautiful and wondrous than the first two, who were her sisters. After she had welcomed him and they had talked for a while, she gave him a hen with twelve chicks as a sign of their betrothal because she, too, wanted to marry the man who would slay the dragon. Then she took him into the den of the dragon, who had not yet returned.

As he waited and pondered on how best to slay the dragon, he saw a crowd of people in the distance who were weeping and lamenting. They were accompanying the king's daughter who was to be offered to the dragon, for the country was forced to offer one maiden a day to the dragon as payment for the water which it owned. The maidens were chosen by lot and that day the lot had fallen to the king's daughter. The crowd brought the poor maiden to the dragon's den and left her there. When the scurfhead saw the maiden sobbing and weeping, he felt sorry for her and asked her what was wrong. She told him her sad tale and he replied, "Don't be afraid, I'll save you."

At last the dragon arrived, still covered with blood from the wound it had received in the garden. The scurfhead had fallen asleep with his head in the maiden's lap. When she caught a glimpse of the dragon covered with blood from the wounds it had received in the garden, she began to tremble and warm tears welled up in her eyes. One of the tears dripped onto the scurfhead's face and woke him up. He sprang to his feet and asked the frightened maiden what had happened. Although she was speechless with fright, she managed to show by her glance that the dragon had arrived. The youth set upon the monster like a serpent, mortally wounding it so that it could neither stand nor move, and plunged straight into a well. When the dragon hit the bottom of the well, the water which the townspeople needed so badly began to gush forth. It formed streams which flowed through the villages, still crimson with the blood of the dying dragon. The maiden went to the scurfhead and thanked him on her knees, saying, "I will never forget you for saving me!" Then she filled her jug and returned to the palace.

When the king and queen saw their daughter return safe and sound, they were overjoyed and asked with great astonishment how she had escaped from the monster. The maiden recounted everything that had taken place and how an unknown hero in the dragon's den had saved her. The king immediately gave orders for the hero to be summoned, for he was anxious to meet the man who had slain the dragon and saved his daughter. The youth was brought in and the king rose to welcome him, offering the boy a seat at his side. The king praised the scurfhead's bravery and added, "Tell me what you would like to have. Don't be afraid to ask, even if it is half my kingdom! I'll give you whatever you want to pay you back for the service you have rendered us by ridding our kingdom of the dragon and by saving my daughter. I would also be very pleased if you would have my daughter for your wife." The hero replied, "The honour and tribute you have paid me have made me very happy. I need nothing at the moment, but if I should ever be in need, I will gladly call on you for help." He then departed content.

From there, our hero returned directly to the three Earthly Beauties who were impatiently awaiting him. They reminded him that they had given him their word that they were willing to marry him. He, too, spoke warmly to them, saying, "I have come to take all three of you with me. The two older sisters I will give in marriage to my brothers and the youngest one I will marry myself." The three maidens made themselves ready and the four of them set off to return to the surface of the earth. The maidens took all of their belongings with them and went to the opening of the cave. There the scurfhead called his two brothers and they let down a rope. The scurfhead tied the rope around the eldest sister and shouted to his brothers to pull her up, explaining that she was to be the wife of the eldest brother. When they let down the rope again to pull up the second maiden, he explained that she was for the second brother. As soon as the two elder sisters had been pulled up, the youngest maiden, who was the prettiest of all, said, "I have an inkling that something terrible is going to happen to you. Your brothers have wicked intentions. They want to leave you down here forever and have me, the prettiest one, for themselves. But don't be afraid. If they do leave you here, run back into the dragon's den. There you will find two rams, a black one and a white one. You must seize the white one, which will take you back to the surface of the earth. Be careful not to seize the black one, because if you do, you will have to remain here and will be lost forever. I will never belong to your brothers, even unto death. I will wait for you until you come." The two brothers then lowered the rope for the third time and pulled the maiden up. When they saw how beautiful she was and heard the scurfhead say that she was for him, they decided to abandon him in the cave below.

The scurfhead remembered what the maiden had advised him to do and ran back to the dragon's den. There he found the two rams, the black one and the white one. But to his great misfortune he seized the black ram instead of the white one and was thus condemned to remain in the depths of the earth.

The poor lad wandered off, downcast and despondent in his misfortune. He happened upon an oak tree where he sat down in the shade. There he heard birds chirping and, looking upwards, he saw a nest of young eagles. He also noticed a snake slithering up the tree to devour the eaglets. The birds cried out as if begging him to save them from the snake. Taking pity on them, he jumped up, drew his knife and slew the snake. Then he returned to his resting place under the tree and fell asleep. When the mother eagle returned and saw the sleeping hero in the shade of the tree, she imagined that he intended to kill her babies, and set upon him. But the babies, by means of sounds and signs, made it clear to her that he had been their saviour, not their attacker. She flew off to the sea to moisten her wings and returned, sitting at the youth's head with wings outstretched to protect him in his sleep. When he awoke, he saw the eagle hovering over him with its wings outstretched and thought that it intended to kill him. But the eagle calmed his fears, telling him in a gentle and soothing voice, "You saved my children. I am therefore indebted to you. I beg you to regard me as your servant and tell me freely what wish of yours I can fulfil to repay you." The hero replied by asking, "But how could you repay me? You are a bird." "I will do whatever you want," responded the eagle. "All right," declared the scurfhead, "I'd like you to take me back to the earth if you can. That is my only wish." The bird replied, "That's easy enough for me. But you must bring with you an oven full of bread, two roasts of mutton and a barrel of water for the journey. Pack everything on my back, climb on and we will fly back to the earth."

The scurfhead recalled the promise of the king whose daughter he had saved from the dragon, went to him and asked for the things the eagle had demanded. The king was surprised at how little the scurfhead wanted in compensation for his great deed, but ordered that he be given everything he needed. The scurfhead then loaded everything onto the eagle, climbed onto its back and they took off, soaring into the air. They flew for a long, long time through wind and rain and finally, after great exertions, they arrived on the earth.

The youth was overjoyed at having escaped from the underworld and asked first of all whether his parents were still alive and how they were faring. When told that they were well, he thought it was high time that he made some money for them. The next morning he went for a walk and, lost in thought, came upon three feathers. He singed the tip of one of the feathers and suddenly three mares appeared, saying to him, "What is your command, master? We are here to serve you." Although he was particularly delighted to have found a source of income, he told them after a moment's thought to go their way and that he would call on them if ever he needed them.

He still wanted to find work and went to see a silversmith, asking if he could serve as the man's apprentice. He said that he wanted no wages, only food and some old clothes. The silversmith saw that the youth was dressed like a noble and accepted him as an apprentice. One day, a herald arrived from the palace and told the silversmith that the king wished to see him. The silversmith was quite alarmed and went to the palace. There the king ordered him to make a spindle which could make gold. He said to the silversmith, "I want to marry off my eldest son, but his bride wants a spindle like the one she had when she was a child. I summoned you because you are the best silversmith of all. Have the spindle ready for me within three days or you will lose your head!"

Though the silversmith was very talented, he had no idea how to make such a spindle. Fearing for his life, he said nothing and returned home in dismay. The scurfhead, sitting at his work, saw his master returning in distress from the palace and asked him why he was so upset. The silversmith replied, "Hold your tongue! It is not your place to ask such questions." But the scurfhead asked again and again until finally the silversmith told him about the spindle. The scurfhead allayed the silversmith's fears and boasted that he could make such a spindle in one night. He would need only five kilos of nuts and plenty of good wine. Although the ill-fated silversmith found this hard to believe, he took heart and went out to buy what the scurfhead had asked for.

The scurfhead locked himself in his room and began cracking open the nuts and drinking the wine. His frightened master tiptoed up to the door and looked in through a crack to see what the apprentice was doing. The sly fox, however, frightened his master even more by calling out, "Be off with you or you'll ruin my work with your evil eye!" The next morning he gave his master the spindle he had received as a gift from the first Earthly Beauty. The silversmith was overjoyed and relieved when he saw the wonderful craftsmanship, and ran off to the king with it. The king, too, was very satisfied with the spindle and gave orders that the silversmith be given five cartloads of gold for his work. The silversmith accepted them and returned to give half the reward to his apprentice. The scurfhead, however, simply replied, "It is enough for me to know that my master is pleased with me."

The next day, the eldest son was to be married and the silversmith was invited to the wedding. He wanted to take his apprentice with him, but the youth would not go. A lofty pole had been set up on a hill outside the town, with a golden apple and a bag of money hanging from it. The king sent heralds all over the kingdom to proclaim that anyone who could jump high enough to reach the apple would receive a royal gift. Many brave men arrived from all corners of the earth, but none could reach the apple. When the scurfhead heard of the proclamation, he singed one of his three feathers and one of the three mares appeared on the spot with garments of gold for him. Dressed in his golden garments, he mounted the mare and rode off to the pole where a large crowd had gathered. He called to them in warning and, taking a mighty leap, plucked the apple from the pole. Everyone was amazed at such bravery. And so, the struggle between the scurfhead and his brothers ended and he was rewarded with the prettiest of the three Earthly Beauties.

3.   The Three Friends and the Earthly Beauty

A man died leaving his wife with child. Six months later she gave birth to a son. Though they were very poor, the woman raised the son well. When he turned fifteen, the youth asked his mother if she had any souvenirs to remember his father by. The mother replied that his father had left many things, but that she had been forced to sell everything off in order to raise the boy. Still the youth continued to pester his mother to find out whether there wasn't something left over of his father's. Finally she replied, "I have the feeling that his sabre may still be under the roof." The youth asked his mother to lift him up onto her shoulders so that he could reach under the roof. There he found the sabre which, after such a long time, was now covered in rust and dirt. He cleaned the sabre and polished it until it shone again. He then slung it over his shoulder and said to his mother, "I am off on a journey to foreign lands." His poor mother began to weep and lament and begged him not to leave. The next morning she said to him, "Take your father's sabre, son, but cut my head off before you go!" The youth replied, "Which son has ever cut off his mother's head? I beg you, mother, do not make it difficult for me and break my heart. Wish me good luck so that, God willing, I may return as soon as possible."

Thereupon he changed his name, calling himself Kordha the Sabre, and inscribed this name on the sabre itself. Then he hugged his mother, and they kissed because they were to separate and wept many tears. Once they had said their good-byes, the youth kissed his sabre for luck and departed, saying, "Farewell and please wish me well for I will not be back for six months." After leaving the village, he wandered through the countryside for five or six hours until he came to a mountain. There was not a soul to be seen. The youth sat down on a flat patch of ground, drew his sabre, kissed it and placed it on his lap. Hardly had an hour passed when another youth of his age came by and greeted him. "Hello," answered Kordha, "Where do you come from and where are you going?" "I am in search of my fortune," replied the other. "I, too, am in search of my fortune. Let us become brothers and travel together." They hugged and kissed and told one another their names: one was called Kordha and the other Ylli the Star. Then they set off together and walked until it got dark, when they lay down and went to sleep without dinner.

The next day they set off again in the same direction and after a while met another youth of the same age. They greeted one another and inquired of one another where they had come from and where they were going. The youth asked Kordha and Ylli if he could become their brother too. And so they became brothers, and the new boy said that his name was Deti the Sea. They all hugged and kissed and swore that they would be faithful to one another and that if anything should happen, they would all die together.

The three set off and arrived at a city. The king of the city had just had a wide moat dug and announced that he would give his daughter's hand in marriage to the man who could jump over the moat, but that those who tried and failed to jump over the moat would have their heads chopped off. Many men had already attempted to jump over the moat and had fallen in, and the hangman had come straight away and chopped off their heads. When the three friends approached and found out that they had to jump over the moat, they thought for a while. Finally they agreed to take courage and jump, or all die together, though Deti had doubts, "Look how wide the moat is! I'm afraid we won't be able to jump across it." Kordha then picked up a stone, gave it to Deti and told him to throw it across the moat. Then he asked, "Was it difficult to throw the stone over to the other side?" "No, but it weighed less than a hundred grams." "Well, it won't be any harder for me to jump across," said Ylli. And in the twinkling of an eye, he grabbed the other two and, using all his strength, jumped with ease across the moat.

The people who had gathered on the other side were amazed. The king then ordered that the three of them be brought to him. They were put in a coach and driven to the king's palace. "Which of you is to marry my daughter?" asked the king. Kordha replied, "Ylli will marry your daughter." The king then ordered the marriage to be arranged and asked Kordha and Deti what their wishes were. Kordha replied that he wanted nothing for himself but that the king should give Deti a gift. A few days after the wedding, Kordha asked his brothers for permission to set off again. They were very sad and said to him, "Is our friendship to have lasted such a short time? How can you have the heart to set off and leave us?" Kordha replied, "Our friendship is eternal, but I must depart. I will leave a feather over your doorway. Pay attention to it, for if the feather ever drips with blood, you will know that I am in danger. You must set off immediately to find me, for I will be in great need of your help." Then he kissed them and departed.

After travelling alone for several days, he came to a place where the road divided into seven. At the crossroads was a cottage in front of which sat an old woman. Kordha asked her to tell him where the roads led. One of the roads, said the old woman, led to the Earthly Beauty. Kordha immediately prepared to set out in that direction. But the old woman said to him, "No, my boy, you'll lose your head there, and that would be a shame because you are still so young. Many kings with mighty armies have taken that road and never got to the end of it, and you want to go all by yourself?" He wrote something on the wall of the cottage and asked the old woman to point it out to the two brave young men who would come by and inquire about him, and to show them the road he was now taking. Then he set off down the road which led to the Earthly Beauty.

After continuing for a while, he came across a Kulshedra with six young. The Kulshedra charged and wanted to devour him, but the boy drew his sabre and slew it and all its young. Suddenly Kordha saw the palace of the Earthly Beauty rising before him. On his way up to it, he came across a spring of cool water at the side of the road and sat down for a rest. From the window of the palace, the Earthly Beauty caught sight of him and said to her Kulshedra, "Look there's a brave young man coming all dressed in white." The Kulshedra replied, "Look out the window and see whether he drinks the water with his hands or on his knees?" The boy knelt down, bowed his head and drank the water without using his hands. The Kulshedra said, "I fear this person." Beside the palace was an apple tree with fruit on it. When Kordha got closer to the tree, the Kulshedra looked out to see if he would jump up and pick the biggest apple. And Kordha jumped and plucked the apple off the tree, but did so by using his teeth and not his hands. When the Kulshedra saw this, it said, "Alas, there is no salvation from this boy!" Kordha approached the gate of the palace and entered straight away, calling out, "Hello to those within." "How dare you enter here!" said the Kulshedra menacingly. And the boy answered angrily, "Why shouldn't I? After all, you dared to enter!" The Kulshedra was furious and set upon Kordha, but he drew his sabre quickly and slit the Kulshedra into two pieces. And so he won the Earthly Beauty.

Several weeks passed and the kings heard that a brave young man had killed the Kulshedra and had married the Earthly Beauty. They set off in haste and arrived at the place where the road divided into seven. There they asked the old woman who it was that had travelled down the road leading to the Earthly Beauty. When she told them that the brave young man was but a youth sixteen years old, they took counsel and decided to attack him by surprise. They set off and did battle with him for twenty-four days, but they could not defeat him and returned home having achieved nothing. After this initial failure, the kings went back to the old woman and asked her to go to the Earthly Beauty and inquire as to what power the boy possessed or what feats he had accomplished to win her. The Earthly Beauty recounted to the old woman what had happened, "He arrived in a fury," she said, "slew the Kulshedra and won me." Then the old woman told her to ask the boy what the source of his heroic power was. A few days later, the Earthly Beauty asked Kordha where he got his power, and the poor boy, because he loved her, revealed to her that it came from his sabre. If anyone were to take his sabre away from him, he would be lost. When the old woman heard this, she stole the sabre and threw it into the sea. Kordha became ill and lay down to die. The old woman returned gleefully to her cottage and announced to the kings that they could now win the Earthly Beauty easily without an army and without doing battle at all.

As the kings were about to begin their attack, Kordha's friends noticed blood dripping from the feather and set off right away in search of him. Ylli took Deti by the arm and in no time they were standing beside Kordha, long before the kings arrived. They asked the Earthly Beauty where the sabre was. She told them that someone had stolen it and thrown it into the sea. Deti then rose and plunged into the sea, found the sabre and brought it back. As soon as the sabre was put in front of him, Kordha opened his eyes and said, "Look how long I've been sleeping!" But when he saw his brothers, he realized that he was in danger.

At that moment the kings arrived to do battle once again. They set upon him furiously but since Kordha had regained his health, he managed to fight the kings off once more and they returned home, vanquished. Kordha took the Earthly Beauty and all her possessions and set off with his friends to return home to his mother. When they arrived at the place where the seven roads met, he gave the old woman a present, saying to her, "This is for you because you did me a good deed by throwing my sabre into the sea. Please tell the kings who did battle with me that I have gone away and taken the Earthly Beauty with me. I am going home and if they still miss me, they can come and do battle with me again. I will be waiting for them. Farewell, old woman!" And so they parted.

First they all went together to the king who was Ylli's father-in-law and asked his permission to take his daughter back to their country. The king replied, "You can go wherever you wish, but my son-in-law and my daughter must remain here." "You can think whatever you want, but we're going anyway!" Kordha retorted. And Ylli said to the king straight off, "I am not going to abandon my friends for the sake of the king's daughter." The king was furious and shouted, "I don't care what he wants. You will have to leave him behind!" Kordha, too, became furious. "What do you mean, you don't care? Do you intend to keep our brother Ylli here by force? The man who can keep one of us by force has yet to be born!" The king gave orders to his guards, saying, "Arrest the three of them and throw them into prison!" But Kordha asked the king to call his daughter first so that everyone could hear what she thought about this. The king ordered his daughter to be brought forth. Kordha said to Ylli, "Put one arm around your wife and the other arm around Deti, say farewell to the king and take off." Astounded, the king called his guards and ordered them to post at least four watchmen at every door. Ylli stood up, walked to the middle of the room and said to the king, "Forgive me, father-in-law, and farewell!" Then he jumped out the window with his wife and Deti, and all three disappeared. Only Kordha remained behind. The king rushed to the window to see whether they had been crushed by the fall, because the window from which they had leapt was very high. When he saw that nothing had happened to them, he became so furious that he didn't know what to do. He gave orders to kill Kordha. When Kordha asked why the king wanted to kill him, he replied, "Because it's your fault that my daughter has left me." Kordha then stood up, took the Earthly Beauty by the hand and started to leave. When the watchmen refused to let him pass, he drew his sabre and slew all four of them. And so he escaped and soon joined his friends.

When the king realized what had happened and that his watchmen had been killed, he ordered the army to pursue the brothers and bring them back dead or alive. When the three brothers saw that the army was following them, they stopped and waited for it to approach. The warriors sent a herald to tell them that it would be better for them to return peacefully to the king, for otherwise all the warriors would attack at once and annihilate them. The three answered, "Do what your king has ordered, for we shall not return." The herald went back and reported that they would not return voluntarily. Then the whole army advanced against the three who were laying in wait for it calmly. When Kordha saw it coming, he rose and shouted, "Hey, wait a moment! What do you think you're doing, friends? You will all be killed if you approach!" Although the soldiers were somewhat put off by his words, they did not believe him and continued their advance.

When Kordha saw that there was nothing more to be done, he told his friends to take the two women and go on ahead. All by himself, he drew his sabre and set upon the army, slaying seven hundred of them including their leader. When the remaining warriors saw that so many men in their ranks had been killed, and that their leader too was dead, they fled in panic. Kordha then departed and soon caught up with his brothers.

They continued their journey and three days later arrived at Kordha's house. "Hello, mother," they said to Kordha's mother. She was confused and asked, "Who are you people calling me mother?" They replied, "Your son, who will arrive any moment, asked us to do so. We made a bet with him that you would not recognize him when he comes." "Oh yes I would," she replied, "I would recognize my son among five hundred men," and began to cry thinking about her boy. Ylli then asked her which of the three was her son. She took a close look at the three boys, compared them and recognized Kordha as her son. She threw her arms around him, kissed him tenderly and embraced the other boys and the two women as well.

The three friends and their wives settled there and after a while, one of them asked, "Are we three friends or just two?" "We are three," Ylli answered. "If we are three, then why do we have only two wives?" Deti jumped up and declared, "That doesn't matter!" But Kordha responded, saying, "We will make you king of the whole

26

country."

And so Deti became king and reigned over the land for a long, long time. And the three remained the best of friends and loved one another like brothers for as long as they lived.

4.   The Three Brothers and the Three Sisters

Once upon a time there lived three brothers and three sisters. The brothers married their sisters off, one to the sun, one to the moon and one to the south wind. After the sisters had been married for some time, the brothers said to one another, "Let us go and see how our sisters are faring." And so they did. They took some food with them for the journey and set off. After they had gone a ways, darkness fell while there were crossing a plain at the foot of a mountain. They sat down, took out their food and made a fire. When they had finished their meal, the eldest brother said, "You two go to sleep and I will keep watch so that no one comes to rob or kill us." The two younger brothers lay down to sleep and the eldest kept watch.

A Kulshedra, attracted by the light of their fire, approached, was delighted to see the humans and set upon the eldest brother keeping watch, to eat him up. The eldest brother shot and killed the Kulshedra, took out his sabre and chopped off its head, stuffing it into his bag. Then he threw the Kulshedra's body into a ditch so that his brothers would not see it. He sat there for a spell, then he woke his brothers and they set out on their way. They spent the second night at a different place, made a fire again, ate supper and two of them lay down to sleep. That night the second brother kept watch and slew a Kulshedra, too. The third night, the youngest brother said he would keep watch. The two older brothers told him he should sleep instead because he was still too young, but he insisted and finally they allowed him to keep watch. A Kulshedra approached to devour the youngest brother, too. He shot at it but missed, for he was too young. The boy then drew his sword and slew the Kulshedra, but as the beast lay dying, it swished with its tail and put out the fire. The boy tried to relight the fire but did not know what to use. Finally, spying a small fire at the top of the mountain and set off for it.

On his way, he met the Mother of the Night and asked her where she was going. She replied that she was on her way to the dawn.

He said to her, "Wait for me to light my fire." She agreed, but he didn't believe her and tied her up so that she could not let the day break. When he got to the fire, he saw a huge cauldron with twelve handles on top of it. He lifted the cauldron off and lit his fire. At that moment the thieves who owned the cauldron arrived. They asked him who he was and he replied, "I am a traveller. My fire went out so I came here to relight it." "How did you manage to lift the cauldron off?" they asked. "There are twelve of us and when we want to lift the cauldron off the fire, each of us has to take a handle and we still have to strain with all our might." "It doesn't seem very heavy to me," retorted the boy and lifted the cauldron again. "You are a good lad," they replied. "We are off to rob the king and you're just the one we need."

So the thirteen of them set out. They broke a hole into the palace wall and entered the courtyard to steal the king's horses. The boy remained outside and thought to himself, "I have never stolen anything. It would be better for me to slay the thieves instead and escape." So he shouted to the thieves, "Come out quickly. Someone has betrayed us." As they crawled through the hole, the boy chopped their heads off one by one. Then he threw his knife into the middle of the king's courtyard, ran away, relit his fire, freed the Mother of the Night, awakened his brothers, and they set out on their way once again.

When the king got up the next morning, he saw the dead men and the knife in the courtyard and wondered what had happened. He gave orders that an inn be built at a crossroads. Anyone who stopped there was not to pay for the night but was instead to tell the story of all the good and bad deeds he had done in his lifetime. Many people stayed at the inn, eating and sleeping there without paying a cent. One day the three brothers happened by and stayed overnight at the inn. When they went to pay the next morning, the inn-keeper said to them, "No one pays here. Instead, everyone must tell a story from his life." The eldest brother told the story of what he had done with the Kulshedra. The second brother also told the story of how he had slain a Kulshedra. The youngest brother then began to tell the story of the Kulshedra and the twelve thieves who had wanted to rob the king. The inn-keeper cried out, "So you're the one the king is looking for!" The two older brothers continued on their way and the third brother was taken to the king. When the king had heard the story, he gave the boy his daughter in marriage.

There was a wedding custom in that land to release a lot of prisoners from jail. One of the prisoners was half man, half iron. When many of the prisoners were released and he was not, the half-iron man began to weep. The king's son-in-law took pity on the man and begged the king to release him, too, but the king had had him imprisoned for life. The son-in-law begged the king again and finally he gave way and freed the prisoner from his chains. The king's daughter was standing nearby, and the moment he was released, the half-iron man devoured her and disappeared. The king was so furious that he drew his sword to slay the son-in-law who was to blame for this misfortune. But the son-in-law declared, "I'll find your daughter and bring her back. But first let me make some iron shoes and an iron cane because I have a long way to walk. Once I am equipped, I will return in one year and bring you your daughter." When everything was ready, he set off.

That evening, he visited his sister who was married to the sun, and knocked at her door. She approached and asked, "Who is there?" "It is a human," he replied. She opened the door and rejoiced to see her brother. After a while, her husband the sun arrived. Because the sister was afraid that the sun would devour her brother, she hid him in a chest. When the sun entered, he asked his wife what she had been cooking. "The same as always," said the wife. "But I can smell meat," said the sun. "No," she replied, "there is no meat." The sun, however, stood up and began looking around for the meat. The wife then said to him, "Eat me rather than my brother who arrived just before you came in." "Let him out, I won't eat him." She got her brother out of the chest and the sun, too, rejoiced at meeting his brother-in-law. Then the brother asked the sun if he knew where a being who was half-man, half-iron lived. "We don't know," the two of them answered, "but go and ask the moon."

The next evening the boy visited the second sister who was married to the moon, but they knew nothing of the half-iron man either.

Then he visited the third sister who was married to the south wind. He asked again if they knew where the half-iron man lived. The south wind answered, "I don't know, but if you take this road before daybreak tomorrow, you will come across a falcon so huge that it cannot fly. Steal up to it, seize it by the head and say: I'll kill you if you don't tell me about the half-iron man. Then it will tell you where the iron man lives and what you must do." The brother set out at dawn and found the falcon. He did just as his brother-in-law, the south wind, had told him and the falcon said, "I know where he is, but first you must serve me many okas of meat and wait until my wings have grown back, for I am very old." And so the boy waited until its wings had grown back. He prepared a lot of meat to feed to the falcon on their journey. Their destination was a mountain so high that no man had ever climbed it. The mountain was in another world, and it was there that the half-iron man lived with the king's daughter.

When they were finally ready, the boy climbed onto the falcon's back, taking the meat with him, and the bird flew off. They flew higher and higher and he kept feeding the falcon pieces of meat until they got close to the mountain. When the meat was all gone and he had nothing more to feed to the falcon, the bird croaked, "Give me more meat." "I haven't got any more. It's all gone." "If you don't give me more meat, I'll throw you off." Not knowing what else to do, the boy cut a piece out of the calf of his leg and gave it to the falcon. The next time the bird demanded meat, he cut a piece out of his thigh. Once they had arrived, he clambered off the falcon. When the falcon saw that the boy was covered in blood, he spit out the pieces of meat and the boy recovered immediately. The boy then went over to one of the palaces nearby and knocked at the door. His wife, the king's daughter, opened and recognized him right away. "My husband!" she exclaimed joyfully. "How did you get here? Who brought you here?" He recounted all he had been through. As they were talking, the half-iron man approached so she quickly hid her husband in the attic. The half-iron man entered and asked, "What have you been cooking?" "The same as always." "But I can smell meat." By chance, he noticed the boy through a hole in the ceiling, went upstairs and sucked his blood out, picking up the skin and bones and throwing them outside. The falcon saw them, recognized them and exclaimed, "That's the boy I carried here! I'll go and get some swallow's milk to bring him back to life." Without delay, it flew off to a place between two mountain peaks where swallow's milk was to be found. It landed, filled its beak and returned, pouring the milk into the boy who recovered immediately. The boy stood up, went back to his wife and told her that she must pretend to be sick. She was to say to the half-iron man, "We have been together for such a long time now and you have never told me the source of your power. I am at death's door. You have nothing more to fear from me." Then he would tell her the source of his power. The boy went off and hid so that the half-iron man could not find and devour him again.

The king's daughter did as they had planned. She pretended to be sick and asked the half-iron man what the source of his power was. "It is in my broom," he told her. The next day when he was out, she burned the broom, but his power remained untouched. The wife pretended to be sick again and asked him once more about his power. This time he said, "My power is in a boar up on the mountain over there. The boar has a silver tusk and in it there is a hare. In the hare's belly are three doves. There lies the source of my power." The half-iron man went back to work. The wife ran out, called her husband and told him what she had heard. The boy climbed the mountain where he met a shepherd tending his sheep and inquired about the whereabouts of a huge boar. "Don't speak so loudly," replied the shepherd. "If the boar hears us it will come and devour us." The boy began talking even louder until the boar heard them and charged into their midst to devour them. But it could not assail the boy because he was carrying a knife. The boar said, "If only I had a stalk of arum to sharpen my teeth with, you'd see something happen!" Then the boy said, "If only I had some fried fish, cake and a cup of wine, you'd see something happen, too!" The shepherd immediately brought the boy and boar what they wanted. When the boar had eaten its arum and the boy his fish and cake, they set upon one another and battled until the boy had slain the boar. He examined its tusks and saw that one of them was indeed made of silver. Breaking it open, he found in it a hare, which he killed, and in the belly of the hare he found the three doves.

The moment the boy slew the boar, the half-iron man fell sick. When the boy killed the hare, the half-iron man became so ill that he could not get up. Then the boy killed two of the doves, took the third one and returned to the iron-man's bed. When he saw the boy approaching, the half-iron man tried to get up but was not able to. And when the boy killed the third dove, the half-iron man died.

The boy took his wife, mounted the falcon, flew back and returned to the king. The king rejoiced to see the two of them and had a splendid feast prepared in their honour.

5. The Youth and the Maiden with Stars on their Foreheads and Crescents on their Breasts

Once upon a time there was a king who had three daughters. When he died, another man mounted the throne and ordered that no one in the country was to leave a light burning on the night of his coronation. Then the new king put on a disguise and went out into the streets alone. As he was walking through the streets of the city, he passed by the house of the three daughters and heard them talking to one another. The eldest daughter said, "If the king were to marry me, I would weave him a carpet so great that the whole army could sit on it and there would still be room left over." The second daughter said, "If the king were to marry me, I would make him a tent with room for the whole army and more." The youngest daughter said, "If the king were to marry me, I would give him a son and a daughter with stars on their foreheads and crescents on their breasts." When the king heard this, he had the three maidens called to him the next morning and married all three. As they had promised, the eldest wove a carpet so great that the whole army could sit on it and the second daughter made a tent with room for the whole army.

After some time, the youngest wife became pregnant and the moment approached for her to give birth. On the day of the birth, the king went out riding. When he returned, he asked what his wife had given birth to. The two sisters answered, "A baby kitten and a baby mouse." When the king heard this, he ordered his youngest wife to sit on the stairs so that everyone who passed by could spit at her. The sisters put the boy and the girl, to whom the youngest wife had given birth, into a box and sent a servant off to throw them into the river. There was a strong wind blowing that day and it carried the box to the other side of the river. On the bank of the river there stood a mill inhabited by an old man and old woman. The old woman noticed the box, took it into her cottage, opened it and saw the youth and the maiden with stars on their foreheads and crescents on their breasts. In great awe and amazement, she took the children out of the box and raised them.

After some time, the old woman died, and it was not long until death overcame the old man too. On his deathbed, he called the youth, saying to him, "My son, in the cave over there I have a bridle. But you must not enter the cave until forty days have passed." When the forty days had passed, the youth entered the cave and found the bridle. The moment he put his hands on it and said, "I wish I had two horses," the two horses appeared before him. He and his sister mounted the horses and rode back into the city where their father lived. There, the youth opened a coffee-house and the maiden lived at home all by herself.

One day the king came to the coffee-house because it was the best one in the city and saw the youth with the star on his forehead. He was so taken by the boy's beauty that he returned home later than usual. When he got home, the sisters asked him why he was so late. He replied, "There is a youth who has opened up a coffee-house. I have never seen such a beautiful boy in all my life. But the most amazing thing is that he has a star on his forehead."

When the sisters heard this, they knew right away that it was the son of the youngest sister. They were furious and pondered on how to kill the youth. So they sent an old woman to the youth's sister and she said to the maiden, "Your brother doesn't love you at all. He sits in the coffee-house all day, has fun and leaves you here all alone. If he loved you, he would bring you a flower from the Earthly Beauty to play with. That evening, the brother returned home and found his sister looking unhappy. He asked her, "Why are you so sad?" "Why shouldn't I be," she replied, "I am shut up here all day long. You can go out. If you loved me, you would go to the Earthly Beauty and bring me back a flower to make me as happy as you are." The brother replied, "All right, you mustn't be sad because of me." He picked up the bridle and a horse appeared. He mounted it and rode straight off in the direction of a Kulshedra.

When the Kulshedra saw him coming, it said, "You are so handsome that it would be a pity to devour you. I will let you live." The youth then asked the way to the Earthly Beauty. The Kulshedra replied, "I don't know where she is. You will have to go and ask my older sister."

The youth continued on his way and finally reached the Kulshedra's older sister. It, too, wanted to devour him but, seeing how handsome he was, it set him free and asked where he wanted to go. The youth told the monster everything, but the Kulshedra did not know the way to the Earthly Beauty either and sent him on to the eldest sister. The eldest sister prepared to set upon the youth to devour him, but when she saw how beautiful he was, took pity on him and let him go.

The youth again asked the way to the Earthly Beauty and the Kulshedra replied, "When you get to her house, rub the door with your scarf and it will open. When you enter, you will see a lion and a lamb. Throw some brains to the lion and some grass to the lamb." The youth went off and did exactly as the Kulshedra had told him. He rubbed the door with his scarf and it opened. He threw some brains to the lion and some grass to the lamb, and they let him pass. He then went into the house and removed a flower which he took back home to his sister. She was delighted and played with it.

Hardly had another day passed when the sisters sent the old woman to see the maiden again. "Did he bring you the flower?" the old woman asked. When the maiden told her that her brother had indeed brought her the flower, the old woman said to her, "That's very nice, my maiden, but if you had the Earthly Beauty's scarf, you'd be even happier."

When the brother came home, the maiden was weeping and lamenting. He asked what was wrong and she replied, "How am I supposed to be happy with a simple flower if I don't have the Earthly Beauty's scarf?" The youth didn't want to see his sister unhappy, so he mounted his horse and hurried off to find his sister the scarf.

The next morning, when the youth had gone to the coffee-house, the old hag appeared again. She said, "You can consider yourself very happy to have such a brother who brings you whatever you wish. But you would be without equals if he brought you the owner of the scarf." Once again the youth set off and went to the oldest Kulshedra who said to him, "Oh, young man, to go there and get the Earthly Beauty herself is not an easy task. You must keep your eyes open and try to find her ring, since the ring is the source of all her power."

The youth departed once more, passed by the lion and lamb and entered the chamber of the Earthly Beauty. As he got closer, he saw that she was asleep. He approached her silently. As soon as he had slipped the ring off her finger, she awoke and realized that he had her in his power. So she accompanied the youth and in no time they were back at home and his sister was again delighted.

The next morning, the king entered the coffee-house and when he returned home, he ordered that a feast be held in honour of the youth and his family. The two sisters, however, ordered the cooks to poison the food. That evening, the youth arrived with his sister and with the Earthly Beauty who was now his wife. The youth, his wife and sister ate nothing at the feast, although the king urged them to, for the Earthly Beauty had noticed that the food was poisoned. They had only two spoonsful of the king's stewed prunes.

When they stood up to leave the table, the king suggested that everyone tell a story. When the youth's turn came, he told the story of his life, and the king recognized that he was the son of his youngest wife whom he had repudiated. He had the youngest wife brought back to him and had the two older sisters drawn and quartered. Then he made the youth his successor and they all lived happily ever after.

6.   The Shoes

Once upon a time there was a king who had a wife and a daughter. When his wife became ill and knew that she was going to die, she called her husband and said to him, "Order a pair of shoes from the shoemaker, not too big and not too small. Tell him to come and measure my feet. When I die, send a servant from town to town with the shoes and marry the girl whom they fit.

When his wife died, the king sent the servant off with the shoes but he could find neither a woman nor a girl whom the shoes fit. The servant returned to the king and said to him, "We have found no women whom the shoes fit, their feet were either too big or too small."

One day, the king's daughter tried the shoes on to see if they would fit, never dreaming that the king would marry her. She slipped the shoes on and to her surprise they fit perfectly. At that very moment, the king called his daughter to bring him a glass of water. She arrived wearing the shoes, never thinking that her father would marry her, his own daughter.

When the king saw that she was wearing the shoes, he said to her, "I am going to marry you. Your mother said in her hour of death that I should marry the woman whom the shoes fit." The daughter replied, "Well, if you really want to marry me, first have two big lamps made, about as tall and as wide as I am, and fashion them in such a way that they can be opened and closed with a screw." He immediately gave orders that the lamps be made and three days later they were ready. The girl had the lamps set up in her chamber and hid in one of them. When her father arrived for the wedding, he could not find his daughter anywhere. He never thought of looking in the lamps. He was very upset that his daughter had escaped from him and therefore summoned the town crier, saying to him, "Take these lamps away and sell them. You can keep the money. I don't want them anymore."

The town crier went off to the next town to sell the lamps. There he saw a prince sitting at a window gazing out. The prince asked how much he wanted for the lamps. "Whatever you wish to give me, my lord." The prince gave him a gold coin, took the lamps and set them up in his chamber.

This prince, who was engaged to the daughter of a king, had a habit of getting up in the middle of the night to eat. For this reason, various plates of food were always brought to him. That night, when he was sleeping, the maiden snuck out of the lamp and tried all the food. After she had finished eating, she washed her hands, went over to the sleeping prince and stroked him. Then she climbed back into the lamp. The youth awoke, stood up, noticed the soap suds and saw that all the food had been touched. The next morning he asked his servants, "Did you try my food, or was there a cat in my chamber nibbling at it?" "No," they replied, "no cat entered your chamber. Why do you ask?" He ordered them to keep watch so that no cats entered his chamber. The next night, he found to his amazement that his food had been touched again. The third night he went to bed, but only pretended to sleep. The maiden crept out of the lamp, began to eat, and when she was finished, went over to his bed to stroke his hands. At that moment, the prince sat up and declared, "So you're the one who has been trying my food! Although I am already engaged, I shall marry you because you are very beautiful." And he married her, though without a wedding celebration.

A time came when the prince had to go off to war. He said to his wife, "I must go to war now. You stay here in this chamber and don't go out. When I return after a long time, I want to find you here. I will order the servants to bring you food and whatever else you need. But you must hide in the lamp so that no one can see you." And so he departed.

One day, the youth's future father-in-law appeared. He entered the groom's chamber and, finding the girl, asked her what she was doing there. Full of anger, he ordered the servants to throw her out of the palace and toss her into a patch of nettles so that she would burn herself and, not be able to stand up anymore, would die.

An old woman who used to visit this patch to gather nettles saw the maiden and asked what she was doing there. The maiden said to her, "They threw me into this patch of nettles so that I would burn myself because they are jealous of me. Please, oh please take me home with you, old woman. I will do all your housework, for you are very old." "I can't take you home with me for I am too poor," the old woman replied. "That doesn't matter," said the girl, "I am willing to live anywhere you live."

Sometime later, the prince returned from the war. He waited for his wife to come out of the lamp but she was no longer there. He loved his wife so much and was so full of longing for her that he fell ill. Despite his illness, he got hungry, so he ordered his servants to call on everyone in the town to bring him pastry. The old woman, too, brought him some pastry which the girl had baked and in which she had hidden a ring he had given her as a wedding present. When the prince ate the pastry, he found the ring and recognized it immediately. He said to the old woman, "I will call upon you tomorrow." "As you wish, my lord," she replied, "but we are poor people."

When he arrived the next morning, he looked all around at everything until he noticed a kneading trough leaning against the wall. He asked the old woman what was in it. "Cakes, my son, but please do not touch them because they haven't risen yet." "All right, I won't," he said, "just take them out so that I can see them." He moved the kneading trough to one side and found his wife standing there. "What are you doing here?" he asked. "Didn't I tell you not to leave the lamp?" She told him what had happened and how his father-in-law had had her tossed into a patch of nettles, how the old woman had found her, taken her home and become like a father and a mother to her, and how she had baked the pastry with the ring in it. Then she asked him to make the old woman rich with gifts, because she had saved her from death. The prince gave the old woman two sacks of silver coins and took his wife home. Then, he called on his would-be father-in-law and said to him, "Because of the wicked things you have done to my wife, I am breaking off my engagement to your daughter and won't marry her anymore." Then he showed everyone the girl who was already his wife.

7.   The Girl Who Became a Boy

Once upon a time there was a man who had three daughters. When the king called up soldiers for the war, the man had no sons to send. As he sat and pondered what to do, his eldest daughter approached him and inquired, "What are you thinking about, father?" He answered, "Leave me alone, daughter. The king has called up soldiers to go to war and I have no sons. I only have you whom I can't send to war." To this she replied, "Marry me to someone!" Later the second daughter gave the very same answer. The youngest daughter, however, replied, "Don't worry, father, I'll go to war. Have a uniform made for me and cut off my hair so that no one will know that I am a girl. Then give me your horse and weapons." Her father did as she had requested and she set off with the other young men of the village. Everyone who saw the new young man was surprised. And so they departed.

That day, the king had ordered his own son to be taken out of the town to be eaten by a Kulshedra. Every year the Kulshedra would come and devour a number of people. One day the Kulshedra said, "If you don't want me to come back ever again, give me the king's son." And so they brought the king's son to the Kulshedra. When the boy was outside the town, the townspeople all watched the Kulshedra setting upon him to devour him and they were all so frightened that no one even thought of going to his assistance. The disguised girl, however, drew her sabre, slew the Kulshedra and saved the king's son. The news that the Kulshedra had been slain spread immediately to the king who was so overjoyed that he gave orders for a banquet and a gun salute. When the young man entered the palace with the king's son, the son whispered, "My father will offer you a kingdom, but ask only for his horse, because it can think and talk like we do."

When they got to the king, he asked, "Which kingdom would you like to have as your reward?" The young man replied, "My only wish is not to go to war." "Fine," said the king, "I will gladly free you from military service, but which kingdom do you want?" "Well, if you really want to give me something, give me the horse you're sitting on." The king refused, however, and so the young man departed. The king's son followed young man and when the people asked where he was going, he replied, "I am going away with my new father. He saved my life and now he is like a father to me. If my real father cares more for his horse than he does for me, his son, then it is better for me to depart."

When the king heard what his son had said, he changed his mind. They brought the young man the horse and placed a golden saddle on it. The young man (we will call him so though he was actually a girl) mounted the horse and rode off to another kingdom.

When he arrived, he saw a crowd of people standing before a moat. The young man's horse saw the crowd in the distance and asked its master, "My lord, can you see what they are doing?" "I can see them all right, but I cannot make out what is going on." "The king had the moat dug because he wants to marry his daughter to someone," replied the horse. "The person who can jump over the moat with his horse and catch an apple can have the king's daughter for his wife. It looks, though, as if no one has yet succeeded. I'll jump over the moat. You just hold on tightly. Don't be afraid, and keep an eye out for the apple. When I jump, I'll stumble at the edge of the moat, so grab my mane and hang on." As they talked, the horse approached. Then it took a run at the moat and leapt over it. When it reached the other side, it stumbled on one leg. The young man seized the mane and the horse leapt into the air again so that the young man was able to catch the apple.

Everyone was surprised because many people had tried to jump the moat, but no one had ever succeeded in catching the apple. The king immediately arranged for the wedding and gave his daughter away in marriage. When the marriage ceremony was over, the bride and the groom went to bed, though of course both of them were girls. The next morning, as is custom, the wife was asked how she had spent the night. "Nothing happened," she replied. The second and third nights were the same. The people at the court decided that they would have to kill the young man, but somehow they felt sorry for him. "I know what to do," said one courtier, "we'll send him into the forest to take food to the woodcutters. There is a Kulshedra in the forest who will come and devour him." The groom, however, was standing

41

behind the door and overheard everything. He went back to his horse and sat down despondently. "Why are you so sad?" asked the horse. "Why shouldn't I be?" he replied, "The king wants to send me into the forest so that the Kulshedra will devour me." "Don't be afraid," declared the horse, "Ask him for a cart to carry the food and for a team of oxen, and I'll tell you what to do when we get there." A little later, the father-in-law summoned the young man and said to him, "Go into the forest and take the woodcutters something to eat." "All right," replied the young man, "but I will need a cart to carry the food." So they gave him what he needed and he set off.

On their way, the horse explained to him, "When we get to the middle of the forest, release one of the oxen and call the woodcutters. The Kulshedra will hear you and rush forth to devour you. But don't worry! Seize it by the ear and put it to the yoke." Hardly had the horse finished explaining when they found themselves in the middle of the forest. The young man released an ox and called the woodcutters. The Kulshedra heard him calling and set upon him, but the young man simply seized it by the ear and put it to the yoke in place of the ox. Then they returned quickly to the king. When the townspeople saw the Kulshedra under the yoke, they were horrified and hid in their houses. The horse then told the young man to release the Kulshedra, which he did.

The bride and groom slept with one another again, but the bride admitted that she had spent the night the same way as she had spent the others. This time the courtiers said, "We'll send him to water the wild mare who devours all living creatures. She will devour him too." The young man overheard everything again and returned despondently to his horse that asked him why he was so sad. The young man recounted, "I escaped from the Kulshedra, but now I am supposed to water a mare which devours all living creatures." "Don't be afraid," said the horse, "she is my mother. Just ask the king for two pails of honey." A little later, the king summoned him and told him to water the mare. The young man then requested two pails of honey, which he received, and set off with his horse.

On their way, the horse said to him, "When we get to the well, draw two pails of water out, pour the two pails of honey into the well and mix everything well. Then hang your saddle nearby so that the mare can see it, and climb up a tall tree. When the mare arrives, she will drink the water, see the golden saddle and say, 'Such sweet water and such a golden saddle! I need a human to sit on me and play with me!' You shout down, 'Here I am, but I'm afraid you will eat me.' She will say, 'No, I won't', and you reply, 'Swear by the head of Demirçil the horse.' She will swear by my head and you can then climb down and mount her."

The young man did as the horse had told him. The mare arrived, drank some water, looked at the golden saddle and said, "Such sweet water and such a golden saddle! I need a human to sit on me and play with me!" The young man shouted, "Here I am, but I'm afraid you will eat me." "No, I won't." "Swear by the head of Demirçil the horse." She swore and he climbed down the tree, mounted the mare and rode around with her. The mare then said, "I would be even happier if Demirçil were here." "I have your son here too," said the young man, called his horse and they all frolicked together.

After a while, the young man and his horse returned to the town and the mare accompanied them. When the townspeople saw the wild mare coming, they scream at it to frighten it off. But the mare would not leave. Finally her son begged her to return home and promised her that he would come to play with her again. And so she departed.

The groom returned to the king and slept with the bride once more. Again nothing happened. This time the king resolved to send the young man to a church full of snakes to collect the taxes which the snakes had not been paying for years. The young man overheard everything from behind the door and returned despondently to his horse. The horse asked, "Why are you so sad, my lord?" "This time I am really going to die," he replied, "the king is going to send me to a church full of snakes." "Don't worry," responded the horse, "ask for a waggon covered with bells and for some donkeys to transport the money." The young man did as the horse had said and his father-in-law told him that he would have to go to the church. When they left, they took the wild mare with them, and the horse and mare explained to the young man what he had to do. "My mother and I," said the stallion, "will guard the doors and neigh loudly. You climb in through the window with all the bells and ring them. The snakes will then cry out and ask whether we are gods come to torture them. You demand the king's taxes and say that God will destroy them if they don't pay up."

When they got to the church, they did everything as planned. The snakes were so frightened by the bells and the noise the horses were making that they brought out heaps of money. When the three were on their way home, the snakes slithered after them and set upon the young man, but were unable to do him any harm.

Then they cursed him, saying, "If you who have taken our money away are a boy, may you be transformed into a girl, and if you are a girl, may you be transformed into a boy," and the girl suddenly realized that she had been turned into a boy.

They returned to the king and when the bride and groom got up the next morning, the young woman, on being asked how she had spent the night, replied, "You don't need to ask any more questions. I spent a wonderful night."

The fairy tale is over and wishes you all the best.

8.   The Maiden in the Box

Once upon a time there was a poor old woman who had one son. When the boy grew up, she said to him, "We are poor folk, my son. Now that you are grown up, you will have to look for a job so that we can live. I cannot feed you any longer." The son realized that his mother was right and said to her, "Mother, I am not fit for hard work. Let us write to my godfather, the merchant in Smyrna. Let him take me on. Then I can send you money so that you will be cared for." So they wrote to his godfather who agreed right away to take the boy on. The mother made him some clothes and sent him by ship to Smyrna. When he arrived, his godfather received him kindly and gave him a job in his shop. And since the godfather had no wife, he gave the boy money so that he would go to market and cook the meals.

One day, when the boy was sitting in front of the shop, he saw a porter carrying a box, shouting: "Box for sale! Whoever buys it will regret it, and whoever does not will regret it too." When the boy heard this, he was intrigued for a long time by the strange words and then asked the porter how much he wanted for the box. "Five hundred piastres, my lad," he replied. The boy, who had managed to save just that amount of money from his wages, paid the porter and took the box. He placed the box in a corner of the shop, hidden from his godfather. The following day was a Sunday and the boy went to market. Afterwards, he went to church, intending to make dinner as soon as he got back. When he left the church and went home to the shop, he found that dinner had already been prepared, a meal as good as any cook could make. He thought to himself, "Well, well, my godfather made the meal himself because I wasn't here." When the godfather arrived, the meal was served and they sat down to eat. The godfather tasted the delicious food and said to Constantine, as the boy was called, "I bet you, my son, that not even the king is enjoying such a wonderful meal today. You are the best cook in the land." The boy, who thought that his godfather had cooked the meal and was just making fun of him, blushed and said nothing.

The next day, he bought some fish, took it home and went off to work. He intended to cook the fish for lunch. When he finished work, he returned home and found that the fish had been cooked already, and in such a delicious manner that the whole neighbourhood was enticed by the smell. "Oh," he thought, "my godfather has done my job once again." The godfather arrived and they sat down to eat. The godfather found the meal so delicious that he did not know how to praise the boy enough. Now the boy realized that his godfather had not made the meal at all and he was completely confused.

The next day he took home all the food he had bought, but instead of going to work he hid in the cupboard. All of a sudden, he saw a maiden step out of the box he had bought. The whole house radiated with her beauty. She immediately put on an apron and began to cook. He crept out of his hiding place, knelt before her and asked her if she was a human being or an angel. She answered, "Fear not, I am a human being. I am the daughter of the King of Egypt. One day, while spending the summer in Smyrna, I saw you and immediately fell in love with you because you are so handsome. When I returned to my father in Egypt, he wanted to give me away in marriage. But since I loved only you and knew that my father would never give me to you, I said to him, 'I shall not marry.' He became furious and ordered his servants to put me in a box and sell me secretly far away from Egypt. I asked the man to take me to Smyrna and sell me to you. So let us wait and see what my father intends to do, for he has no other children."

When the boy heard that she was the daughter of a king, he fell to his knees again. But she caused him to rise and kissed him. Then they got married in secret, without telling his godfather. The next day, Constantine went in search of a ship and spoke to its captain, saying, "I am going to bring you a box. Take good care of it, as you would of your own eyes, and take it to my mother." He then brought the box with the maiden in it to the captain who transported it with a letter to Constantine's mother. In the letter, Constantine wrote that the woman in the box was his wife. The old woman received her with great love and kindness.

One day, a Jew came to the old woman's house and, seeing the beautiful maiden, was seized with a passion to win her. Whenever he saw her at the door, he would immediately go up to sell his wares, but the maiden always went back into the house right away. The Jew returned day after day to see her, but she hid from him. He sent people to talk to her, but she refused to see them. Then the Jew became frustrated and wrote a letter to Constantine saying, "Your wife lets young men into the house without your mother's knowledge. She is a wicked woman."

When Constantine read the letter, he was so angry that he left Smyrna immediately and returned home. From her window, the maiden saw him coming. She ran down the stairs to open the door and gave him a kiss. There was a large river next to the house. When Constantine saw his wife, he was so furious that he did not wait to ask whether what the Jew had written him was true or not. Instead, he seized her and threw her into the river. Then he entered the house and asked his mother about the maiden. The mother told him everything the Jew had done to win the maiden and that she had always rejected his advances.

Constantine was so grieved that he wanted to die. He ran down to the river and had people search everywhere to see whether his wife had drowned. As she was nowhere to be seen, he took flight, like a madman, to the mountains.

Some fishermen were just spreading their nets when the maiden fell into the river and they fished her out of the water, half drowned, and wrapped her in a cloak. A Turk came along to buy fish. The fishermen said that they had caught nothing but a woman. When the Turk saw her, his heart was ablaze and he bought her from the fishermen for fifty thousand piastres. When the young woman woke up, she found herself beside the Turk. She recalled what had happened to her and asked the Turk, "What are you going to do with me now? If you take me with you and another man stronger than you sees me, he will take me away from you. Do you know what we should do? Give me some of your clothes so that I can dress up like a man. Then no one will know I am a woman and you can keep me." He agreed. She took the clothes, went behind a bush and got dressed. The Turk's horse was grazing nearby and, when she had finished changing, she mounted it and rode off. When the Turk wondered why she had not come back, he went in search of her, but she was gone. The poor man then set off too, half-naked and without his horse.

The maiden rode for hours on end, from mountain to mountain, all through the night, until she arrived, without knowing it, in Egypt where her father reigned. Since the gates of the capital city were already closed and it was raining, she sat down outside.

At that time in Egypt, the king had just died and, since he had left no heir, his ministers took counsel and sent emissaries off in search of his daughter, who according to the king was lost. They searched for days but could not find her, and because the country needed a new king, the ministers said, "Since we have no child of the king, we shall, after this dreadful night of wind and rain in which anyone outside would have perished, take as our king the first person we see outside the city gates tomorrow morning."

The next morning the maiden, still dressed as a man, almost dead from the cold and unaware of what was to happen, saw the gates being opened and the guards marching out. She mounted her horse and rode to the side to let them by. When they saw the handsome young man, they knelt at his feet, brought him into the palace and made him king.

The maiden ruled wisely and no one knew that she was a woman. She reigned over the kingdom so well that everyone loved her. Indeed, she was so loved by the people that they put her picture up at every public fountain in the country so that everyone fetching water would see her. The girl secretly ordered her servants to watch out for anyone who sighed on seeing her picture. They were to arrest him, take him to the palace and keep him there as long as she wished.

One day the Jew who had written Constantine the letter came by and, seeing the picture, sighed. When the royal servants noticed this, they arrested him and took him to the palace. The next day, the fishermen came by and sighed too when they saw the picture. So they were also taken to the palace. Then the Turk came by and he too was arrested when he sighed. Sometime later, the husband happened to pass by a fountain and, seeing the picture, cried out, "It looks just like her. Oh, how I wish I hadn't lost her!" He broke into tears and was therefore taken to the palace, too.

When the maiden saw that all those who had wanted to have her had been gathered together, she ordered her ministers to assemble in order to announce to her prisoners the sentences she would pass. They all assembled and she sat down as king in the middle of the room. She then had all the prisoners brought in and gave orders that none of them should speak without her permission. The king then began by asking, "Jew, why did you sigh when you saw the picture at the fountain? Be careful not to lie or I'll have your head chopped off immediately!" The Jew replied, "What can I tell you, oh king? I saw that it was the picture of a woman." He then proceeded to tell the whole truth, including the letter he had written because the maiden had refused to marry him. When he was finished, the king said to him, "Good, you have told the truth, sit at the side over there." When the husband heard the Jew telling how he had slandered his wife, he rushed forth to strike him, but the king cried out, "Stay where you are, or you'll be sorry!" And he stayed put.

The king then asked the fishermen why they had sighed. They answered that they had fished the woman out of the river and sold her to a Turk. "And you," said the king to the Turk, "why did you sigh?" "I am the one," he said, "who bought her. But she ran away from me before I got a chance to see her properly and took my clothes and my horse." The ministers were puzzled and looked at the king, but she gave a sign that they should remain silent.

Then she asked her husband, "And why did you sigh?" "Oh, what an unhappy man I am," he answered with tears in his eyes, "I was her husband and now I have lost her." "No," she replied, "you haven't lost her at all. Wait for a moment until I come back."

She went out of the room, changed into the women's clothes she had worn when she was living with her husband and came in again. When the men saw her, their eyes bulged in amazement. The ministers recognized her as the daughter of the king, and her husband and the others recognized her as the maiden. First her husband came up to her, fell to his knees and asked for forgiveness. She caused him to rise, kissed him and had him sit at her side. She gave money to the fishermen and to the Turk. She pardoned the Jew whom the minister wanted to hang, but ordered him to leave her kingdom within twenty-four hours. The heralds then announced that the king's daughter had been found and there was great feasting. Constantine was made king and they have been feasting right up to the present day.

9. The Tale of the Youth Who Understood the Language of the Animals

Once upon a time there was a youth who was neither poor nor rich. He owned a team of oxen and a herd of sheep and had a garden with many different fruit trees growing in it. Whenever the young man was in his garden and people passed by, he would invite them in and allow them to pick and eat whatever fruit they liked.

One day, when the young man was in his garden, a monk came by, so the young man invited him in, saying, "Won't you come in and have something to eat?" The monk entered the garden and ate all he wanted. As the monk was about to leave, the young man said, "Take some fruit with you so you'll have something to eat on your way." The monk replied, "I am full. I don't need anything more, but I would like you to tell me your wishes so that I can give you something too." The young man retorted, "What could you give me?" "Whatever you want," said the monk, "I can make you very rich. I can make you king. Or do you want the trees and stones to talk to you? I can give you honours, or would you like to learn the language of the birds and the animals? Which of these things would you like? Tell me and I will give it to you." The young man answered that he would like to learn the language of the animals. The monk replied, "Then you will be able to understand their language, but don't tell anyone or you will die." The young man agreed, saying, "I won't tell anyone. Please teach it to me!" All the monk then said was, "May you know it!" On hearing these words, the young man could suddenly understand what the animals were saying. He got up, went home and could now understand everything the birds and animals were talking about.

One evening he went out for a walk with his wife. They passed by the stable where the oxen, a mare, a donkey and other animals were kept. As they passed by, he overheard an ox talking to the donkey. The ox said to the donkey, "You don't have any problems. You eat the same grass as I do and they leave you alone. As for me, the master

50

yokes me to the plough and I have to pull it all day long. They don't give me any food either. I have to forage for myself. They leave you alone and bring you food." The donkey replied, "The humans are right when they say that oxen are stupid. God has given you horns instead of brains." "Well, let me ask you a question," said the ox, "if you are so clever. Tell me what I can do so that I won't have to work." "Tomorrow morning," replied the donkey, "when the stable-boy comes to take you out to the field, pretend you're sick. Drool and don't eat any grass this evening and the stable-boy will think you really are sick. Then he'll leave you alone."

Thus spoke the donkey and the master heard everything from outside where he was sitting and listening. The wife asked him what he was listening to. "I'm only looking to see if the oxen are all right," the man replied, and they went back into the house. The next morning the stable-boy went out to get the oxen and take them to the field, and found that one ox was sick. He ran to his master right away and reported what had happened. The master replied, "Let the ox be sick. Leave him alone today. Take the donkey instead and yoke him to the plough with the other oxen." So the stable-boy went back, took the donkey and yoked him to the plough. The donkey had to work all day long until the sun set. He was so exhausted from his work that he could hardly walk. When he got back and they put him in the stable, the master went out to hear what the donkey would say to the ox. The donkey asked the ox, "Are you all right?" "I did what you told me," replied the ox. "Well, get up quickly," stated the donkey, "and eat your grass. You'll have to be in good health by the time the stable-boy gets back. Our master has been talking to the butcher, and if you're still sick, they're going to slaughter you tomorrow."

When the ox heard this, he got up and began eating. He gobbled up the grass in front of him all at once. When the master, standing outside the stable, heard the nonsense the donkey had told the ox and saw how the ox was eating everything up, he had to laugh. His wife noticed him laughing and said, "What are you laughing about all by yourself like an idiot?" "Oh, I was just thinking of something," said the man. But she would not give up and said, "No, you're not thinking about anything. I think you can understand the language of the animals." "No I can't," he replied, "I just had to laugh."

A few days later, the lambs were to be separated from the mother sheep and taken up to the mountain pastures according to custom. And so the young man, his wife and their little son set off. The wife was pregnant again. Before they set off, she packed all sorts of things onto a mare which the man mounted, setting his son in front of him. When they had gone a ways, the wife said, "Let me ride too. I am getting tired." So she mounted the mare too, although it was in foal. When they had gone a bit further, the mare's foal, plodding along at its mother's side, said to its mother, "Pull me. I'm getting tired." The mare replied, "You're walking all by yourself and you say you're tired? I have four humans and a lot of baggage to lug and I'm carrying another foal. I can't allow myself to get tired. I can't wait for you any longer. Keep up with me if you want or fall behind."

Since the man understood what the mare had said to her foal, he had his wife dismount. But his wife was still tired and was unwilling to get off. Indeed she got very angry. Finally they arrived at the mountain hut. The shepherds were busy catching a little lamb to slaughter and eat when they saw the man coming. The little lamb bleated, crying to its mother, "They're going to get me, they're going to slaughter me!" The sheep replied, "Alas, what can I do about it, my son? There's nothing I can do! The jackals devour some of us and the humans eat the rest. Now they've got you too and the master is going to eat you. Just let them do what they want. We are in their hands." The master said to one of the shepherds, "Let that little lamb go, and catch another one." So they let it go and caught another lamb. But the second one began to cry too, calling for help from its mother, who answered, "May the master spare you! They've killed all the other lambs I've given birth to. And now they've got you, and will get me and all the other sheep too. There's nothing I can do about it. The master does as he wishes." The man told the shepherds to let the second lamb go, so they caught a third one which began to cry. Its mother replied, "I still have all the five lambs I've given birth to. The master hasn't eaten any of mine. One of them will have to be sacrificed." The master then told the shepherds they could roast the lamb. And so the shepherds slaughtered it, roasted and ate it. Afterwards they separated the little lambs from the mother sheep. The master remained in the mountain pastures, sleeping in a hut with his wife.

In the night, jackals and wolves appeared, surrounding the sheep and howling. They said to the dogs, "Stay where you are. We're coming to get meat, but we'll leave some for you." The man owned two young dogs whom the shepherds cared for with love and affection and fed well. They got everything they wanted to eat. He also owned an old dog who had only two teeth left. All the others had fallen out. Sometimes they only gave the poor old dog a slice of bread, other times they gave him nothing at all. When the jackals and wolves ordered the dogs to stay put, the two young dogs replied, "We will bark, but we won't come near you. Leave a sheep here near us tomorrow so we will have something to eat." But the old dog said to the wild animals, "I am going to drive you away. I have two teeth left, and I'm going to sink them into your hides. My master has just arrived and I would be ashamed of myself if I didn't. I have been living off his bread."

The master understood what the two young dogs and the old one had said. The next morning he got up early to return home. On departing he said to the shepherds, "Call the dogs!" They assembled the dogs and the masters gave orders, saying, "Kill the two young dogs and give the old one some meat and milk." The shepherds thought they had heard wrong and asked him, "We are to kill the young dogs and let the old one live?" The master replied, "Do as I have told you. Kill them right away in my presence." So whether they wanted to or not, the shepherds had to kill the two young dogs and let the old one live.

When they had been home for some time, the wife began to weep and lament. Every time the husband gave her a chore she would groan and refuse to do it. Finally he asked her what was wrong. She replied, "What do you mean? I can see that you don't love me the way other men love their wives." "What kind of love do you mean?" asked the man, "I love you. We eat together, we drink together, we sleep together. What more do you want?" "If you really loved me," she retorted, "you would tell me everything you know." "What do you mean?" he inquired, and she said, "You were out two nights at the stable listening and laughing to yourself. Then, when we went up to the mountain hut, I had to get off the mare when it started neighing with its foal. Up in the pastures you only let them slaughter the third lamb. Yesterday morning, you had the two young dogs killed and let the old one live. You know something you're not telling me about."

Finally, the man said to her, "All right, I'll tell you, though I'll suffer greatly for it, because it will be the death of me." The wife replied, "Go ahead and tell me, then you can die as far as I'm concerned." The man said, "Get some bread and porridge ready, because I know I shall die as soon as I've told you." While he talked, she got the food ready. She baked a loaf of bread, cooked the porridge, waiting impatiently for her husband to tell her everything, and was quite willing to let him die.

There was a dog in the house who understood what was happening and began to whimper. The man also had a lot of hens, and with them was a rooster. While the dog was whining, the rooster called the hens to him and beat his wings proudly so that the hens began to tremble and ducked down, pecking at the ground. The rooster gathered all the hens around him and then took his pleasure with them. The dog said to the rooster, "Aren't you ashamed of yourself, rooster? Don't you feel sorry for our master? He is about to die and you have no sense of shame. You are crowing and taking your pleasure with the hens!" The rooster replied, "For heaven's sake! I love our master because he gives grain to me and my wives. I have forty wives and only have to beat my wings for them to tremble. But he has only one wife and this wife has persuaded him to reveal his secret. And now he is to die! He should do something!" "What should he do?" asked the dog. The rooster replied, "If our master would listen to me, he would take his wife and lock her up. Then he would take a club of young hornbeam and beat her black and blue. That's what he should do!"

The master understood what the rooster had said and did just that. He called his wife but instead of telling her his secret, he gave her a sound thrashing, threw her out and found himself another wife.

10.   The Stirrup Moor

Once upon a time there was a king who owned a mare. It was his own personal mare and no one else was allowed to ride it. The mare had never had a foal. Nor did the king have any children. One day, he saddled the mare and rode out to find a potion so that his wife could bear children and the mare could have a foal. On his way, the king met an old man who asked him where he was going. The king replied, "I have set out to find a remedy because my mare, which I've had for ten years now, is infertile and my wife hasn't had any children either." The old man said, "Here, take this apple. Go home and peel it, and give the apple to the queen and the peelings to the mare. Then they will both become pregnant and give birth." The king took the apple and returned to his palace. He gave the apple to the queen and the peelings to the mare, as the old man had told him to do. Both became pregnant and gave birth: the queen had a son with a star on his forehead and the mare had a foal with a star on its forehead. The king gave the stallion to his son and no one else was allowed to ride it. Everyone marvelled when the two rode out together.

Time passed and the youth turned twenty. He loved to hunt and went out every day with his stallion. One day, he lost his way and came to a river as big as the Vjosa. As he was riding along the bank of the river he saw a beautiful maiden on the other side who was also out hunting with her servants and hounds. The maiden was the daughter of a king, but her father was king of the jinns. She was therefore a jinn maiden, not a human being. When the youth saw the beautiful maiden he fell in love with her and returned day after day to the same place to see her. One day, he could stand it no longer. He spurred on his stallion and they leapt over the river to the other side. He then approached the maiden and spoke to her. The maiden asked him, "What are you doing on my land?" "I want to ask you a question," replied the youth, "I am so full of longing for you. Do you love me or not?" The maiden looked at the handsome youth and fell in love with him, saying, "I love you five times more than you love me, but nothing will come of our love because of our families. Your father is a king and my father is a king, but your father is king of the humans and mine is king of the jinns. It simply won't work out." "But what can we do to stay together?" pleaded the youth, "for I will never give you up." The maiden took a piece of toast out of her pocket and said to the youth, "Take this piece of toast and go back home. When you get there, pretend you are deathly ill and don't eat anything they give you. Eat this toast instead when no one is watching. Then they will ask you what you want. Whenever they ask you, say you want nothing at all. In the end, they will ask you: Wouldn't you like a girl? Just sigh deeply and they will understand that you love me and that we can't be together." Then the two separated.

The youth went home and became ill. They brought him food, but he would eat none of it. The king sent for all his physicians, for he had only one son, and he had no peer on earth. But however much the physicians examined him, they could not find out what was wrong. At that time, one of the king's shepherds was on his way to bring the king a lamb and a gardener was on his way, too, to bring the king a melon. The two met on the road and asked one another where they were going. "I'm going to see the king," said the first one. "So am I," said the second, "because his son is ill." They continued on their way and arrived at the palace where they offered their gifts. On seeing the youth, the gardener realized immediately that he wasn't ill at all, but was in love. So he said, "Send all the people out of the room. You go too, my lord. Leave me alone with the youth. I think I can cure him." The king replied, "I do hope so," and sent everyone out of the room, leaving the gardener alone with the youth.

The gardener began by asking the youth what he wanted and mentioned all sorts of things. The youth replied time and time again, "There is nothing I want." Finally the gardener asked, "Would you like the daughter of the king of the jinns?" The youth sighed deeply and replied, "Yes, indeed I would." The gardener then said, "I will tell the king and when you get up, everything will be arranged." The gardener went back to the king and said to him, "The youth is now in good health and has gotten up. As you can see, he has gone out to see his stallion. He had simply fallen in love with the daughter of the king of the jinns. You must bring her here as a bride for your son, otherwise he will be so distraught in his longing that you will lose him." The king agreed right away. He sent a message to the king of the jinns inviting him to a banquet.

When the king of the jinns arrived, they celebrated for a whole week, eating, drinking, listening to music and playing games. Then the king of the humans said to the king of the jinns, "We have finally gotten to know one another and from now on we shall be friends. But I would like to go even further." "As you wish," replied the king of the jinns. "Give me your daughter as a wife for my son," said the king, "then we will be relatives." "Fine, I agree," said the king of the jinns. And so, the two kings became relatives and exchanged rings. When the king of the jinns returned home, his wife greeted him and asked him, "How was it at the king's banquet?" He replied, "They received me with hospitality and great honour and then we became relatives, for I have given our daughter in marriage to the king's son." When the queen heard this, she screamed, "You want me to give my daughter to the humans? Never! If you agreed to that, you did a very wicked thing!" She then stood up, took her daughter by the hand and went off to another corner of the world where another king of the jinns lived. She took her daughter there and left her with the other king of the jinns. Later, the mother died leaving the maiden all alone.

When the son of the king of the humans heard that the maiden had been taken away, he became ill again and went to his stallion to tell him his tale of woe. The stallion said to him, "Since you are going to die of longing for the maiden, go to your father and ask him to have his servants bring you your best clothes and to have them saddle me with two pouches of money. Then say to him: I want to go out into the courtyard and ride my stallion before I die, because I cannot give up the ghost without have ridden my stallion one last time with my best clothes on." The youth did as the stallion had told him. Though the king agreed to all his son's requests, he had guardsmen posted and locked the gates so that the youth couldn't ride away. The youth went out of the palace, mounted his stallion and rode around in the courtyard for a while and then, suddenly, he shouted, "Farewell, father!" His father hardly had time to shout, "Catch them!" before the stallion and the youth had leapt over the walls and galloped off.

On their way, they arrived at a house with no doors or windows. A beautiful maiden who had seven brothers lived there. The brothers were off fighting with the king of Russia because he wanted to marry their sister and they had refused to give her up. They had therefore gone to war and had been fighting for five years. When the youth approached the house, which was more like a fortress, he took out his sword and struck the wall with it. A doorway opened where he had struck and the youth went through. On entering the house, he encountered the maiden all alone. She asked him, "Who are you and how did you get in here? There is a mighty king who has been fighting with my brothers for five years. No one is allowed to enter here." The youth replied, "I haven't come to do you any harm. I just want to see what's going on. Tell me where your brothers are and I will go and make friends with them." She replied, "My brothers are at the beach because some ships full of soldiers are coming tomorrow to do battle with them. The youth went out and struck the wall again, and the doorway disappeared. He went off to find the seven brothers. When he found them, they sat down to talk and he asked what they were doing there. They told him their problem, "Ten ships full of soldiers are coming tomorrow and we will have to fight." The youth replied, "Don't be afraid. I will stay here and fight with you."

The next day, the ships full of soldiers arrived and the seven brothers got up to go into battle. The youth, however, said to them, "Wait a moment, let them get off the ships first, then we will charge and do battle with them." "But there are so many of them," said the brothers, "and only a handful of us. Once they get off the ships, we are lost." The youth retorted, "Stay here and don't worry." So they let the soldiers get off the ships. The king's son got up and mounted his stallion, stroking its mane and the forehead with a star on it. Then he took off his fez and set upon the soldiers. The two of them shone so brightly that the soldiers were blinded, and the youth was able to charge into their midst and slay almost all of them. He let a few of them live so that they would return home with their ships to tell the tale of their disaster. Then the youth returned to the brothers who took him home to their house nearby.

The soldiers who had survived reported to the king of Russia, "You have lost many soldiers, for there was a man there who shone as bright as the sun that we couldn't see to fight him." When the king of Russia heard this, he decided to give up.

The seven brothers took the king's son home with them and kept him there for a month because they were afraid that the enemy would return. But no one came. Then they said to the youth, "You have saved us. Let us become brothers. We will give you our sister in marriage." The youth replied, "All right, but I actually love the daughter of the king of the jinns and have set off to find her. When I return, I will take your sister with me." And so they exchanged rings. The youngest of the seven brothers said he would accompany the youth. They kissed one another, said farewell and the two of them departed.

On their way, they saw an inn in the distance. The stallion said to the youth, "Do you see that inn? A Moor lives there who always sets a table at the roadside, but no one stops there to eat because everyone is afraid of him. His table is made of gold and so are the dishes, the plates, the spoons and the forks. You won't even see that much gold at the king's table. "Now," continued the stallion, "we are getting closer to the inn. We'll leave the boy here at the river so that no one can see him and go on ahead. When we approach the table, you get off and eat. But you'll have to be quick and get back on me right away because the Moor has a mare that is swifter than any stallion on earth. We are now approaching someone selling hides. Buy five buffalo hides and cover my body with them, and put the saddle over them." The youth did as the stallion had told him. He went over to the tanner, bought the hides, put them on the stallion and rode to the inn. There he found the table, got off and had something to eat. The Moor went over to the window and asked, "Who is down there?" The youth continued eating and didn't answer. Then the Moor went out and mounted his mare. The youth finished eating and jumped on his stallion. When the Moor's horse passed through the entrance to the inn, it neighed and the whole place was transformed into a lake so that the youth's stallion and the mare were up to their bellies in water. The mare immediately set upon the stallion and the stallion upon the mare. The mare bit into the stallion and ripped off a whole buffalo hide in one piece. The stallion bit into the mare and broke one of its ribs. By the time the five buffalo hides had been torn off, the stallion and the mare were both exhausted. All the mare's ribs had been broken and the two horses fell to the ground. The Moor and the youth fought with their swords. But no matter how often they struck one another, neither one was ever wounded. After the sword-fight, they wrestled with their bare hands, but neither of them could win. When they got tired and had no energy left at all, the Moor said, "You are very strong indeed. Let us become brothers. I have seen the whole world, but I have never seen a person like you." The youth replied, "All right, let us become brothers, although I don't really trust you yet." So the Moor gave his word and they trusted one another. The Moor took the youth with him and they went back to the inn. They called the other boy, took the horses with them and all went in together.

The black man, however, was not a real Moor, but the Earthly Beauty. When they entered the inn, the Moor went into another room to make coffee. There he took off his black skin and became the Earthly Beauty he actually was. Then he brought in the coffee, shook hands with everyone and welcomed them. When the men saw the beautiful girl, they began to tremble. The girl went back into the other room, put on the black skin again, and returned as the Moor, saying to the king's son, "Did you see my sister who brought you the coffee?" "Yes, I did," said the youth. The Moor continued, "I would like you to have her for your wife." "All right, I'll take her," said the king's son, "but first I have to find the daughter of the king of the jinns, then I'll come back and take her with me." And so they agreed and exchanged rings. Then the Moor said, "It is I who am the girl." He took off his black skin and everyone could see that he was the beautiful girl. The Moor, who was now called the Stirrup Moor, said to the youth, "You won't be able to find the maiden you're looking for all by yourself." He replied, "You are right. Let us go together if you it's all right with you." And so they spent a month at the house of the Stirrup Moor and, once the mare had recovered, the three of them set off.

They travelled a long, long way and eventually they arrived in another world. There, they came to a big river that was spanned by a bridge made of two parts. One part of the bridge was on one side of the river and the other part was on the other side. When they got to the bridge, the Stirrup Moor said, "We have arrived, so listen to what I have to say because you will have to repeat it to cross the bridge. Otherwise it will collapse and you will drown." The Stirrup Moor went up to the bridge and said, "It's me, bridge. I want to cross, but I can't cross you like that." The two parts of the bridge then rose and joined to make one bridge. The Stirrup Moor walked onto the bridge and crossed over. The others said the same thing and they too were able to cross to the other side.

Finally they reached the place where the daughter of the king of the jinns was living and entered the house of an old woman to spend the night. There they heard music, gun salutes, songs and dances as if a marriage were being celebrated in town and asked the old woman if someone was getting married. She replied, "Oh yes, the daughter of the king of the jinns is getting married. Another king is taking her away with him." The Stirrup Moor asked, "When is the bridegroom coming to get her?" "In three days," answered the old woman. The Moor then addressed the old woman again, saying, "Here is a handful of money for you. Go to the maiden and whisper in her ear that the son of the king of the humans has come and wants to meet her. And bring us her answer." The old woman agreed, saying, "All right, I'll go," And off she went.

When she got to the palace gate, she began to prattle with the maiden's servants the way old women do, "I want to see your mistress. Let me through." But the servants wouldn't let her in, and she began to shout. The mistress overheard her and asked her servants why the old woman was shouting. On hearing the answer of the servants, the maiden said, "Let her in."

And so the old woman went in to see the maiden, kissed her and whispered in her ear, "The son of the king of the humans has come to meet you." The maiden then gave orders to her servants, saying, "Go and cut off a branch from the big apple tree at the end of the little garden." And they went and cut the branch off, and the maiden began beating the old woman with it. The old woman screamed and ran home lamenting and cursing, "You go and see her yourself. The king's daughter has beaten me because of you." When the Stirrup Moor heard what had happened, he calmed the old woman down and asked her what the maiden had said. He gave her more money and she told him, "The mistress sent for a branch from the big apple tree at the end of the little garden." The Stirrup Moor then took the youth aside and said to him, "Go and sit under the big apple tree tonight. I'll come too, so don't be afraid. I'll wait outside and keep watch." And so the youth entered the garden that evening and sat down under the apple tree. At midnight, the king's daughter arrived and found the youth asleep. She said nothing, but put a handful of sweets in his pocket and departed.

Next morning, the Moor came and asked the youth, "What did she say?" "She didn't come," he replied. The Moor examined the youth, took a look at his pocket and saw the sweets. "What did you put in your pocket last night?" he asked. "Nothing," replied the youth. "What are those sweets you have in your pocket then?" When the youth noticed the sweets, he was amazed. The Stirrup Moor then said,

"She was here, but you were asleep. If we want to win her, we will have to send the old woman to the king's daughter again to find out what she has to say." And so they went back to the old woman, and with great difficulty the Stirrup Moor managed to persuade her to return to the maiden. He gave her a great deal of money and sent her off. The daughter of the king of the jinns was already waiting at the window. When she saw the old woman coming, she gave orders, saying, "Let the old woman in." The old woman entered and repeated what she had said the first time. The mistress then sent for a rod from a little apple tree in the middle of the big garden and used it to beat the old woman who fled home once more screaming.

The Stirrup Moor asked the old woman what had happened, and she explained about the rod the maiden had used to beat her. The Moor then took the youth to the little apple tree in the middle of the big garden. The king's daughter got up at midnight and found the youth asleep again. She took his fez, left him hers and departed. When the youth got up the next morning, he met the Stirrup Moor who asked him about the maiden. "She didn't come," said the youth. The Stirrup Moor then asked, "Which fez were you wearing last night?" "My own," replied the youth. "Look at the fez you're wearing now," said the Stirrup Moor. The youth looked at the fez and was amazed.

So they went back to the old woman and forced her to return to the maiden again. What did the mistress do this time? She sent for her servants saying, "Bring back a bunch of nettles from the end of the big garden." When the servants brought the nettles, she took them, threw the old woman to the ground and beat her with the nettles until she was covered in blisters from head to toe. The old woman fled home screaming and cursing, saying that she was going to throw all of them out of her house. The Stirrup Moor calmed her down again and gave her more money. The old woman then told him where the nettles had come from.

The Moor took the youth, set him in the place where the nettles grew, grabbed a bunch of them, shook them and stung the youth so that he could not sleep. At midnight, the king's daughter appeared and this time found the youth awake. "What are you doing here?" she asked. He replied that he had come to marry her. She retorted, "I would like to marry you, but it wouldn't be that easy. There are jinns here too. I could get away; they couldn't catch me. But you would never get away." "What should we do?" inquired the youth. She explained, "I must leave tomorrow morning because the groom's attendants are coming to get me. There is one thing you could do to save me, but someone would have to sacrifice himself." "Tell me what it is," said the youth, "what can I do?" She replied, "When I leave tomorrow morning, there is a mosque at a certain point along the road. There I will tell the groom's attendants that I promised my mother I would go into the mosque to pray before getting married. They will let me enter the mosque alone. If someone else were already in the mosque, I could give him my clothes and he could put them on and go back out as the bride. Then we would be able to flee together." She then promised that she would return to him from the mosque.

The youth went back to the Stirrup Moor and told him everything. "Where can we find someone willing to sacrifice himself?" asked the Moor. The little boy, the youngest of the seven brothers, interrupted saying, "I'll do it, I'll sacrifice my head. If I survive, I survive; if not, then I won't." The boy departed for the mosque. When the maiden arrived the next morning, she gave him her clothes, and he put them on and became the bride. The king's daughter met the Stirrup Moor and her new husband and they left together for the Moor's inn to await news of the boy dressed in the bride's clothes.

The false bride was brought to the king's palace to be married off. When the time came for her to be brought to the groom, she became ill and couldn't go. She stayed in her room all night in the company of the groom's eldest sister. The following night, the groom's youngest sister said that she too wanted to spend the night with the bride and her request was granted. She visited the bride, but soon discovered that she wasn't a real bride, but a young man. The girl said to him, "They haven't come for you yet... but if you want to marry me, we could escape together." He replied, "I would like to all right, but how can we escape?" "Let me worry about that," replied the girl. They got up and went off to the king's stable. There they chose the swiftest horses and mounted them. She tied the boy to the horse and to herself so that he wouldn't fall off.

One day, while the Stirrup Moor and the king's son were still at the inn, the boy and his bride arrived. The five of them then set off: the king's son with his two wives, the Stirrup Moor who was actually the Earthly Beauty and the daughter of the king of the jinns, and the boy and his bride, and returned to the other brothers who had remained at home. They were received hospitably by the brothers and stayed at their house for some time. Finally, the king's son took the sister of the seven brothers and set off together with his other wives. The youngest of the seven brothers still wanted to accompany them and the other brothers agreed. So he too set off with the king's son. The Stirrup Moor rebuilt his palace with everything in it right across from that of the king, the youth's father, and they all went to live in it: the youth with his wives and his brother-in-law with his wife.

One morning the king got up and was surprised to see a palace right across from his. He asked which palace it was and who had built it. His courtiers went out to have a look and reported, "That's the palace of the king's son." Later the son invited the father and all his courtiers to a banquet. While they were celebrating, the father fell in love with the son's young wives and said to him, "Let me have one of your wives." The son replied, "You already have a hundred wives and if you need more you can get them. I only have these three and don't want any more because I won them after great perils." And he would not give the king any of his wives.

The king returned to his palace and invited the son to a banquet. The youth arrived with his wives, his brother-in-law and wife and was received as hospitably as he had received the king. Once they had eaten, the king suggested, "Shall we play cards?" "All right," replied his son, "what shall we play for?" The father said, "If you win, you can put out my eyes, and if I win, I can put out your eyes." And so they began to play. The son won the first game and his father said to him, "You've won. Put out my eyes." "I don't want to deprive you of your eyesight," responded the youth, "let's play once more." They played once more and the son beat his father again. The father repeated, "Put out my eyes. You have won." "I can't put out your eyes. You are my father," replied the son. The father then declared, "If I had won, I would have put out your eyes, so blind me if you want to, because you have won."

They began to play again and this time the father beat the son saying, "Now I've won and I shall put out your eyes." The youth replied, "I beat you twice and didn't blind you and you want to put out my eyes after winning just once?" The king insisted that he had won, and because he wanted his wives, he had his son's eyes put out. The youth's three wives were away at a dance at the time. As the boy's eyes were being put out, the daughter of the king of the jinns realized what was happening and said to the Stirrup Moor, "What shall we do?

The king has blinded our husband to take us away from him." The wives and the youth's brother-in-law got up to return to their palace. When the king saw that they were going, he rushed to try and stop them. But the Stirrup Moor was so strong that he was able to fight the king off and even the whole army couldn't stop them.

After the king's servants had blinded the son, they threw him into a ravine for the birds to eat him. When they left, the youth managed to climb an oak tree to protect himself from the birds. There was a spring nearby where devils were gathering. The head of the devils asked the other devils, one after the other, what they had accomplished. The first one he asked was the devil who had possessed the king and made him blind his own son. He replied, "Today I made the king have his son's eyes put out." The head of the devils was very pleased and made him an officer. He then asked another devil who replied, "I went out today and peed on the sheep of a shepherd tending his flock up in the mountains. The sheep have fallen ill and will all die." The head of the devils made him an officer too. He then asked the next devil what he had done. He answered, "I tried the best I could, but I didn't accomplish anything." The head of the devils got angry and started to beat him. The devil began to sob and cried, "How is the king's son supposed to know that he must come to this spring, sprinkle sand from the spring in his eyes and rinse them with the water in order to regain his sight? And how is the shepherd to know that if he comes to the spring and sprinkles the water over the sheep, they will all get well?" Then a rooster crowed and the devils all disappeared.

When they were gone, the youth climbed down from the tree and walked in the direction of the voices. He got closer to the spring and, hearing it bubbling, groped forward to find it. Then he sprinkled sand in his eyes, scooped out some water, rinsed his eyes with it and regained his sight. Near the spring he found an empty gourd which the devils had left behind. He filled it with water and went off to the shepherd whose sheep were all dying and who was at the verge of killing himself. The youth asked the shepherd what he would give him if he saved his sheep. The shepherd replied, "Whatever you want. Just bring the sheep back to life. I only need to see them once and I'll give you whatever you want." "All I want is for you to make me some shepherd's clothes," said the youth, "but they must be fine-looking. I will give you my own clothes in exchange." Then the youth sprinkled water over the sheep and they came back to life. The shepherd took the youth home, gave him something to eat, made some fine clothes and presented them to him.

The youth then returned to his father who was in a very sad way because the Stirrup Moor had killed all his soldiers and because he hadn't gained the wives. The youth asked the king what was wrong and why he looked so despondent. The king replied, "What do I have left, shepherd? Don't you see that I have lost all my soldiers and that I can't have the wives I wanted?" The youth then asked, "What would you give me if I were to win them over all by myself?" The king replied, "I would give you half of my kingdom and we would reign together." "All right" responded the youth, "you give me half of your kingdom, but you must also give me one of the wives, any one you wish." "I agree," said the king.

The youth then went across to the Stirrup Moor's palace. The Moor had put on his black skin and was waiting for the enemy to come so that he could vanquish them. When the youth arrived, the Moor lunged at him with his lance. The youth deflected it with his hands and grappled with the Moor who began fighting with his bare hands too. The youth got closer and the Moor lunged at him again. When the Moor realized he couldn't win, he shouted to the others, "Now we are lost. This one is just as strong as our husband and will take us." The daughter of the king of the jinns took a look at him, and recognized the crooked tooth that showed when he laughed. She shouted, "Stop, it's our husband". Then they all recognized him, opened the door and let him in.

A little later, the youth sent a message to the king to tell him to come over because he was in the palace. The king happily rushed over to the palace and hugged and kissed the shepherd, still not knowing that it was his own son. The king and the son then went into a room, sat down and sent for the women. The king was overjoyed when they arrived. The shepherd declared that he now owned half of the kingdom and one of the wives, one that the king did not want. The king replied, "Which one should I give you? This one? Fine. Or that one? All the better. Or shall I give you the third one? She would be best. But no, I'll give you one of my nieces." "No," insisted the youth, "I want one of the wives. That's what we agreed to." The king could not bring himself to give one of his wives up and said to the shepherd, "Let us wait for a moment. Before we decide, we'll go through the rooms and see how they are decorated. If this palace if more beautiful than mine, I'll live here and you can have my palace." So they got up and visited all the rooms.

The Stirrup Moor had put the oven on and by the time they had gone through all the palace, it was very hot indeed. When they had seen all the rooms, the youth said, "Now, let's have a look at the kitchen," and they entered the kitchen where the oven was. Immediately, the Stirrup Moor seized the king and threw him into the oven where he was burnt to ashes. Thus, the king's son kept his three wives and became king. And so they lived and reigned happily ever after.

11.   The King's Daughter and the Skull

Once upon a time there was a king who had three daughters. One day he went out riding on his horse and rode past a palace surrounded by a moat. The horse got one of its legs stuck in the mire and could not extract it. A number of people happened by, but no one could help. As nighttime approached, the king swore, "I will give my eldest daughter to anyone who can get my horse's leg out of the moat!" The moment he swore the oath, the horse was able to extract its leg, though there was no one to be seen around them. The king rode home and told his daughter that she was to be married. He was quite sure that someone from the palace behind the moat had freed his horse and therefore took his daughter there.

The maiden entered the palace and waited a moment in the hall. A horrible Moor came out, opening a large door. And what did the poor girl see through the door but a skull! She went in trembling feverishly and the Moor said to her, "This is your husband. You must spend the rest of your life with him." The poor maiden was in the depths of despair and began to weep. What a sorrowful life with a skull!

The next morning, the father sent the old governess to the maiden to ask her how she was. When the maiden saw the governess, she threw her arms around her, weeping and begging to be taken home because she could not stand another minute. So the old woman took the daughter back to her father without saying a word. The king then sent his second eldest daughter, but she came back just as the first one had because she could not live with the horrible skull either. When the third daughter saw that her two sisters had returned home, she went to her father and said, "Father, send me to live with the skull. It doesn't matter what happens to me." "My dear daughter," replied the king, "you are the pet of the family and you are willing to marry the skull? Do you want to throw your whole life away? But go if you want!" "Yes, father, I'll go and try my luck," said the pretty maiden. And so, the old king sent his daughter off and was very sad to see her go. She too entered the hall where the Moor was waiting. Once again the skull came into the room, but the maiden was not afraid. She took the skull in her hands and stroked it, saying, "What a lucky girl I am to have such a wonderful husband!" Then she laid the skull in the corner of the room.

The next morning, the king despatched the governess who asked the maiden, "My girl, how did you spend the night? What was your husband like?" "It couldn't have been better, nanny, I have a husband without equals!" The governess returned home and reported what she had heard. The king was delighted, and the sisters were very curious. "Is it possible," they wondered, "to be happy with a skull?" Some time later, they sent the old governess back with a diamond brooch and had her ask their sister to buy it. The old woman went off to the happy maiden and asked her, "My girl, wouldn't you like to have this beautiful brooch?" "Oh yes I would, nanny," the clever maiden replied, "but I'll have to ask my husband, because he must like it too." Having said this, she accompanied the governess to the door, went up to her room and began to weep because she didn't know where to get the money to buy the brooch. The Moor came in as she was weeping and asked what the matter was. She told him her problem and the Moor went off to the skull which ordered, "Tell the mistress to get the key near the chimney, go into the other room and take as much money as she wants." The Moor reported what the skull had said and the maiden went off happily to the room and filled her pockets with money.

The next day, the governess returned and asked the maiden on behalf of her sisters, "Did you speak to your husband? Did he like the brooch?" "You know, nanny dear," the maiden replied, "he doesn't want to spoil my happiness. Look at all the money he's given me." The old woman's eyes opened wide. She was astounded, and all the more so because she knew the girl was married to a skull. Bewildered, she returned home. When the sisters heard what had happened they were green with envy. The next day they invited their sister to go to the baths with them. The old woman brought the sisters' invitation and the maiden replied that she would first have to ask her husband. She returned to her room again and began to weep because she didn't know what to do. Again the Moor came in and asked her why she was weeping. She told him what had happened and he went off to the skull which declared, "Tell the mistress to take these crumbs and scatter them outside." The maiden did as the skull had told her and what did she see? The whole road was full of coaches and one of them was made of gold. Standing in front of them were servants waiting with everything she needed to go to the baths. The sisters were stupefied when they saw her and began to regret their decision. "We were stupid not to have stayed at the palace," the wicked sisters thought.

The third day, they sent the governess off again to say that they wanted to come over for a meal. When the governess had returned home, the maiden went back to her room and began to weep. The Moor appeared once again, found out why she was weeping and hurried off to the skull. The skull ordered the maiden to scatter the crumbs in the kitchen, which she did. To her surprise a pantry appeared full of all sorts of food, with servants standing at attention. Just before the sisters were to arrive, she arranged for the servants to say to her from time to time in her sisters' presence: "Could you come out for a moment? The master wishes to speak to you." The sisters arrived and were quite taken by the delicious meal. The servants did as they were told and asked the maiden to come out of the room, which she did. She spoke to herself so that the sisters would hear her and think she was talking to her husband. But still they were not satisfied. Now they wanted to meet the husband.

This time the maiden didn't know what to do. While she was weeping, a black cat appeared and enticed the maiden into following it into a beautiful garden. There she saw a girl and a boy under a rose bush. Beside them was a baby lying directly in the sun. The maiden felt sorry for the baby and covered its head with a towel. Then she noticed that the girl's long blonde hair was entangled in the thorns of the rose bush, so she began extricating the strands one by one, careful not to hurt the girl or disturb her sleep. When the girl awoke, she was surprised and woke the boy up to ask him what had happened, but he had no idea either. Then the girl with the long blonde hair said, "Let the person who has been so kind to me come forth and I will make all his wishes come true."

The maiden with the skull came out from behind the rose bush where she was hiding and said to the blonde girl, "I beg you, sister, save me from the predicament I'm in or I am doomed. My father married me to the skull of a dead man, and now my sisters want to meet my husband face to face because they are green with envy. Do you know how they can meet him the way he was before he died? If you can help me, I'll never forget you." Thus spoke the maiden and touched the girl's heart. "Here is the man you are looking for," she replied. "This is your husband!"

And at that moment, the skull was transformed into a human being. The blonde girl, radiant and fair, was actually the Earthly Beauty. She had earlier changed the man into a skull to keep him for herself and not to let him into the world of the living.

The maiden was overjoyed and returned to the palace where her sisters were waiting. They were overwhelmed when they saw the husband alive. The couple reigned a long, long time and are still living happily ever after.

12. The Bear and the Dervish

Once upon a time there was a shepherd who tended a flock of sheep. He was bothered day after day by a bear who would come along and steal five or six of his sheep. One day, a dervish came by. The shepherd greeted him and told him his tale of woe about the thievish bear. "I'll slay him for you," said the dervish. "I just need three pieces of goat's cheese." The shepherd gave him the cheese and the dervish went off to meet the bear who was on his way as usual to steal some sheep. The dervish pretended that he wanted to make a bet with the bear to find out who was the stronger of the two. The bear said that he was the stronger but the dervish replied, "I can crush you like this rock," put his hand into the basket and took out the first piece of cheese, then the second, and then the third, crushing them all until they were nothing but crumbs. The bear was amazed, picked up a white stone but couldn't crush it as the dervish had done, so the two decided to make friends.

After a while, the bear became hungry and asked the dervish to bring him an ox while he cut wood in the forest. The dervish replied, "You go ahead and get your ox, that's nothing for me. I want a lion." With this trick, the dervish succeeded in not having to get the ox, and went into the forest to cut wood. The bear sauntered off to a herd, seized an ox and heaved it over his shoulder. The dervish went into the forest, took a rope and tied all the trees up into one as if he wanted to pull them all out together. The bear waited for the dervish, but the dervish didn't come, so he went into the forest himself and came upon the dervish who was pretending to pull out all the trees at once. The bear was astounded and thought to himself that the dervish must be a thousand times stronger than he was. He said to the dervish, "What are you going to do with all the trees you're pulling out?" A couple of branches would be enough." The dervish replied: "I'm not the sort of person to take just two pieces of wood. You take them if you want them." The bear immediately broke off two branches and returned to

72

his ox.

Now the ox had to be roasted. The dervish said to the bear, "I'll go and fetch some water. You turn the meat on the spit, but don't weary yourself." The dervish only said this because he couldn't turn such a huge ox on the spit himself. He took a goatskin bag and went off to the spring at the foot of a cliff. There he filled the goatskin bag and wanted to heave it over his shoulder, but it was so heavy that he couldn't even lift it. The bear waited for an hour, two hours, and finally set off for the spring. When he arrived, he found the dervish and asked, "What are you waiting for?" The dervish replied, "I keep wondering whether I shouldn't bring the whole spring with the cliff, because it fills up so slowly. I would be ashamed of myself to bring back just the goatskin bag, so you carry it." The bear heaved the goatskin bag over his shoulder and they set off. On their way back, the bear said to the dervish, "Let's have a wrestle!" The dervish replied, "What? You can't match your strength with mine." But they wrestled nevertheless. The bear hugged the dervish with such strength that the dervish's eyes bulged out of his head. When the bear saw the dervish's blood-red face and his bulging eyes he asked what was wrong. The dervish replied, "Oh nothing, I just don't know what to do. If I throw you to one side, it would cut you to pieces. If I throw you to the other side, it would be even worse." The bear then said to him, "Take pity on me, let me go!" And the dervish let him go.

They carried on to the place where the ox was roasting and sat down to eat. After a couple of bites, the dervish was full and the bear asked why he ate so little. The dervish replied that he had just eaten a huge mutton on leaving to get the water. Once they had finished their meal, the bear said, "Let's go to my place because we are friends now." When they arrived, the bear ordered his mother and sister to sharpen the axe because he wanted to kill his new friend to get away from him, since the dervish was stronger than he was.

But the bear's sister overheard everything and warned the dervish. After they had finished dinner, they all went off to sleep. But the dervish just pretended to go with them to the place where they slept and instead hid under a donkey's saddle. At midnight the bear got up, took the axe and struck the dervish three or four times with it. Thinking he had killed the dervish, he returned to bed and went back to sleep. At the crack of dawn, the bear went out to gather wood. When he returned he saw the dervish coming out of the house. His eyes opened wide in astonishment and he asked the dervish how he had slept. The dervish declared, "I slept very well, except for a couple of fleas that bit me at midnight."

The bear was astounded once again that the dervish had felt the axe as if it were a fleabite. It was all too much for him, so he told the dervish what he had done in the middle of the night. He then begged the dervish to make him just as strong as he was. "That's easy," said the dervish, "All I need is some milk." The bear went off to the herd of the shepherd who was sorry indeed to see him come back alive. The bear returned with a goatskin bag full of milk, and on the orders of the dervish he lit a fire and placed a cauldron of milk on it. When the milk began to boil, the dervish said, "Stick your head into it and you'll be strong." The bear stuck his head into the cauldron a first time and burned himself; he stuck his head in a second time and then a third time, whereupon the dervish gave him a kick and he fell into the cauldron and boiled to death.

Thereafter, the dervish return to the shepherd and told him that he had slain the bear. The shepherd didn't know how to repay the dervish and asked him what he would like. But the dervish wanted only a little kid-goat and taking it with him, he departed. He spent the night in a valley of wolves. While the dervish was sleeping, a wolf seized the kid-goat and gobbled it up. Furious, the dervish took off his trousers and hung them in front of the wolf's den. When the wolf then tried to leave his den, he tangled himself in the trousers. The dervish wrapped the wolf up in the trousers and set off with his bundle.

He arrived in a village on a Sunday. The priest was just coming out of the church when he saw the stranger and asked him where he had come from and what he wanted. The dervish replied, "I have come here to sell a shepherd. He is very good. He just eats too much. But aside from food, he asks for no wages." The priest asked where he had the shepherd. "Here in my trousers," replied the dervish and gave the trousers to the priest who took them home. The dervish departed leaving the priest his shepherd. The next morning the priest opened his window to see if the new shepherd had already taken the sheep out to pasture. But there was nothing to be seen, because the shepherd, who was of course a wolf, had not left behind a single sheep. The priest went out to the pen where he kept his animals, but there were no more sheep there either. He slung a rifle over his shoulder and set off in search of the dervish.

On his way, the dervish had met up with some thieves who were fighting over how to divide the money they had stolen. When they saw the dervish, they gave him the money to divide. The dervish declared, "I don't like squabbling, so I am going to tie you all to a tree." He took the first thief's money and put it in his pocket, then he took the second thief's money and put it in his pocket, and then he took the money of all the other thieves, put it in his pocket and fled.

A short while later, the priest arrived at the place where the dervish had tied up the thieves. "Has a dervish passed by on this road?" he inquired. "He sold me a shepherd who ate all my sheep." The thieves replied, "He was just here and tied us all up." So they set off with the priest in search of the dervish, but he was nowhere to be found. Finally they went to his house and surprised him there. When the dervish saw them coming, he called all the people in the village. As soon as the villagers heard that the dervish was being attacked, they rushed forth, seized the thieves and the priest and thrashed them to bits.

13. The Snake and the King's Daughter

Once upon a time there was an old woman who had no children and owned nothing but the little cottage she lived in. Every day, she would go into the forest to gather firewood. One day a little snake slithered into her bundle of wood. Not noticing it, the old woman heaved the wood over her shoulder and returned home. When she dropped the wood on the floor, the snake crawled out and began to play with the cat. The old woman left the snake alone and kept it for a son because she had no children. The snake grew and grew and one day it said to her, "Old woman, go to the king and tell him to give me his daughter in marriage." She replied, "All right, my son, but how do you expect the king to give you his only daughter. You're a snake!" "That doesn't matter, mother, go anyway and we'll see what he says."

The old woman did as the snake had said and went to see the king. But the guards at the palace gate, having asked her what she wanted and what her business with the king was, would not let her enter. The old woman, nevertheless, refused to be turned away and insisted on seeing the king alone, until finally the guards allowed her to pass. She went up to see the king and said to him, "I am very embarrassed about this, but I promised to ask you, so I will. My son is a snake and wants to marry Your Majesty's daughter." When the king heard this, he became furious and kicked the old woman down the stairs, breaking her leg. She limped home, cursing the snake because she was now a cripple. The snake said to her, "Don't worry about your leg, I'll heal it. But you must not give up yet!"

The snake then produced a ring, blew on it and said, "Heal the old woman's leg!" Immediately the leg was healed. The next morning the snake sent the old woman back to the king and the very same thing happened. After being kicked and beaten, she swore she would never again set foot in the palace again.

The third day, the snake said to her, "Go back to the king again. This is the last time I'll send you." The old woman was unwilling at first, but since the snake promised that it was the last time, she went back to the king and said to him, "Your Majesty, I must have your daughter as a wife for my son. Otherwise I will be in great trouble." The king chuckled and replied, "I will give my daughter to your son under the following conditions. Your cottage must be a palace as big as mine by tomorrow. The path from your door to my door must be spanned with silk and four hundred attendants must be waiting on horseback, one for every hue and colour on earth. If you can do all that by tomorrow morning, I will give my daughter to your son in marriage." When the old woman heard this she departed, happy this time not to be kicked and beaten about. She reported to the snake what the king had said and the snake simply replied, "Everything will be ready in time."

At the stroke of midnight, the snake blew on the ring and said, "May the old woman's cottage turn into a palace bigger than the king's!" And at once the cottage became a palace. The old woman, who was sleeping on a mat on the floor, suddenly found herself in a real bed complete with a bell for the maid. The snake then blew on the ring again and said, "May the path between our door and the door of the king's palace be spanned with silk!" And so it happened. Then the snake blew on the ring a third time and said, "May four hundred attendants on horseback, dressed in every hue and colour, await our command!" And they too appeared. When the snake was finished, he lay down to go to sleep. Before doing so, however, he ordered the attendants on horseback to keep guard around the house.

When the king got up the next morning, he looked out the window and saw a huge, magnificent palace and wondered whom it belonged to. He called his wife over and asked her, "Is that really a palace, wife, or are my eyes deceiving me?" "It is a palace all right," she replied. "Yesterday there was a cottage there belonging to an old woman." Then the king remembered the conditions he had set the old woman and the two of them, the king and queen, began to lament the fate of their poor daughter. Now she would have to marry the snake because they had given their word and could not break it. The time came for the bride to be fetched and the horsemen were readied. They mounted the snake in the saddle with them and, singing a ballad, rode off to the king. There they lifted the snake off the horse and took it to the king and queen. The two were most distressed and thought to themselves, "It would be better for us to kill our daughter. What a dreadful fate to have a snake for a son-in-law!

The attendants picked up the bride and the wedding took place. After the festivities, the time came for the groom to be led to the bride's chamber. When the girl saw the snake, she screamed in horror. The snake, however, shed its skin and turned into such a handsome young man that she was completely overwhelmed. Then he said to her, "My dear wife, never tell anyone that I am a human being by night and a snake by day. For if you do I will disappear and you will never find me again!" She replied, "All right, dear husband, I won't tell anyone. But tell me at least what your name is!" He told her he was called Swift. The next morning the king sent someone to the snake's palace to find out whether his daughter was still alive. When he was told that she was fine and there was no need to worry, he became suspicious and didn't believe what he had heard.

The next week, the king sent a servant to invite his daughter and the snake to lunch. When his daughter and his son-in-law arrived, the girl's mother began to weep, saying, "Oh, my poor daughter. We have caused you such grief! How miserable you must be!" But the girl replied that she felt very lucky.

A few days later, a great wedding was to be held in another part of town, to which the king and his daughter were invited. The snake said to his wife, "You go ahead. I'll come later this evening so that no one will know that it is I, turned into a human being. And remember, you mustn't tell anybody what you know because you won't see me again if you do." The girl went off to the wedding alone and when darkness fell, the snake shed its skin, put on some splendid garments and followed her. When the two arrived, everyone rose in awe because they thought an angel had just come in. A little later, he began to dance so gracefully that everyone stood still in amazement and thought, "That is no being of this world. He must be from heaven!" The girl's mother, sitting beside her, said, "My dear girl, how lucky you would be if you had a man like that for a husband!" The girl couldn't stand it any longer and burst out, "That is my husband, mother. That is Swift, the man I love." The moment she spoke, Swift became invisible and no one understood where he had disappeared to so swiftly. The girl looked around, could not see him anywhere and broke into tears. "Now look what you made me do, mother!" she sobbed. "He warned me not to tell anyone who he was or he would leave me forever! I must set off in search of him. He told me that if I tried to find him I would need iron shoes, an iron staff and a travelling case." Her parents gave her what she needed and she set off in search of her husband.

She roamed for days and nights and finally went to seek the advice of the sun. Only the sun's mother and children were at home and the children immediately set upon the girl to devour her. The mother, however, stopped them and invited the girl in. "Why have you come here?" she asked. The girl told her everything that had happened and said, "I would like to ask your child, the sun, whether he has seen my husband anywhere in the course of his travels." The old woman replied, "The sun isn't back yet, but we can ask him when he gets in. I fear though that he will eat you up when he comes back all tired and smells a human being." "He won't eat me if you don't want him to," countered the girl. The old woman felt sorry for her and hid her. When the sun came home for dinner, exhausted from his long journey, he said to his mother the moment he sat down, "I smell human flesh. Bring me some of it to eat, because I'm terribly tired." The mother replied, "There is no human here, my lad. Who would possibly come to visit us?" "Oh yes there is," said the sun, "Bring me the human. I won't eat him, I'll just ask what he wants." The old woman made the sun promise not to eat the human, brought the girl out of hiding and took her to the sun. The girl said to the sun, "I'm looking for Swift, my husband. I've come to ask Your Majesty if you've seen him anywhere in the course of your travels." The sun replied, "No, I haven't seen him anywhere. But go and ask the moon if he's seen him at night."

The poor girl continued on her way, wandering for many days and nights until she finally reached the moon. The moon could not tell her anything either and sent her on to the wind. Once again she set off, this time in search of the wind. By now she was exhausted from walking and, with the last ounce of her energy just managed to reach the house of the wind. There she met the wind's elderly mother and the little wind children who came blowing around to devour her. The old women stopped them, however, and invited the girl in.

"Why have you come here, my daughter?" she asked. The girl told her the reason for her journey and where she had been. The wind's mother said, "We'll ask him. I'm afraid though that he'll eat you up on the spot when he comes back all tired and smells a human being." But the girl insisted once more, saying, "He won't eat me if you don't want him to." The old woman took pity on the girl and hid her.

When the wind came in for breakfast, he could smell human flesh right away and said to his mother, "I smell human flesh. Bring me some of it to eat, for I am very tired." The mother replied, "How could there possibly be any humans here?" But he insisted that his mother bring forth the human and finally promised, "I won't eat the human, mother, but bring him out so that I can ask him a few questions." The mother made the wind give his word of honour and brought the girl out. The wind asked her why she had gone to all the trouble she'd been through. "I am in search of Swift, my husband," said the girl, "It has been a long time since he disappeared and I haven't been able to find him." "Your husband is being held prisoner by a Kulshedra beyond the sea. He's a long, long way from here," said the wind. The girl implored him, "I must find him, no matter how far away he is. I beg Your Excellency to take me with you across the sea." The wind replied, "I would gladly take you with me, but I'm afraid you would fall off along the way, because I am very swift." "No, I won't fall off," she assured him. "Please take me with you."

The wind took pity on the girl and lifted her up on his back, saying, "Hold onto my hair and don't look down or you'll get dizzy." The wind gave out a strong gust and carried the girl across the sea, depositing her beside a spring. The poor girl had just sat down for a while to rest when suddenly a terrifying roar echoed from the mountains. A Kulshedra appeared at the spring and, catching sight of the girl, began to hop around on one leg, chanting, "First I had one, now I have two, my precious one." It seized the girl and took her to its home where Swift was being held prisoner. He recognized his wife at once, but didn't dare say anything because he was frightened of the Kulshedra. Making sure the Kulshedra would not notice, he threw his ring into a jug that the wife had to wash so that she would know he was there. And it worked. As she was washing the jug, the ring fell into her hands and she recognized it as her husband's. Later when they had an opportunity to see one another, he whispered to her, "Don't talk to me when the Kulshedra is present or it will devour us."

The Kulshedra fed the two of them well so that it could devour them later, the wife first and then the husband. It had also overheard them talking. One day the Kulshedra said to the wife, "When I get back for dinner, my girl, I want to find the house swept in certain parts and unswept in others." As the poor wife was wondering what to do, her husband woke up and asked what she was thinking. She told him about the Kulshedra's orders and that she was wondering how to carry them out. The husband said, "Let me take care of things! Look for a bread crust and bring it here. Use it to sweep the floor and draw it behind you when you put it away. That way some parts of the house will be swept and others unswept." And so the wife did what her husband had suggested. When the Kulshedra came home that evening and asked the wife whether she had done her chores, she replied, "Yes, I've finished, mother." The Kulshedra looked around and saw that everything had been done exactly as it had wanted. "That wasn't your idea," shouted the monster. "It was your husband's!"

The next day the Kulshedra said to the young woman again, "When I get home this evening, daughter, I want to find two cauldrons of tears here and if I don't, I shall devour you." When the Kulshedra had left, the girl took out the two cauldrons, placed them in front of her and began to weep to fill them up. But in vain - the cauldrons would not fill up. When her husband got up, he found his wife weeping and asked her what the matter was. She explained that the Kulshedra had demanded two cauldrons full of tears the night before and that otherwise she would be devoured. The husband said to her, "What a fool you are! Do you think you can fill these cauldrons with tears! Rest for a moment and let me handle this. Take the cauldrons and fill them with water, add a handful of salt and cover them up." The young woman did as her husband had said.

When the Kulshedra got back that evening and asked whether she had done her chores, the woman replied, "I finished everything, mother." The Kulshedra went over and saw that the cauldrons were indeed full of tears. Tasting the liquid with the tip of its tongue, the Kulshedra realized that it was salty like tears, and said to the woman, "I know very well, daughter, that this wasn't your idea, but Swift's." Following this, the Kulshedra began to hate the young man and planned how it would eat him.

But the young man sensed the danger, so he put on some old clothes and went out to one of the Kulshedra's forests to chop wood. The Kulshedra searched through all its forests but could not find him. One day, however, the Kulshedra happened by while the young man was still chopping wood and, hearing the sound of the axe, shouted, "Who dares to chop wood in my forest?" He replied, "I am a poor man and am making a coffin for a young man who just died." The Kulshedra asked who the young man was. "A handsome lad whose name was Swift," the man replied. The Kulshedra was delighted when it heard that Swift had died, and said, "Oh, how happy I am!" It approached the coffin. The young man asked, "Did you know the lad?" "Yes," it replied. "Take courage then, Your Majesty," said the young man, "and climb in and see if I've done everything properly." "I'm so happy that he's dead," said the Kulshedra again, and climbed into the coffin. The young man shut the coffin right away, locked it and set it on fire.

When he had made sure that the Kulshedra had been burned to ashes, he returned home and said to his wife, "The Kulshedra is gone forever. Pack your things and let us return home." So they gathered up all their things, went back home and lived happily ever after. The man who had once been a snake in the daytime and a human being at night was now a human being forever.

14.   Gjizar the Nightingale

Once upon a time there was a king who had three sons. The only thing the king cared about was praying at the mosque. So he had a beautiful mosque built and when the workers had finished it, he went there to pray. While he was praying, a dervish entered and said to him, "The mosque is indeed beautiful, but your prayers are in vain." When the king heard this, he had the mosque razed to the ground and had another more beautiful one built on another spot. When the second mosque was finished, he went there to pray. The dervish entered again and said the same thing as the first time: "The mosque is indeed beautiful, but your prayers are in vain." The king then had this mosque, too, razed to the ground and another one built. He wasted so much of his money that his fortune was all gone and the kingdom became poor. When the third mosque was finished, he went there to pray. While he was praying, the dervish entered again and repeated what he had said earlier. The king got up and returned to his palace, where he sank into a state of profound dejection. He had no more money to have the mosque razed to the ground and another built, and yet when he went to say his prayers, he knew that they were in vain.

His sons noticed that he was lost in thought and worried, asking him, "What is wrong, father? Why are you so sad? We have our fortune, we are royalty. Why are you so lost in your thoughts?" The king replied, "I have spent my whole fortune on building mosques and I cannot even pray in them." "But why not?" the sons asked. He answered, "Every time I say my prayers in the mosque, a dervish comes by and tells me that my prayers are in vain." The sons then replied, "Go to the mosque tomorrow morning and pray. We will wait outside for the dervish to see what he has to say." And so it happened. The dervish entered as usual and said, "The mosque is indeed beautiful, but your prayers are in vain." As the dervish was going out the door, the sons took hold of him and asked him, "Why do you always say, 'The mosque is indeed beautiful, but your prayers are in vain?'" The dervish replied, "This mosque is indeed beautiful, there is none more beautiful on earth. But it needs Gjizar the nightingale to sing in it for the mosque to be one of a kind on earth." The sons inquired, "Where is this Gjizar the nightingale?" The dervish replied, "I have simply heard of it, but I do not know where it is." Then they let the dervish go, ran back to the palace and said to their father, "The dervish told us that Gjizar the nightingale is missing from the mosque, but he does not know where it is to be found. Let us go and see if we can find it." So the three sons set off to find Gjizar the nightingale. When they had journeyed for about twenty days, they came to a spot where the road divided into three. At every fork there was a stone with an inscription on it. At two of the forks, the inscription read, 'Whoever takes this road will return'. The third inscription read, 'Whoever takes this road will never return'. The three brothers stood there for a moment and took counsel. The youngest of them said, "Let us separate here. Each of us will go his own way. We'll leave our three rings here, and the first one to get back will go and look for the others." So they left their rings all under one stone, kissed one another and separated. The youngest brother took the road with the inscription 'Whoever takes this road will never return' and the other two took the roads on which one could come back. One of the two older brothers reached a city and became a barber, the other reached another city and opened a coffee-house. There they remained and looked after their businesses.

The youngest brother, who had taken the road marked with the inscription saying that he would never come back, got lost in a wilderness in which there were no villages, inns or people, only wild animals and other savage beings. On his way he met a savage woman who was combing her hair with the branch of a gorse bush. The youth went up to her and combed her hair with a comb, picking out all the lice. When he had got all the lice out of her hair, she said to him, "What can I do for you, now that you have done such a good deed and rid me of the lice?" He replied, "I need nothing anything. I would just like to ask you a question, and if you know the answer, tell me." She replied, "What would you like to know?" The youth said, "I am looking for Gjizar the nightingale. You may have heard of it since you live here in the mountains." She answered, "The bird you are looking for is not here. Go back, for there are only wild animals here. Even I, a savage, have never been over these mountains because the land beyond is full of huge beasts." The youth replied, "I am going.

84

Whatever happens is God's will."

And so he left her and climbed up into the mountains. There he saw a house. It was the house of a tiger. He went in. The tiger was not at home, but his wife was there baking bread. The youth addressed her and she answered, "What are you doing here? My husband will be returning any moment now and will devour you." He replied, "Well, since I am already here, do whatever you want with me." When the moment came for the tiger's wife to put the bread into the oven, she had to fan the embers of the fire with her breasts. Each time she did this, she burned herself and was sick for ten days. When the youth saw what she was doing, he said to her, "Let me do it." He took some leaves and fanned the embers with them. When the wife saw that she could bake bread without getting sick, she was very happy. But she was sorry for the youth, because her husband would come and devour him. When she took the bread out of the oven, she gave some to the youth and then hid him in a trunk.

Presently, the tiger came home and saw that his wife was not sick, but up and about, and snarled, "Why didn't you bake any bread today?" "I did," she replied. He retorted, "You used to get sick when you baked bread. Why aren't you sick now?" She replied, "I found a way of baking bread without burning myself." She showed him how. She fanned the embers with the leaves and said, "If there were a human being here who had shown me how to do it, what would you do with him?" The tiger replied, "I would make friends with the human being." So she let the youth out of the trunk and said to her husband, "This is the one who taught me how to fan the embers." The youth and the tiger kissed one another and became friends. The tiger asked him, "Why have you come here?" "I am looking for a bird called Gjizar the nightingale," the youth replied. "Have you ever heard of it?" The tiger said, "There is no bird like that here, but I have a brother who is very old. His eyelids have fallen down over his eyes so he no longer sees anything. Go and pay him a visit." He showed the youth the road to the house, saying, "When you get close to the house, you'll see the wife of my brother the lion. She is old and has just turned around and is looking towards the house. You must go there backwards and take her breast into your mouth. She will then ask you, 'Who are you sucking at my breast,' and you must answer, 'I am your son. I recognize you as my mother.' Then my brother inside the house will ask who is there. You must reply immediately, 'I am a friend of your brother the tiger who has sent me to you with a problem,' and he will say, 'Come in then'. You go inside and raise his eyelids so he can see you. He might know where Gjizar the nightingale is. If he does not know, you must not go any farther, but come back here." Then the tiger and the youth kissed one another and separated. The youth arrived at the lion's house and did as the tiger had told him, asking the lion if he knew where Gjizar the nightingale was. The lion replied, "The bird is nowhere to be found. Go back because from here on, there are only savage creatures from the realm of the jinns. Even I do not go there, though I am king of the wild animals."

But despite what the lion had said, the youth did not go back. He said good-bye to the lion and set off down the road which the lion had told him not to take. After he had gone quite always, three eagles flew over him, opening up their beaks to devour him. But the youth simply drew his sabre and chopped off the wing of one eagle, the leg of another and the beak of the third. The birds flew off and the youth was able to continue down the road. After he had gone a bit farther, he saw a house in the middle of a wide field and walked up to it. There he met an old woman who had just put a cake in the oven to bake. When she saw the youth, she cried out, "What are you doing here, my son? My daughters will be back any moment now and devour you." The youth replied, "Well, since I am already in your hands, do whatever you want with me." The old woman took the cake out of the oven and gave some to the youth to eat. Then she set the table in the middle of the room, placed a bowl of water in the middle of the table, brought out some food and locked the youth in a closet which had a hole in it, so that he could see what was happening. After a short while, the youth saw an eagle approaching, the one whose wing he had chopped off. It flew in through the window to the bowl of water on the table, bathed in it and turned into a maiden. Soon after this, the other eagles he had wounded flew in, bathed and turned into maidens. Then they said to their mother, the old woman, "It smells like a human being here." The old woman replied, "You've just come from the humans, that's why it smells of them." After the maidens had eaten, the old woman asked them, "If I had a man here, what would you do with him?" The eldest maiden replied, "By the soul of the man who chopped off my wing, I swear I would do him no harm." The second said, "By the soul of the man who chopped off my leg, I swear I would do him no harm." The youngest maiden also made the same promise, so the old woman let the youth out of the closet and he said, "I am the one who wounded you all." But they were pleased to see the youth again and asked him, "What are you doing here?" He replied, "I am in search of Gjizar the nightingale and no one I've asked up to now has known anything about it." They replied, "We know where Gjizar the nightingale is. If you are walking, you'll never get there, and even if you did, it would take three years." He then said, "Well, what should I do?" "We want you to do a good deed," they answered, "and then we'll take you there in an hour and you can find the nightingale." The youth replied, "What is it you want; what is the good deed I can do for you?" They answered, "We want you to stay with us for three months and sleep with each of us for one month."

After the three months were over, they took him to the place where Gjizar the nightingale was. In that region the Earthly Beauty reigned as queen. She had five hundred guardsmen at her court. A wolf kept watch at the outer door, a tiger at the second door and a lion at the door to her chamber. The three maidens took the youth there and left him in the courtyard just after all the guardsmen, the wolf, the tiger, the lion and the Earthly Beauty had gone to sleep. The youth went straight to the chamber of the Earthly Beauty. In her chamber she had four lighted candles and another four unlit on the table. The lighted candles were just about to go out. When the youth entered the chamber, he lit the four new candles and put out the burning ones, took the cage with Gjizar the nightingale in it and left. When he went out the door, everyone woke up. But before they could catch him, the three maidens grabbed him and took him off to their house.

There they remained together for quite a while, until the youth said, "Take me back to my country now," and they took him back to the place where he had left his brothers. He went over to the stone where they had left their rings, found his brothers' rings and set off down the roads they had taken. He found one brother working as a barber and the other in his coffee-house and said to them, "Come, let us go back to our father. I have found Gjizar the nightingale and brought it back." And so the three brothers set out to find their father.

On their way they got thirsty. Though they could find no spring to drink from, they did come across a well, but had nothing to draw water with. The two older brothers said to the youngest, "You climb down into the well and draw some water so that we can drink." Then they attached a rope to him, lowered him into the well, cut the rope and ran off. At that moment, Gjizar the nightingale stopped singing. The water in the well was not very deep, however, so the youth did not drown. It only reached up to his neck and his head remained above the surface. The two brothers took the bird and brought it to their father. He asked about the youngest son, "What have you done with your brother?" They replied, "He has turned into a scoundrel and makes trouble everywhere from town to town."

Now the queen, the Earthly Beauty, set out to do battle with the king and to find the man who had taken the bird. The eldest brother went to see her and she asked him, "Did you take Gjizar the nightingale?" He replied, "Yes, I did." "Where did you find it?" she asked. "In a cypress tree," he replied. So she had him flung to the ground and ordered her servants to beat him with a cane until he died. Then she had her cannons set up to fire at the city and had destroyed half the king's palace, when the second brother, hearing that she had killed the first, became afraid. He ran off to his father and told him the truth that they had thrown the youngest brother into a well. The king sent his servants out immediately and they pulled the youth, half dead, out of the well. He could still breathe, but was unable to speak.

A few days later he was feeling better and was able to speak again. The moment he spoke, Gjizar the nightingale began to sing and indeed sang so beautifully that everyone marvelled. When the Earthly Beauty heard the nightingale's song, she sent her servants to lay out a red cloth from the palace gate all the way to her ship. Then the king's son mounted a horse, took the nightingale in his hand and rode out on the cloth. When the people saw him riding, they were very frightened and thought to themselves, "Now the Earthly Beauty is going to turn the city inside out." But they were wrong. When the king's son approached the ship, the Earthly Beauty came out and welcomed him. As they boarded the ship she asked him, "Where did you take the nightingale?" He told her exactly how he had found the bird, and so they became friends and got married.

And that is how the king's son won the Earthly Beauty and lived happily ever after.

15.   Half Rooster

Once upon a time there was an old man and an old woman who owned nothing but a cat and a rooster. One day they got into a terrible argument and shouted at one another so furiously that they decided to separate forever. The old couple divided everything they had and the woman got the cat and the man got the rooster. The cat caught birds every day which the old woman cooked, so that she at least had something to live on.

But the old man had nothing to eat. So one day he said to the rooster, "Dear rooster, I am so sorry, but I really don't know what to do. I am going to have to eat you." The rooster understood and nodded. The old man sliced the rooster into two halves, cooked and ate one half and kept the other. From then on the second half of the rooster was known as 'Half Rooster'.

Half Rooster decided that it was time to go on a journey and earn some money. And so he set off, hopping on one leg. At the edge of a pond, he met a frog and said to it, "Frog, why don't you come with me. I'm on a journey to earn some money." "All right, I will," said the frog. It had a last drink of water, as much as it could swallow, and leapt into Half Rooster's belly. Half Rooster continued on his way and met a fox. "Fox, let us become friends." "All right, little Half Rooster," replied the fox, "but where are you going?" "I'm off to see the world. Do you want to come with me?" "Sure, I'll come," said the fox and crawled into Half Rooster's belly.

After continuing on his journey for a short time, Half Rooster met a wolf who asked him where he was going. "To make some money, dear wolf. Do you want to come with me?" "Oh yes, I'll come," it replied and crawled into Half Rooster's belly too. They all set off and after a while met a mouse. The little mouse laughed and asked Half Rooster, "Aren't you getting tired, Half Rooster, if you have to hop on one leg all the time?" "Not at all," replied Half Rooster. When the mouse asked where he was going, Half Rooster replied that he wanted to see the world and make some money. Half Rooster persuaded the mouse to come along too, and the little mouse jumped into his belly, which was now almost bursting because it was so full.

One day Half Rooster got hungry. He hopped into a vegetable garden and began to crow, "Cock-a-doodle-doo! Look, I'm here!" The king heard him and gave orders that the rooster be caught. The servants rushed out and surrounded the garden. But though Half Rooster was still crowing, they could not find him, so they cut off all the heads of cabbage in the garden to see where he was. Finally they found him in the last head of cabbage, seized him and stuck him in the oven to roast.

Half Rooster was in a desperate situation and cried out, "Frog, if you've ever been my friend, help me now!" The frog leapt out right away, spewed out all the water it had swallowed and put out the fire. Then the servants locked Half Rooster in a stable so that the horses would trample him to death with their hooves. "Wolf," Half Rooster cried out, "if you've ever been my friend, help me now!" So the wolf leapt out and bit all the horses until they died. The king's servants seized Half Rooster for the third time and locked him up with the geese so that they would peck at him with their beaks. But Half Rooster called his friend the fox who leapt out and ate up all the geese.

The king's servants did not know what to do, so they locked Half Rooster up in a chest of gold, the strongest one they had. Half Rooster swallowed as many pieces of gold as he could and then called the mouse, "Mouse, if you've ever been my friend, help me now!" The mouse leapt out of his belly and gnawed a big hole in the chest so that both of them could escape.

Half Rooster hopped home quickly. On his way, he lost a piece of gold. When he got back to the old man, he said to him, "Master, from now on give me enough to eat and a soft place to sleep. Take the rod and hit me on the back with it every day." The old man did as the rooster had told him. Every day, Half Rooster got plenty to eat and a soft place to sleep and every day the old man hit him on the back with the rod. Every time he hit the rooster, a piece of gold fell out and with the money the old man was able to live a good life.

When the old woman found out what had happened, she was furious and green with envy. She screamed at her cat, "Go on, you good-for-nothing! Go on a journey and make some money!" The cat obeyed, and on its way found and swallowed the piece of gold which

Half Rooster had lost. It also found a lot of insects, salamanders, snakes and mice and ate them all, returning home to its mistress with a full belly. Just as Half Rooster had done, the cat said to the old women, "Give me enough to eat every day and a soft place to sleep, because I was on a journey and have made money."

The old woman did as the cat had said and hit it on the back with a rod every day. The first day, a piece of gold fell out, but on the days that followed, only salamanders, snakes, mice and other little creatures came out to the fury of old woman. In her rage, she killed the cat and then died herself of anger and envy.

16.   The Boy with No Name

Once upon a time there was a man and a women to whom God had given no children. One evening the man was returning from the fields with his team of oxen when he met a dervish who was leaning against the wall of his house. The dervish asked the man to invite him in because he had been travelling for quite a while. It was the fifth day of Ramadan and after some time had passed, the wife beat the drum to show that the time had come for the Ramadan supper. Once they had eaten, the dervish asked the couple whether they had any children. The husband answered, "No, my dear dervish, I am already fifty and my wife is forty. God in his greatness has given us no children, although I don't think we are such bad people." The dervish then brought out a book in which their fate was written. After he had leafed through it, he predicted that God would give them a son, but he added that they must not give the boy a name until he returned to them.

Less than two years later, the couple did have a son, just as the dervish had predicted, and they gave him no name. The boy grew up and turned fifteen. His friends would taunt him by shouting, "Ha, Ha! You're nameless! Boy without a name!" One time the boy got so upset that he sent all his friends to his father to ask the father to give him a name. But the father refused, for he remembered the words of the dervish and was afraid of losing the child. The boy therefore decided not to stay with his father any longer and ran away. He hiked into a forest and came to a cliff. In the cliff was a cave in which an old blind man lived tending his sheep. The boy asked the old man if he might enter the cave because otherwise he would have to sleep outside. The old man welcomed the boy hospitably and slaughtered a sheep for their evening meal. When they had finished eating, the boy inquired whether the old man had any children. The old man said no and asked the boy if he might look after him as his child instead. The boy was happy and agreed to the proposal. The next morning the boy told the old man he should stay at home because he was blind and said he would take the sheep out to pasture himself. At first the old man refused, but when he saw that the boy really wanted to, he consented. But before the boy went out, he warned him, "Not far from here, my son, there is a garden surrounded by orange trees. There are jinns living there, and you must not take the sheep there or you will lose your eyesight as I did."

The boy took the sheep out to pasture and led them straight to the garden. There he sat down on a wall and began playing his flute. After a while, the jinns came out and began to dance. That evening when he took the sheep back to the cave, the old man came out to stroke a black ram. He noticed that the boy had taken the sheep to the garden after all and warned him a second time. Nevertheless, the boy took the sheep there day after day. One day, the king of the jinns appeared in the garden and said, "I cannot go on like this, these wars are tiring me out. What can I give you to take over my job?" The boy replied that he wanted nothing but a potion to cure his father's blindness. The king assembled all the jinns and asked if any of them had caused the old man to go blind. They all said no, but the king of the jinns said they must wait for a crippled jinn who was still on his way. When the crippled jinn arrived, the king asked him the same question. The crippled jinn replied that he had punished the old man by blinding him in both eyes. For this reason, the king of the jinns gave the boy an eye potion.

When the boy returned home that evening, he rubbed the potion on the old man's eyes, and suddenly the old man could see again. He took the boy by the hand and showed him seven rooms in the cave. The rooms were furnished with everything one could possibly need and one of them was full of gold. The old man showed the boy all the rooms but one. Pointing to it, he said "That is your room, but the time has not come for you to use it." The boy could hardly conceal his curiosity. One day, he went back to the garden and played his flute, and the jinns came out to dance. When they tired of dancing, they asked him to stop for a rest. "We aren't stopping," said the boy, "unless you tell me where I can find the key to the room my father didn't show me." Finally the jinns told him that the old man had hidden the key in his beard. That night when the old man was asleep, the boy removed the key from his beard and the next morning said he was too sick to take the sheep out to pasture.

When the old man had left the cave with the sheep, the boy took the key and opened the door. As soon as he did so, a horse in the room neighed and asked the boy whether he was a man or a ghost. When the horse heard that he was not a ghost, he told the boy to put on a coat and a sword. Then he told him to fetch a mirror, a comb and a ball and to fill the pouches of the saddle with diamonds. When everything was done, the horse said that they could now go out for a ride. As they were riding out of the cave, the tip of the sword brushed against something. At that moment the black ram which the old man had been stroking began to bleat and said, "The boy has taken the horse away!" The old man stroked his beard and realized that the key to the room was gone. He mounted the black ram and set off after the boy.

On their way, the horse asked the boy whether he could see anything behind them. The boy answered that he could see a black cloud coming over the mountain. The horse then told the boy to throw the comb onto the ground. Immediately the road behind them became covered in trees and the old man could hardly make his way through. Then the boy threw the mirror onto the ground and the road became so icy that the old man and his ram could hardly proceed another step. The horse again asked the boy whether he could see anything. He answered, "Now I can see a big wolf who is about to set upon us." At that moment the boy and the horse came to a big river which the old man could not cross because it was the border. The old man stopped on the river bank and called to the boy who had leapt across the river with his horse. The boy came to a stop and the two of them, one on one side of the river and the other on the opposite side, began to talk. The old man said to the boy, "That horse was meant for you, but I couldn't give it to you because the time hadn't come. Take it now, but let me give you a piece of advice: if you continue down that road, you will find a dead horse. Strip its hide off and take it with you. And wherever you spend the night tonight, cover yourself and the horse with it, otherwise the king of that country will kill you." The boy took what the old man had said to heart and did as he was told.

They rode on until night fell and came to a city where he covered himself and his horse with the hide of the dead horse. He entered an inn and asked the inn-keeper to let him stay the night. Although the inn-keeper did not really want to because the horse hide looked so mangy and he was afraid it would infect the other horses, he finally agreed, giving him a room of his own. When the boy spread out the hide, the whole room began to shimmer and he and the horse were covered in garments of gold.

At that time there happened to be a farmer bringing three melons to the king of the country. One of the melons was over-ripe, the second one was very ripe and the third one had just ripened. The king asked his counsellors the meaning of the three melons. The counsellors answered that the melons signified the king's three daughters. The first melon stood for the eldest daughter who should have been married long ago. The second one stood for the second eldest daughter whose time to marry had already come too. The third melon stood for the youngest daughter who had just become of marriageable age. At this, the king ordered all his subjects to assemble on a square and took his daughters there. The eldest daughter chose the son of the vizier for a husband. The second eldest chose the son of a minister, but the youngest could find no one to choose. The king then asked if all the young men were present. The inn-keeper where the boy was staying replied that there was still a scurfhead at his inn.

The king sent the inn-keeper and three guards to fetch the boy, but the boy was ashamed to appear before the king and would not go with them. Ignoring his protests, the inn-keeper and the guards seized him and brought him to the square. When they arrived, the youngest daughter threw an apple and hit the boy with no name. The king, however, did not want to give his daughter to the boy and told his subjects that she had made a mistake. The youngest daughter threw the apple three more times and each time it hit the boy with no name. Finally they agreed to give the girl to the boy even though he looked like a scurfhead because the boy was still wearing a piece of hide from the dead horse. The king wanted nothing to do with his daughter anymore because she had chosen the scurfhead for a husband, and he refused to let her visit him, though he still treated the two other daughters well.

One day, when the king was going to war with his enemies, he called on his two older sons-in-law for help. Although he had not asked the help of the youngest son-in-law who looked like a scurfhead, the boy rode out with them anyway. Once they were some distance from the city, the boy with no name stopped at a stream and took off the horsehide he was wearing. Then he took the hide off his horse and told it to charge into the midst of the enemy. The horse did as its master had ordered. The boy slew hordes of the enemy with his sword and the horse trampled hundreds of them with its hooves. Each time the boy charged into the field, the king won the battle against his enemy. In one of the pitched battles the boy with no name lost a finger. He went to the king, who did not recognize him without the horsehide and asked him to bind it. The king bound the boy's finger and bestowed upon him three apples and a scarf for his heroism. The boy took the apples and the scarf and put them in his pocket.

In the next battle, the king got gunpowder in his eyes and went blind. Several people told the king that the only thing that would help him recover his sight was deer's milk. The king therefore called the husbands of his two eldest daughters and asked them to fetch some deer's milk, which was to be found at a place where two mountains met. The sons-in-law agreed. The boy with no name heard this and he, too, set out the same day that the two husbands left, even though they had made fun of him. When the boy reached a stream, he took off the horsehide and rode ahead with his horse. At the place where the two mountains met, he tied his horse up and so, displaced one of the mountains slightly and found the deer's milk he was seeking. Then he built himself a little hut of branches. Nearby he came across some wild mares whose milk he put in bottles. Then he sat down in front of the hut and waited for the other two husbands to come by. They arrived after a while, still laughing, but they did not recognize him, and asked what he was selling in the bottles. When he replied that he was selling deer's milk, both the king's sons-in-law rejoiced at having found what they were looking for so easily. The boy with no name sold them the wild mare's milk and they departed happily.

After waiting for a while, the boy too set off and soon caught up with his brothers-in-law who were still making fun of him. "You wanted to find deer's milk and you can't even get rid of the scurf on your head," they laughed. They returned to the king and gave him the milk which he applied to his eyes. But because they had given him mare's milk, his eyes began to sting even worse. Then, the boy with no name asked his wife to beg her mother to have the king receive them. Though the mother had little hope that the king would agree, she asked him anyway and finally, after much persuasion, he consented. The boy with no name told his wife to go straight to her father, the king, and rub his eyes with the deer's milk, and she did as her husband had told her. Immediately the king opened his eyes and could see again. He asked his daughter who had given her the remedy. She made no reply, but gave him instead the three apples and the scarf that the king had given her husband during the war.

The king made some inquiries and eventually came to realize that it was his third son-in-law, whom he had never seen, who had healed him. He also realized that it had only been with the help of this son-in-law that he had won the war. He commanded that the son-in-law be sent for, but the boy refused to go. Finally the king said, "Either you come to see me or I will go to see you." The boy replied that he would only go if the king met him halfway, and so the king, intent on meeting his son-in-law, set off. On his way to meet the king, the boy ordered his horse not to ride through the gate, but to leap over the walls. Then he rode through the market square, but no one recognized him without the horsehide. They all marvelled at the wondrous horse. The palace itself trembled as the mighty horse advanced. When it leapt over the walls, all the palace windows shattered. The king welcomed the boy with open arms and asked him to sit down, but the boy remained standing. After a while, the king put his hand in his pocket and pulled out the scarf he had given to the boy during the war. In the middle of the scarf was stitched the name Suleyman, and so the boy finally had a name. When the king tired of reigning over his kingdom, he abdicated and made his third son-in-law his successor. The two other sons-in-law who had made fun of the boy with no name became his servants. And his wife's two older sisters became her ladies-in-waiting.

17.   The Barefaced Man and the Pasha's Brother

Once upon a time there was a widow who had two sons. The older of the two was a pasha in Baghdad. When the younger son grew up, people said to him, "Aren't you lucky to have a brother who is Pasha in Baghdad?" The youth replied that he had no brother. "Oh yes you do," they persisted. "Your mother just hasn't told you about him because she is afraid that you will leave her too." The next morning he asked his mother, "Mother, do I have a brother?" "Yes you do, my son," she replied, "but the people who have told you about him do not have your best interests at heart." Every day after that the youth asked his mother, "Mother, please let me go and see my brother," until she could do nothing but reply, "All right, my son. But swear to me that you will come home immediately if you meet a barefaced man on the road."

The youth set off on his way. After travelling for three days he did indeed meet a barefaced man on the road and so he went back home. A few days later he set off again and had travelled for six days when he again met a barefaced man, but this time he did not return home. The barefaced man asked him where he was going. The youth mentioned carelessly that he was off to see his brother who was Pasha in Baghdad. The barefaced man then said, "I too am on my way to Baghdad. Let us go together."

They travelled together and had walked a long way when the youth became thirsty. The barefaced man led him to a well which had neither a pail nor a rope and said to him," I'll tie you to my belt and lower you into the well so that you can drink." And so he did. When the youth had had enough to drink, he shouted, "I'm finished. Pull me up." But the barefaced man shouted back, "I will pull you out of the well only if you promise that from now on you will be the barefaced man and I can be the Pasha's brother." The youth had no choice but to give his promise. The barefaced man pulled him out of the well and they continued on their way to the palace of the Pasha who received the brother with great joy.

The next morning, the barefaced man said to the Pasha, "Are you bored? I can offer you some entertainment, for I have a barefaced man with me who is very brave. He will slay anything, no matter what it is." The barefaced man wanted to get rid of the brother because he was afraid that he would tell the Pasha the truth. The Pasha replied, "A Kulshedra comes from time to time. Perhaps he could slay it for me." When the youth heard this, all he said was, "Give me two cudgels and have a bonfire laid." The Pasha had everything prepared for him right away and the youth set out. The Kulshedra, attracted by the fire, approached the youth and prepared to devour him. But the youth dealt it a blow on the head with the cudgel and slew it. In no time, the news had spread that the youth had slain the Kulshedra, and the Pasha awarded him a medal for he was fond of the boy. The barefaced man was most upset because he was still afraid that the youth would tell the Pasha which of them was the real brother.

The barefaced man asked the Pasha again, "Have you any other wishes?" "Yes," replied the Pasha, "I am engaged to the daughter of the Shah of Persia, but whenever I send my soldiers there, they are all killed. Send the youth there." So the youth set out with ninety-seven soldiers.

On his way, he happened upon a fellow sitting on the bank of a river who was drinking all the water in the river and then spitting it out again. The youth stopped with his soldiers and watched the young man, for he had never seen anyone swallow so much water before. Finally he asked the fellow, "What are you doing?" "There's nothing else I can do," the other replied. I just sit here all day and play with the water." "Would you like to come with me?" "Yes, I would," the fellow said, and he set out with the youth. They continued on their way and came upon another young man who was playing with some hares. He would let them go and then catch them again. The youth asked the fellow what he was doing and he replied, "There's nothing else I can do but catch hares." "Would you like to come with me?" "Yes, indeed," he replied and they all set off again.

After a while they sat down to rest under an oak tree. In the tree was a nest of baby eagles and a snake was crawling up the tree to devour them. When the youth saw what was happening, he jumped up and slew the snake. The moment the mother eagle arrived, it set upon the youth and tried to gouge his eyes out, but the baby eagles cried out, "No, no, he saved us from the snake!" The eagle said to the youth, "You saved my children from the snake. What can I do for you?" But the youth replied that there was nothing he wanted, so the eagle plucked a feather out of its wing and said, "Take this feather and if you ever need me, burn it and I will come to your aid right away." The youth took the feather and put it in his pocket, and the whole group set out again.

On their way, they came across an ant-hill. They went around it, taking care not to step on it so as not to destroy it. The queen of the ants asked, "Why did you not step on the ant-hill?" "I didn't want to do you any harm," replied the youth, and the queen of the ants declared, "You have done us a great service, and as thanks I will give you one of my wings. If you are ever in danger, burn it and I will come to your aid with all my army."

And so they arrived at the palace of the Shah of Persia and the youth said to him, "I have come to fetch the Pasha's bride." The Shah retorted, "If you can eat three hundred plates of food, you can have the bride." The fellow who had drunk all the water in the river said that he was willing to try. The Shah sent for three hundred plates of food, and the fellow ate everything up, more than the Pasha's whole army could have eaten. There was not a crumb left over. The Shah became worried and declared, "Whoever wins the flag in a race with my swiftest horses can have the bride." The young man who had been catching hares exclaimed, "Don't worry, I'll win the flag for you." When the horses arrived at the racetrack, the young man said to the riders, "I'll give you a head start and then I'll set out after you." So they let the horses gallop away. The hare catcher set out last, caught up with the horses, passed them and won the flag. When the youth showed the Shah that he had won the flag, the Shah was even more worried, but still he would not give up the bride.

Next the Shah declared, "I have a barn full of wheat, barley and millet all mixed up together. You must sort it out for me in three days, otherwise I won't give you the Pasha's bride. This time the youth despaired for he knew it was impossible to sort out that much grain in three days. Then he remembered the ant's wing and threw it into the fire. Immediately the queen of the ants arrived and asked him what he wanted. He told her about the barn full of grain and she summoned all her ants. In three hours they had finished the task. The youth sent a message to the Shah, saying, "The grain has been sorted into three piles. Now you must give us the maiden." The Shah wondered how the youth could have done the chore in three hours. He went out to the barn and saw, to his utter amazement, that the grain had indeed been sorted into three piles.

The Shah then declared, "I have one more request. I want you to bring me a bottle of water from the mountains whose peaks touch. At the foot of the mountains is a cave and in the cave is the water you must bring me. It is a remedy to bring the dead back to life."

The youth remembered the eagle's feather and burnt it. The eagle appeared and asked the youth what he desired. The youth told the eagle about the water he must bring from the mountains. At once the eagle flew off and in no time it brought back the water and gave it to the youth who presented it to the Shah. In the palace, the bride took a flask of the water. She was then given to the youth and together they made their way home.

They were singing and making merry when they arrived at the Pasha's palace. The barefaced man heard their laughter and went out to meet them. When he saw that the youth had returned safe and sound, he was furious. In his anger, he drew his sword and chopped the youth in two. When the Pasha found out that the barefaced man had slain the youth of whom he was fond, he was so despondent that he could neither eat nor sleep. Though he did not punish the barefaced man because he believed him to be his brother, he refused to see him anymore.

Meanwhile, the bride had sprinkled the magic water over the youth and brought him back to life without the Pasha's knowledge. The next morning, the youth went to the Pasha's palace and declared, "I want to see the Pasha. I must talk to him." But the servants did not recognize him and told him that the Pasha was in mourning and would not see anyone. But the youth insisted, and so they finally called the Pasha, "There is a youth here who wishes to speak to Your Lordship," they said. "Let him in," replied the Pasha. When the youth arrived in the Pasha's chamber he began by asking, "If a man has made a promise and has then been cut into two, he can't come back to life, can he?" "No," replied the Pasha, "he can't come back to life." "And if a man is cut into two and then does come back to life, is he still bound to keep his promise?" "No," said the Pasha, "no one is bound by a promise after his death." "Fine," said the youth, "now I can tell you what I couldn't tell you before, for I have died and come back to life. Now I can tell you that it is I who am your brother. The other is a barefaced man whom I promised that I would never say anything as long as I lived." Then he recounted everything that had happened to him on his journey.

The Pasha was overjoyed and embraced his brother, and a great feast was held. Then the Pasha ordered the oven to be stoked up and the barefaced man to be thrown into it. And so it was done.

18. The Foolish Youth and the Ring

Once upon a time there was an old woman with one son who was a fool. The mother was very poor and spun yarn for a living. One day her son said, "Mother, I am going out now to sell the yarn." "All right, my son, see that you sell it quickly and bring back a loaf of bread for dinner." The youth departed and sold the yarn for three piastres. On his way to buy bread, he happened upon a charlatan who was about to kill a dog. The youth begged him, "Please don't kill the dog. It would be a sin." "Well, you take it then," said the charlatan. The youth asked, "Will you sell it to me?" "I will indeed," the other replied. So the youth bought the dog for two and a half piastres and used the other half piastre to buy food for the dog.

The boy returned home and told his mother that he had bought a dog. "You fool," she scolded, "what am I supposed to do with a dog?" The poor mother returned to her spindle and spun some more yarn. When she was finished, she gave it to her son to sell. He sold the yarn, but then he happened on someone who was about to kill a cat. And so he bought the cat, just as he had bought the dog, and purchased some fish for it to eat. He returned home again and said, "Mother, I've bought us a cat." "I hope it bites you in the ear, you fool," said the mother, "we don't even have enough to eat and now we have a cat to feed." She began once more to spin yarn which the youth took and sold. This time, he came across someone who was about to kill a donkey. The youth called out, "Don't kill the donkey. Sell it to me." So the youth bought the donkey for fifty piastres and with his remaining ten piastres he bought some straw. The mother was expecting the youth to return with a loaf of bread, but instead he came back with a donkey. The poor woman almost fainted at the sight, but she quickly spun more yarn and this time she went out to sell it herself.

One day, the youth took the donkey out to gather firewood. When he had finished chopping the wood, he loaded it onto the donkey. On their way home, he saw a fire burning in a garden. As he stood watching it, he noticed a snake trapped in a fig tree. "Save me from the fire, son of man!" the snake pleaded with him. "You're a snake and will bite me. I don't trust you," he replied. "If you save me from the fire," answered the snake, "I'll be of great service to you." So the youth went into the garden and rescued the snake from the tree.

When they were out of danger, the snake said, "Come back with me to our cave where my mother and my brothers are." The youth agreed and, on their way, the snake advised him, "Don't accept anything from my mother but the ring she keeps under her tongue." When they arrived at the cave, the mother darted forward to bite the youth, but the little snake called out, "Mother, don't touch the boy. He saved me from the fire." And so she did him no harm. The little snake continued, "Mother, give him something as a reward because he saved my life." She asked the youth what he wanted and he replied, "All I want is the ring under your tongue." She gave him the ring and explained, "The ring will grant your every wish. But take care that you never lose it!"

When the youth returned home, he called out, "Mother, it's time for supper!" "There's no supper, my son. We have nothing to eat," she replied. "Come over here then and you'll see the table laden with lots of delicious foods." The mother was curious to see what the youth had set the table with. But he simply said to his ring, "Ring, oh ring, bring me a table laden with delicious food!", and immediately his wish was granted. When they had finished their meal, the son said to his mother, "Mother, I want the king's daughter. Go and tell the king that your son wants to marry his daughter." The mother went to the king and told him her son's wish. "If he can build a palace better than mine," replied the king, "he can have my daughter."

The old woman returned home and told her son what the king had said. The youth asked the ring to build him a better palace than the king's. Immediately a palace appeared, and was indeed more magnificent than the king's. The mother returned to the king and asked for his daughter's hand, saying, "My son has built the palace and now he wants your daughter." But the king said, "First he must build a road of silver plate leading from my palace to his. Then he can have my daughter." The mother told her son what the king had said. The foolish youth once again asked his ring to do his bidding and at once the road was built. When the mother asked for the hand of the king's daughter for the third time, the king replied, "If he can furnish his palace more grandly than mine, we will give him our daughter."

The youth ordered the ring to fill the palace with elegant furnishings and the mother returned to the king to tell him everything was ready. The king went over to see for himself, and as the youth's palace was indeed furnished more grandly than his own he gave the youth his daughter's hand in marriage.

A few days later, the young wife stole the ring and said to it, "Ring, take me to the other side of the Black Sea and leave my husband in the little cottage where he began." Immediately she was transported to the other side of the Black Sea with the ring and the husband was back in his old cottage. He searched everywhere but could not find the ring. The dog and the cat said to him, "Let us go and look for your ring." "All right," replied the youth, and they set out together.

After travelling for some time, they arrived at the Black Sea. There, the cat climbed on the dog's back and they swam across to the other side. They continued their journey until night fell. They came to a house and went in to spend the night. At the stroke of midnight, the cat heard scampering sounds and hid behind the curtains. The king of the mice was getting married and the mice were celebrating his wedding. When the mouse king's bride entered the room, the cat leapt into their midst and frightened them out of their wits. But the cat said to the mice, "Don't be afraid. I won't do you any harm. I want you to help me find me a ring and if you don't, I'll eat the bride."

The mice scurried about in all directions in search of the ring and finally found it with the king's daughter, who was asleep. She had stuck the ring in her nostril which made it very difficult to steal. What could they do? One of the mice stuck his tail into the girl's nose and tickled her, making her sneeze. The ring flew out and the mice caught it and took it back to the cat.

The dog and the cat set off immediately for the sea where the cat climbed onto the dog's back once more. When they were in the middle of the sea, the dog said, "Let me carry the ring for a while." "No," said the cat, "I won't give it to you." They began to argue and while they were fighting, the ring fell into the water. When they reached land, the cat lay down on the beach. It had not waited long before a little fish swam by. The cat caught the fish and inside it was the ring. The dog and the cat took the ring back to their master who ordered, "Ring, bring me back my palace with all its furnishings, and throw my wife into the sea."

The tale is over and wishes you health and happiness.

19. The Princess of China

Once upon a time there were a king and a queen who had one son. One day the youth went hunting with the son of the Grand Vizier. In the course of the hunt, they killed a magpie and a drop of its blood fell onto the snow which had fallen heavily that winter. At that moment, a dervish happened by and, seeing the red blood in the snow, declared, "This blood is as red as the cheeks of the king of China's daughter."

When the youth heard this, he was filled with such longing that he fell ill. He had to see the king of China's daughter and find out if she was really as beautiful as the dervish had said. The queen noticed her son was ill and that he was moaning and sighing all the time. She therefore asked him, "What is troubling you, my son? What has made you so sad?" He replied, "I am so full of longing for something that I have fallen ill. If you promise me that I can have the thing I want, I will get better and not die." The mother asked what it was that he wanted. The youth called the son of the Grand Vizier and secretly asked him, "What do we need to travel to China?" He replied that they would need three baskets full of gold and three horsemen. The son then turned to his mother and said, "Give me three baskets of gold and three horsemen and I promise to return, no matter where I go." The mother went to the king and said to him, "Our only son has fallen ill. He wants to go on a journey because he is suffering from a great longing for something. He will return in two or three years, but he needs three baskets of gold and three horsemen." The king had everything readied and the youth set off with the son of the Grand Vizier.

When they reached China, the three horsemen returned home. The two young men looked for an inn and asked an innkeeper, "How much money do you earn in a day?" "Two hundred pence," replied the innkeeper. "We'll give you three hundred pence," they said, "if you promise not to let anyone else into the inn." The innkeeper gave them a room which was usually reserved for three. They bought some women's clothes and a couple of days later the son of the Grand Vizier went off to the barber for a shave. When the barber had shaved him, the young man gave him one piece of silver. Two or three days later he returned to the barber for another shave and gave him five pieces of silver. The third time he gave him ten pieces of silver and then asked, "Where is the Turkish girls' school here? I have a sister whom I must take to school." The barber dispatched a young lad to show him where the school was, and the two of them returned to the inn where the king's son was waiting. There, the son of the Grand Vizier dressed in the women's clothes. Then he said to the lad, "Show me where the school is and then go home. I will go in by myself."

When they arrived at the school, the lad departed and the son of the Grand Vizier rang the bell at the door of the school. A girl came out and he said to her, "Here are ten pieces of gold. Take them to the teacher with this note and give her my greetings." The girl went back inside, gave the coins to the teacher and said, "There is a lady at the door who gave me these coins and told me to give you her greetings." "Did you see who she was?" asked the teacher, but the girl replied that she hadn't.

The next day the son of the Grand Vizier went back to the school at the same time and rang the bell again. The teacher sent the same girl to answer the door and the young man repeated what he had said the day before. The teacher was surprised and did not understand why someone was sending her gold coins, so she ordered the girl not to accept any more gold coins from the woman if she came again, but to have her come into the building.

The following day, when the young man knocked again, the girl asked him to come inside. He sat down on a bench beside the teacher and gave her ten gold coins. Then all the pupils came in to recite their lessons and went out again, one by one. The king's daughter, too, came in and, having recited her lessons, whispered to the teacher that she wanted to invite the lady to dinner. The teacher said to the young man, "The king's daughter would like to invite you to dinner tonight." The young man accepted the invitation, saying, "Let me go home first to ask permission and tell them not to wait up for me because I can spend the night at the home of the king's daughter." Then he returned to the inn and said to the king's son, "Don't be sad any longer. I'll arrange everything so that you can marry the king's daughter. She has invited me to dinner tonight."

And so he had dinner with her and lay down beside her to go to sleep. The maiden however noticed that the woman was really a young man because in his sleep, he threw his leg over her. She asked him straight out whether he was a man and he told her the whole truth. "Yes, I am a man and have I come here with the king's son who is so taken with you that he wants to marry you. I dressed in these women's clothes so as to be able to see you." She asked him if she might see the king's son. Is your mother still alive?" inquired the son of the Grand Vizier. "Not anymore." "When do you go to pray at her grave?" "Every Friday," she replied. Then he suggested that he would go back to the inn and send the king's son to the graveyard on Friday so that she could see him.

On Friday, the maiden went to the graveyard and saw the king's son, who had fallen asleep. He did not wake up as she approached, but she could see that he was very handsome. She picked three flowers buds, laid them on his chest and departed. When the young man woke up and saw the flower buds, he was angry at himself for having missed the maiden. The son of the Grand Vizier later returned to the maiden and asked her whether she had seen the king's son. She replied, "He was sleeping when I saw him, but I would like very much to see him again, for I have fallen in love with him." "Can you go back to the graveyard tomorrow?" "I can go any day I want. No one stops me," replied the maiden. "I'll go too and make sure he doesn't fall asleep," the youth promised.

When she returned to her mother's grave the next day she found the young man there, threw her arms around him and kissed him. "I would like to have you for my husband," she told him, "but I don't know how, because I am already engaged. The attendants of the groom are coming this week to fetch me." The king's son replied, "I don't know what to do either. Let's ask the son of the Grand Vizier and do whatever he says." When the son of the Grand Vizier arrived, he asked the maiden, "Do you like him enough to have him for your husband?" She told him that she did, but that she was engaged and the attendants of the groom would soon be coming to fetch her. The son of the Grand Vizier suggested a plan, "When you depart with the attendants of the groom and pass the graveyard, tell them that you want to get out for a moment to pay your respects one last time at your mother's grave. When you arrive at the grave, I'll put on your clothes and you stay here with the king's son. I will return in your place and you leave the graveyard as soon as you can get away." When the day came for the groom's attendants to fetch her, she asked them to stop for a moment at the graveyard. They agreed and she went in. The son of the Grand Vizier dressed in the maiden's clothes and climbed back into the wedding coach, and the maiden and the king's son married in secret.

When the son of the Grand Vizier arrived, he was led to the house of the groom with all the pomp and ceremony of a royal wedding. It was the custom there for the sisters of the groom to spend the first three nights with the bride, but the three sisters could not agree which one of them was to go first. The queen, the groom's mother, decided that the youngest daughter, whom she loved the most, should spend the first night with the bride. After the first night, the youngest daughter fell in love with the bride and begged her mother to let her spend the second night there too. The second night, she realized that the bride was actually a young man and said to him, "Tell me the truth, are you a man or a woman?" "I am a man," he replied, "and then told her the story of what had happened. She saw that he was very handsome and said, "I'd like to marry you but I don't know whether you want me." "Oh yes, I do. Do you know what we can do to escape tonight? You must say that you want to go out riding and ask for a stable boy and two horses. When we get to the city gates, show the guards something that belongs to your father and they will let us pass."

The maiden went back to her mother and asked for a stable boy and two horses so that she could go riding. Her mother arranged for everything and the maiden secretly took two water glasses with her. When everyone was asleep in the middle of the night, the maiden and the young man rose and crept out, mounted the horses and sent the stable boy home, saying they would be away for two or three days.

When the servants came the next morning to wake the bride and the youngest daughter, the room was empty. The stable boy reported that they had gone out riding and would be back in two or three days. The servants waited for three days, but the couple never returned, for they had caught up with the king's son and had married too.

20.   The Jealous Sisters

Once upon a time there were three sisters, the youngest of whom was prettier than the other two. Her name was Fatima. One day the sisters asked the sun, "Dear sun, which of us is the prettiest?" "Fatima," the sun replied. The next day, the two sisters rubbed dirt into Fatima's face and asked the sun again, but it repeated, "Fatima is the prettiest."

The two sisters took counsel on what they could do to rid themselves of Fatima. They decided that the next day they would pretend to go out for wood. They would leave the house before Fatima and when she tried to follow them, she would not be able to find them in the woods. They thought they had found the solution. The next morning they said to Fatima, "You sweep the house and we'll go out to chop wood. You'll find us near a gourd we will hang in a tree." The sisters departed and Fatima swept the house. When she had finished, she set off to look for the gourd. She searched in one direction and then in the other, but could not find her sisters anywhere because they had come home by another road. Fatima wandered through the forest in circles, looking for a path. When it got dark, she climbed up to the top of a high tree and saw a light in the distance. Frightened as she was, she ran towards it and entered a cottage.

The cottage was the home of forty thieves who went out robbing at night. As was their custom, they returned home the following day and beat with their rifles on the door, which opened and let them in. The thieves sat down at the table, were brought some delicious food and began to eat. At the first bite they noticed that it was not their servant who had prepared the meal, so they asked him if there were anyone else with him in the house. At first the servant did not want to say anything, but then he told them the truth. The thieves thought that one of them should have Fatima for his wife, but they finally decided to marry her to the servant instead so that there would be no fighting among them. The forty thieves came to love Fatima as their sister and brought her many beautiful presents.

When the sisters heard that Fatima was married, they were annoyed and resolved to kill her. One day they sent a maidservant to the house of the forty thieves with a poisoned golden necklace. The moment Fatima put on the necklace, she fell over dead. When the thieves came home and knocked at the door, there was no one to open it. They entered the cottage and found Fatima lying dead in the middle of the room. They shook her, turned her over, and finally took off her new necklace. Then Fatima came to herself and told the thieves how she had died. She promised the thieves not to accept any more gifts from her sisters.

But the sisters found out that Fatima was not dead after all and sent their maidservant off once again with some more poisoned gold. With compliments and flattery she had learned from the sisters, the maidservant persuaded Fatima to accept the present. The moment she put the gold in her dress, she fell dead again. The thieves and Fatima's husband returned home the next morning and again found her dead on the floor. They turned her over, searched everywhere and finally discovered the gold in her bosom. This time the thieves scolded her even more severely and warned her not to accept any gifts that her sisters might send.

The third day, the sisters sent Fatima a ring which, despite all the thieves' warnings, she accepted. The moment she put the ring on, she fell dead a third time. When the thieves returned home from their robberies they found her and searched her again, but none of them thought of looking at her fingers. Finally they gave up and began to weep and mourn the loss of Fatima. They placed her in a coffin, weighed it down with a tree trunk and threw it into a fountain.

One day, the king's stable boy went to the fountain to water his horse. The horse saw the silhouette of the coffin in the fountain and shied away, refusing to drink. The stable boy returned home and told the king what had happened. The king rode out to the fountain himself and saw the silhouette of the coffin in the water. Immediately he gave orders to have the coffin raised and, seeing the beautiful maiden inside it, took her home with him and locked her in a room. With time she got thinner and thinner and the ring fell off her finger.

As soon as the ring fell off her finger, Fatima came back to life again. The king married her and they both lived happily ever after.

21.   The Grateful Snake and the Magic Case

Once upon a time there was a poor man who had one son. One day the son found a snake almost frozen to death and took it home with him. When the little snake had recovered in the warmth of the house, it said to the boy, "I cannot repay you for what you have done but come with me to my father. When he asks you what he can do to repay you, ask only for his cigarette case. In the case is a strand of hair, and when you shake it, it will make all your wishes come true."

They went off to the little snake's parents who were overjoyed to see their son again. The snake's father asked the youth what he wanted as a reward for having saved their son's life and the youth asked for the case as the little snake had told him. The father became angry and refused to part with his cigarette case. He said to the youth, "I'll give you absolutely anything you want, except for this case." When the youth got up to leave and the little snake set out to follow him, the mother began to weep and implored her husband, "It is better to give him what he wants than for us to lose our son." She would not let her son leave and both of them begged the father until at last he gave in. The little snake called the youth back and the father gave him the cigarette case. Then the youth returned home.

At that time, the king had just proclaimed throughout his territories that all the young men of the country were to assemble in front of his palace because his daughter wished to choose a husband. The princess would throw an apple to the man she wanted. So the youth set out for the assembly. On his way, he shook the case and received handsome garments and a white horse. He let all the other young men go before him and was the last to arrive in front of the palace. The maiden did not care for any of the men who were already assembled there and when the youth finally appeared, she threw him the apple. The king summoned the youth and they agreed to hold the wedding celebration in four months' time. A few days later, the youth went back to his home.

As the wedding approached, he shook his case and a palace appeared. When the villagers woke the next morning, they looked at one another in utter amazement and wondered who could possibly have built the palace in such a short time. Finally, one Saturday evening, the youth went to fetch his bride and they celebrated for several days. The bride and groom spent a week with the king and then returned to the youth's own palace.

After a while, the youth's father-in-law went to war with another king and summoned all his warriors. He called his son-in-law too and made him commander-in-chief of the army. While the youth was at war, the king called his daughter to him and asked her whether she was happy with her husband. She told him that she had no maids or butlers and that all her wishes were granted whenever her husband shook his cigarette case. The king convinced his daughter to steal the case from her husband, but she did not know where he kept it hidden.

In this long-ago time all the birds and animals could speak, so the king asked the animals which one of them could find out where his son-in-law had hidden the cigarette case. "I'll find it," promised the mouse. "When you go to bed, just set out a lamp with some petroleum in it." When everyone had gone to bed and was fast asleep, the mouse dipped its tail into the petroleum and stuck it in the son-in-law's nose. The youth sneezed and the case fell out. The mouse seized the case and ran off with it to the king.

The son-in-law understood at once that he had lost the case when he sneezed and immediately got up to look for it. He searched the palace from top to bottom but could not find it anywhere, and thought that it must have fallen into a mouse hole. He knew that without his case he would become poor again.

But the king, who now knew best of all where the case was, summoned his son-in-law and daughter to him and bestowed upon them a kingdom of their own where they lived happily ever after.

22.   The Maiden Who Was Promised to the Sun

Once upon a time there was a queen who had no children. She prayed to the sun and begged it to give her at least a daughter. She promised that when the child turned twelve, she would give it to the sun. Soon after this, the queen gave birth to a girl. One morning, as the maiden was on her way to school, the sun said to her, "Tell your mother to give me the thing she promised me." The maiden went home and told her mother what the sun had said. The mother replied, "Tell the sun that the thing I promised him is still too small." This the maiden told to the sun the next time she was on her way to school.

But one day, after the maiden's twelfth birthday, the sun abducted her and took her home with him. The mother waited and waited, and when the maiden did not return, she knew that the sun had taken her away in fulfilment of her promise. She had the whole house painted black, locked the door, and would not open it anymore. She sat inside all by herself weeping and lamenting.

In the house of the sun lived a Kulshedra. When the Kulshedra saw the maiden, it exclaimed, "She smells like a child of royalty!" But the sun replied, "She is my child, so don't you touch her." One day the sun sent the maiden into the garden to fetch a head of cabbage. Breaking off the head of cabbage, the girl thought to herself, "My mother's heart has been broken, just like this cabbage," and she began to cry. At the sight of her tears, the sun asked, "Why in heaven's name are you weeping? Is it because you miss your mother?" The maiden replied that she missed her terribly and the sun declared, "Well, if you really want to go home, you must summon an animal to take you." When the maiden began calling for an animal, the sun summoned the Kulshedra for her and asked, "If you were hungry, what would you eat?" "I'd eat her," said the Kulshedra. "And if you were thirsty, what would you drink?" "I'd drink her blood." The sun realized that the Kulshedra was not the right animal to take the maiden home and told her to summon a stag. "Will you take this maiden back home to her house?" asked the sun. "Yes, I will." "If you were hungry, what would you eat?" "I'd eat some fresh grass." "And if you were thirsty, what would you drink?" "I'd drink some cold water," replied the stag. "But if I take the maiden home, her mother must bring me three okas of fresh hay."

The stag then carried the maiden home on its antlers. On the way, the stag became hungry and said to the maiden, "Climb up into the tree over there. If anyone tells you to climb down, don't do it until I get back." The maiden did as she was told and climbed into the tree.

A Kulshedra happened by and, looking around, it spotted the maiden in the tree. "Come on down," it said, "so that we can talk." The maiden replied, "No, I won't come down, because I'm afraid you will to eat me." "I won't eat you," the Kulshedra assured her, but the maiden retorted, "You run home first and I'll climb down when you return." So the Kulshedra departed.

The stag returned and the maiden, who saw the Kulshedra coming back, cried out, "Come quickly! There's a Kulshedra on its way to devour me." The stag took the maiden on its antlers, galloped off and told everyone it met on the way, "If you see a Kulshedra, don't tell it which road we've taken. Tell it that the maiden and the stag have taken another road."

And so they arrived safe and sound at the mother's palace and knocked at her door. When no one opened the door, the maiden knocked again and cried out, "Mother, open the door. It's me, your daughter!" Upon this the mother opened the door and was overjoyed to see her daughter again.

When the friends of the queen's daughter heard that the maiden was back, they went to her mother and asked her to let the girl come out to play. They all went off to a garden with a big gate that would not open. The girls pressed with all their might against the door, but they could not open it. The queen's daughter tried too. She took a run and the moment she touched the door it opened and let her pass, but then it immediately closed again behind her. When the other girls saw that the door would not open again and that the queen's daughter was shut inside, they went back to the maiden's mother and told her sorrowfully what had happened. On hearing this, the queen began to weep and was not to be consoled.

Behind the door, the maiden discovered a garden full of people and animals that had been turned to marble. Among them was a marble king holding a scroll in his hand that said: "I will marry any girl who can spend three days, three nights and three weeks without sleep, for she will bring me back to life." So the maiden sat down with a book and began to read. Three days, three nights and three weeks passed.

One day a merchant happened by with maidservants for sale. The maiden went to the window and asked how much a servant cost. "As much as you wish to give me," replied the merchant. She scooped up a handful of gold coins and tossed them down to him. Then she lowered a rope for the servant to cling to, and heaved her up. She told the servant, "You mustn't sleep for two or three nights so that I can have some rest. As you can see from the scroll the king is holding, I haven't slept for a long time. When the king comes back to life, you must wake me up." She explained to the servant what was written on the king's scroll, and then she lay down and went to sleep.

The servant, however, dressed in the maiden's clothes so that the king would marry her instead. When three weeks were up, the king came to life and asked the servant, "Who are you?" "I am the one who has spent three days, three nights and three weeks without sleep," she replied. And so he made her his wife. "Who is that maiden sleeping over there?" he asked her. "Oh, that is my servant. I brought her along because I was frightened." When the maiden woke up, the king asked his wife, "What shall we do with the servant?" On hearing this, the maiden replied, "Let me tend the geese." So the king made the maiden his goose-girl and she built herself a hut in which to live in. The maiden sat in her hut weeping and recounting her tale of woe.

But the king happened to hear her and came to ask why she was weeping. She told him everything that had happened, and the king made her his wife and had the servant executed and chopped into a thousand pieces.

23.   Muja's Strength

Many years ago there lived a mountain man in Kladusha in the Krahina near Jutbina. He had two sons called Muja and Halil, and a daughter called Kunja. This mountain man was very strong and courageous, as were his two sons. Nevertheless, the father was very poor and had great difficulty making ends meet. Muja had to go to work as soon as he was physically able and entered the service of a rich man to gain his living. He was made a cowherd. He was entrusted with a herd and sent up to the mountain pastures with it.

From then on, Muja would get up as soon as the stars faded and the first rays of dawn began to appear, stick a crust of bread and a few grains of salt in his pocket, take his staff and set out with the cows to climb up into the mountains. There he let the animals graze all day, ate his bread and salt, drank water from a spring and rested in the noonday heat. Muja got to know every path, leading his herd in one direction and then in the other to find the best pastures. In the evening he would take the cows home again. His master was surprised because the cows were producing so much milk that he could not find enough containers in which to store it. But still, Muja received only bread and salt as wages.

Things went well until, one day, Muja lost the cows up in the mountain pastures. He followed their tracks, leaving no stone unturned, and searched until it got dark, but could simply not find his cows. That night he did not return home. How could he go back without the cows? The master would be furious and the other cowherds would make fun of him. Exhausted from his searching and running around, he sat down despondently beside a boulder as the sun set behind the mountains. There, a pitch-black, moonless and starless night overtook him. Muja did not know what else to do so he decided to get a bit of sleep and wait until dawn to start searching for the cows again.

Near the boulder where Muja was resting, he noticed two cradles with crying infants. He went over to have a look and took pity on the infants because they were still very small, rocking them in their cradles until they fell asleep. At midnight, two lights appeared on top of the boulder, bedazzling him with their glare. But in fact they were not lights, but two Zanas bathed in light. The Zanas watched Muja gently rocking the infants' cradles and speaking softly and gently to them. They were surprised to see him and asked, "Who are you? What are you doing here? Have you lost something here and come to look for it?" "I am a cowherd and work for bread and salt," Muja replied, "I wander all day long over the mountain pastures. But today something terrible happened to me. I lost my master's cows and came in search of them. Then night fell and I wanted to get some rest, but I couldn't sleep because of the crying of these infants. I took pity on them and rocked their cradles. They have just fallen asleep... But who are you? I cannot see your faces. Where did the light come from?"

The two Zanas recognized Muja because they had often seen him in the meadows with his cows. "We are Zanas, Muja," they replied. "We go out every night on our wanderings to help the good and the righteous. We left our children here. You are a good man, Muja, and have rocked them to sleep. May you be rewarded! Tell us what you want for having helped us, Muja. Do you want strength? Would you like to be a mighty warrior? Do you want property or wealth? Do you wish for knowledge or to be able to speak other languages? Tell us what you want and we will give it to you." Muja replied to the Zanas, "Fair Zanas, the other cowherds always taunt me and make fun of me. Can you to make me so strong so that I can fight and beat them?" "Is that the only thing you want, Muja?" "That's all."

One Zana then said to the other, "Shall we give Muja some of our milk, sister, so that he will grow strong?" "Yes, let us give him some milk, sister." The Zanas then gave Muja their breasts and he drank three drops of milk. Immediately he felt strong enough to pull a tree out of the ground by its roots. The Zanas said to him, "Let's see how strong you are, Muja. Pick up this rock and raise it into the air." The Zanas pointed to the boulder which weighed as much as three teams of oxen.

Muja knelt, put his arms around the boulder, moved it and eventually managed to lift it as high as his ankles. But he could not get it any higher and dropped it. "We'll have to give him some more milk," they said. Muja had another drink, seized the boulder and raised it as high as his knees. Since he still could not lift it any higher, the Zanas gave him their breasts a third time. His strength grew. Once again he seized the boulder and this time raised it to his waist. As he could not lift it any higher the Zanas gave him even more milk. Muja thus had another drink and was now stronger than a Drangue. He lifted the boulder, rested it on his shoulders and then raised it over his head, standing as firm as a pillar. "Where should I throw the boulder?" he asked the Zanas. "Into the Green Valleys or down onto the Plain of Jutbina?" The Zanas grinned and replied, "We must not give him any more milk or he'll destroy the whole world." Then the Zanas asked Muja all about his father and mother, about his brother and sister and about Jutbina and the Krahina.

In the meantime, a bright moon had risen and was shining down on them. The shadow of the huge boulder grew and darkened the nearby gorges. A cool evening breeze blew over the mountain pastures, the leaves of the beech trees rustled in the wind and the pure spring water murmured. When the Zanas had finished asking Muja all about himself, they said to him, "We would like you to become our blood-brother, Muja. Will you?" "If you want me to be your blood-brother, Zanas, I will," replied Muja, "Once we are related to one another, I can call on your help, and if anyone ever insults you, you can call on me to come and help you." "Fine, blood-brother."

When rosy dawn announced the approach of a new day, the Zanas took their cradles, slung them over their backs and disappeared, leaving behind but a ray of light. Muja rubbed his eyes to make out where the Zanas had gone, but could see nothing but light. He pondered to himself, "Perhaps I was only dreaming?", and went off to a spring to wash. The cold water refreshed him. At the edge of the water was a huge boulder which twenty men could not have lifted. Muja knelt, put his arms around the boulder and lifted it onto his shoulders. He laughed, saying, "It was certainly no dream," and tossed the boulder away. It rolled from cliff to cliff all the way down into the valley below. Its echo resounded through the mountain pastures.

After a while, he departed in search of his cows and eventually found them with their udders full. He herded them together and took them back down into the valley. It was already day when he arrived on the Plain of Jutbina, where all the cowherds had assembled. When they saw Muja coming, they began making fun of him, "Well, you finally got here, did you, sleepy-head?" Muja scowled at them but made no reply. "Didn't the wolves get you and all your cows?" He gave them an even fiercer look but still said nothing. "Shall we have a wrestle?" Muja laughed out loud and replied, "All right, I'm ready for you." "Aren't you afraid we'll pin you to the ground?" "I'm not afraid of you," he countered and hastily rolled up his sleeves. When the strongest of the cowherds approached and tried to grab Muja by the waist to wrestle him down, Muja seized him by the arm, lifted him up, shook him back and forth several times and hurled him into the air. The other cowherds looked on in dismay. "What has happened to Muja?" They backed off, turned tail and fled as fast as they could. "Does anyone else want to fight with me?" Muja shouted. But there was no reply, for they had all disappeared.

Muja led the cows back to his master and said to him, "Here are your cows! You can start looking for another cowherd!" Then he returned to Kladusha, to his father, mother, brother and sister. From then on, Muja worked for himself. He went hunting up in the mountain pastures. The wolves trembled whenever they heard him approach. Muja fought for his country and everyone in the Kingdom of the Christians panicked at the very mention of his name.

24.   Muja and the Zanas

The whole world had heard of the heroic deeds of Gjeto Basho Muja before he had even reached the prime of his life. He had stalked hordes of wild beasts in the mountains and slain many an enemy from the Kingdom of the Christians and from beyond the sea. Muja defended the country and the poor people. His heroic deeds and his courage were famous throughout the Krahina and especially in Jutbina. No foreigners dared cross the border of the Krahina to plunder and maraud. Together with his band of thirty warriors, Muja had conducted many raids in the Krahina and the Kingdom of the Christians, penetrating right to New Kotor and even farther, and every time he returned home victorious. Such a man was Gjeto Basho Muja.

The days, months and years passed until, as is the custom, the time came for him to marry. One day, therefore, Muja mounted his steed as the first rays of dawn struck the peaks, and crossed the mountain passes into the Kingdom of the Christians in order to find himself a bride. He chose a fair maiden from a good family whom his friends had recommended and who was fitting for Muja's lineage.

As soon as Muja had arranged for his marriage, he returned to Jutbina and assembled three hundred attendants to collect the bride, all of whom were his friends. The three hundred shone in their robes of sparkling gold and bore golden swords, arrows and lances. All of them rode white steeds with saddles of gold. All were young with the exception of their leader, an old man with grey hair called Aga Dizdar Osman who was second in command only to Gjeto Basho Muja.

Before the attendants set off to claim the bride in the Kingdom of the Christians, Muja spoke to them, saying, "Listen to my words, attendants! When you reach the mountain pastures, you will come across three shady resting spots. Take care not to revel and not to dismount for a rest. Be careful not to drink from the springs there for it is inhabited by three evil Zanas. They may be having their afternoon nap there or refreshing themselves at the water and you may disturb and upset them. They never let anyone escape unharmed." Muja warned the attendants strictly and they promised to follow his instructions.

The next morning, the attendants saddled and mounted their horses and set off in what was a joyful spectacle for all of Jutbina. They departed for the Kingdom of the Christians to pick up Muja's bride, singing songs and playing music with their horns. When they reached the mountain pastures, they remembered Muja's warning, stopped chanting and making music, dismounted and led their horses by the reins in silence. Nowhere did they pause, nowhere did they drink from the springs, nowhere did they rest in the shade, nowhere did they stop to dance and make merry. They carried on over the mountains and arrived safe and sound on the other side at the bride's home in the Kingdom of the Christians.

Her father welcomed the attendants, giving them food and drink and entertaining them with games and amusements. The music and dancing echoed until midnight. When the stars faded and the next day dawned, the attendants rose, girded their weapons, collected the bride and set off for Jutbina. They continued singing and revelling on their way. The peaks and valleys echoed their mirth.

And so they arrived at one of the three resting spots. Here they remembered Muja's words, stopped singing and revelling and carried on in silence. But then Aga Dizdar Osman, the old man with grey hair, spoke, "Listen, attendants of the bride. I have accompanied many a bride. We have always stopped and revelled at this resting spot and quenched our thirst at this spring. We have always dismounted to dance. Nothing has ever happened to us here. So let us make merry!" When the other attendants heard this, they stopped at the resting spot right away, dismounted and began to sing and dance. They muddied the springs and streams, set up targets and shot at them with their bows and arrows. The mountain pastures echoed with their mirth once again.

Suddenly there was a terrifying clap of thunder. The din resounded through the mountains, a strong gale began to blow through the trees, the mountain pastures thundered and quaked. Hovering over the peaks in the midst of the storm were the three evil Zanas. They gnashed their teeth, spewed smoke and fire and descended upon the resting spot where the attendants of the bride had chosen to stop. In the blink of an eye, the three Zanas turned the attendants to stone and transformed their horses into tree trunks. Where but a moment ago song and merriment had resounded, no human voice or neighing of horses was to be heard. Silence and death reigned. The mountain peaks echoed no more, the wind ceased to blow, the resting spots, the meadows and springs were emptied. Left all alone in her horror and shock was Muja's bride. She alone had survived, but did not know what to do or where to go. The Zanas lunged forth to attack her, seized her by the arm and dragged her off into a cavern deep in the mountains where no human being had ever set foot. There they kept the maiden prisoner, forcing her to feed them and bring them water so that she never had a moment's rest.

Gjeto Basho Muja knew nothing of what had happened. He waited for the attendants to bring him his bride. He waited and waited but they did not come. The longer they were away, the more Muja began to worry. He listened for singing or for the neighing of horses, but there was nothing to be heard. Finally he realized what had happened. The attendants of the bride had broken their word. He was in despair for he knew that the three Zanas were evil to the core and had unimaginable skills.

He waited no longer. Heaving a sack filled with bread and meat over his shoulder, he mounted his steed and set off for the mountain pastures. 'What can all the warriors possibly be doing in their garments of gold and with their golden swords, arrows and lances?' he wondered. 'What has happened to the horses that speed like the wind?' He looked everywhere but could see nothing but stones and tree trunks. Muja approached the stones and recognized their form as that of his warriors. Yes, the white stone was their leader, Aga Dizdar Osman; the reddish one was like Ali Bajraktar and the next was like Butali Tali. One by one, he recognized them all: Basho Jona, Zukut Bajraktar, Shaban Evimadhi, Kazi Mehmet Aga and the rest. Once beings of flesh and blood, they were now turned to stone. But nowhere could Muja find his bride. He was in such despair that he almost broke into tears!

But Muja was a man of courage. He concentrated his thoughts on how to turn the stones and tree trunks into living beings again. He did not restrain his horse or dismount but rode back and forth over the desolate mountain pastures looking for the spring of the Zanas, for their resting spots, and for his bride. He entered a dark grove of beech trees, riding deeper and deeper to where the sun's rays no longer penetrated. He continued on his way until he came to a spring with water as sparkling as tears. There he stopped and dismounted to rest for a while. He took a good look at the beech trees but could find no path through them, only bushes and scrub. Rising above the grove was a cliff covered in grass. At the foot of it he saw a number of boulders buried in scree. The branches of the ancient trees were so entwined with one another that no sunlight or wind could get through. Eternal twilight reigned here.

"This must be the home of the Zanas," Muja thought to himself. He put his horse to pasture among the beech trees and sat down beside the spring, waiting patiently for the Zanas to arrive. Three days passed and no one came. Muja saw deer approach the watering hole but he did not string his bow. He saw fair-feathered birds but he did not shoot at them. He had not come to hunt but for something more important. When three days had passed, he caught sight in the twilight of a young maiden in her bridal gown bearing a water jug in her hands. She was as fair as the moon in May, but so sorrowful. Muja wondered what the young maiden was doing in such a dark and gloomy place. Perhaps she was a vision. But no, she came closer and closer. Suddenly Muja recognized her and his heart began to beat rapidly. The maiden with the jug arrived at the spring, saw Muja but did not recognize him. "Good day, young man!" she said. "Good day, young maid," he replied. She put her jug down to fill it. "Whom are you fetching the water for, maid? Whom are you taking it to?" "Oh, do not ask me, young man. I am of a noble family and have just been married. My attendants were taking me to my husband when..." The maiden proceeded to tell him the whole story of how the Zanas had petrified the men and horses and of how she had been taken prisoner.

Muja asked her, "Who were you marrying, maid? What was the man's name?" "Oh, wretch that I am, I left my mother and father, I left my brothers and sisters to marry a famous warrior. His name is Gjeto Basho Muja. Do you know him, young man? Have you ever heard of him, Gjeto Basho Muja of Jutbina? Muja neither laughed nor responded. He stared at the fair maiden and said, "Do you recognize me, fair maid?" "How could I possibly know you. I've never seen you before. But when I look at you, I am reminded of what I heard of Muja. You could be Gjeto Basho Muja."

Muja could wait no longer and laughed out loud, "I am Muja, fair maid! You have recognized me indeed. But if you are the daughter of a noble family, will you now listen to me and to what I have to say?" "I give you my word," she replied, "by the ruler over the sun and the moon, over heaven and earth, that I will listen to what you have to say, Muja. I would have faith in you even if I knew you were going to behead me." "No, I would never behead you, for I loved you and still do. I am going to try and save you and bring your attendants back to life. To do this, however, I must know the source of the Zanas' power. Therefore, when you return to the cavern, say to them that you know they are very powerful and ask them where they get their power." "Do you really think that the Zanas will tell me the source of their power, Muja?" "Do not lose heart, maiden. Do as I tell you. The sun is now setting behind the mountains and the moon is rising over the beech trees. The Zanas will soon come to the spring to dine in the moonlight. When they sit down to dinner, stand at a distance and do not eat or drink anything. The Zanas will take pity on you and will not want to eat without you. Then, if you remember what to say, they will divulge their secret. Say to them, 'Mountain Zanas, may you always have bread to eat, may you always have the high mountains to live in, may you always have resting spots for your afternoon naps and springs to refresh yourselves in. I have been living with you for some time now and will live with you forever as your prisoner. Why don't you tell me where your power comes from?' Ask them, for there is no reason why they should not believe you. And even if they should turn you to stone, I shall do everything in my power and save you. I will wait for you here tomorrow." "All right, Muja. I will do as you say." The maiden picked up her water jug, said good-bye to Muja and disappeared into the darkness. Muja watched her as long as he could and then returned to the Green Valleys.

The maiden went back to the cavern. The Zanas asked her, "Why are you so late, dear bride?" "The water was muddy, dear Zanas, and I had to wait for it to clear." "You have done well, my dear." The sun set and the moon rose, shining over the tips of the beech trees and spreading its rays into the valleys and gorges. There was a light breeze which caused the leaves to rustle. The birds twittered among the branches. The deer came out of the forest to graze and drink. The mountain Zanas waited no longer. They went off to the spring and set the table to have dinner. The young bride stood near-

126

by, broke the bread for them and brought them their water, but did not sit down with them to eat. She stood there, her eyes downcast. The youngest of the Zanas asked her, "What is wrong, dear bride? Why are you not eating or drinking? You are not ill, are you? Or are you homesick for your fellow human beings?" "No," replied the maiden, "I am neither ill nor homesick. I am content to be here where I am. You love me. That is why you wanted to keep me with you. If you did not love me you would have turned me to stone as you did the others, but I simply cannot eat or drink anymore until you answer a question I have to ask you. Therefore I swear in your presence, dear mountain Zanas, may you always have bread to eat, may you always have the high mountains to live in, may you always have resting spots for your afternoon naps and springs to refresh yourselves in, may you always have the light of the moon to dance by... Why don't you tell me where your power comes from? You have become my sisters. I will always be with you. I can find no better place to live than here with you because nowhere on earth could I find more kind and understanding sisters."

The moment the two elder Zanas heard this they leapt to their feet to turn the poor maiden to stone, but in a flash the youngest Zana intervened, stretched out her hands and covered their mouths so that they could not pronounce the fatal words. She called out, "May God damn you, sisters. What could this young bride possibly do to us if we told her of our power? She is a human, we are Zanas. She is of the earth, we are of the heavens and earth. She is our prisoner, we are the rulers. She has given us her word of honour and we must not doubt it. She breaks our bread for us and brings us our water. We must tell her the truth."

The elder Zanas stepped back. The youngest one turned to the bride and said, "Listen, daughter of man, we have three wild goats with golden horns grazing in the Green Valleys. No one on earth can capture these goats because they are so light-footed and can jump from rock to rock and leap from cliff to cliff. Even the bears and wolves fear them because they attack with their golden horns. But if someone were to capture them - I shudder at the thought - we would have no more power. We would no longer be able to fly and turn humans to stone. We would be women like all the others." When the bride heard this, she smiled, sat down and ate dinner with them as usual.

When the three Zanas had finished their meal, they refreshed themselves in the spring, picked flowers and made wreathes of them which they placed on their heads. Then they sang and danced. The moon and the stars looked down upon them from above. Muja's bride watched them from below. The oaks and beeches made no sound. When the three Zanas had finished singing and dancing they joined hands and returned quickly to their cavern. Silence reigned.

When the new day dawned and the Zanas were still asleep, Muja's bride rose, took her water jug and went to the spring. There she found Muja waiting for her. He was delighted to see her. "You have survived, I see." "Yes, I was almost turned to stone. But ask no more questions. I know you are brave, but they are mountain Zanas and have tremendous power." "And where do they get their power?" Muja asked. The maiden then told him about the three wild goats with the golden horns. Muja listened attentively and said, "I understand, maiden. Now it is my turn. Go back to the Zanas, wait there and do not be afraid. Simply pretend you know nothing. I will return to fetch you safe and sound. I will also bring your attendants back to life and then we will hold our wedding a second time with an even bigger celebration so that the very mountain pastures will resound with the merriment. The Zanas themselves will be your bridesmaids and accompany you in a golden carriage right to my fortress." The maiden looked bewildered and, though she was not too sure, she believed him. She had to smile, however, at the thought of the Zanas with her in the bridal carriage.

Muja waited no longer. He said farewell, mounted his steed and rode off to Jutbina. He stood in the middle of the square and shouted at the top of his voice so that all of the Krahina could hear him, "Listen to me, men! Gjeto Basho Muja is speaking to you. Let all brave hunters come to my fortress tonight with their hounds. I will give you as much to eat and drink as your hearts desire, and tomorrow we will set off for the hunt. Do you hear me?" Then he returned home, slaughtered sheep and lambs, had bread baked and the ovens heated. As soon as they heard Muja's call, three hundred brave hunters gathered with over a thousand hounds and marched towards Muja's fortress. "You called, Muja?" "Yes, my brothers, I called you. Come in!" Muja received them cordially and invited them to dinner. He asked Halil to take out his *lahuta* and play for their entertainment.

At the break of dawn, Muja said to his friends, "Listen,

128

hunters, to why I have called you. There are three wild goats with golden horns grazing in the Green Valleys. I want to take these three goats alive. We will therefore encircle the mountain pastures and hunt them until they tire and fall into our hands. But take care to use neither arrow nor lance, for if you wound or kill them, none of you will ever return to Jutbina alive." "We shall do as you order, Muja," replied the hunters.

Muja then led them into the Green Valleys. There they encircled the mountain pastures and took up their positions. There was no room for even a bird to escape. Muja entered the circle with a few light-footed friends and some of the hounds. The others lay in wait. Then, sounding their horns unceasingly, the hunters pursued the goats from rock to rock and from cliff to cliff. The very mountain pastures trembled. When three days and three nights had passed, the goats grew tired, fell to the ground and lay their heads on the earth to rest. Muja thus captured them alive, took them back to Jutbina and locked them up in a pen, bringing them fresh grass and water from the mountain pastures. He invited the hunters to dine with him once more, gave them presents and bid them farewell.

And what happened up on the mountain pastures? The mountain Zanas suddenly lost their power. They tried to fly but they could not. Their bodies had become stiff and heavy. They ordered the wind to blow through the beech trees, but it refused. They concentrated their thoughts on the wild goats, but the goats did not come. The Zanas then set off to look for the goats; they searched the valleys and the cliffs, but the goats were nowhere to be seen. The eldest Zana clapped her hands and said, "Zanas, my dear Zanas of the mountain cliffs, someone has captured our goats!" Muja's bride smiled. "Listen to me, Zanas, I have something to tell you. Gjeto Basho Muja send his greetings and tells you that since you stole his bride and turned his attendants and their horses to stone, he has captured your goats and is holding them hostage."

When the Zanas heard this, they tried to turn the bride to stone, but they could not for their power had dissipated. They then set off for Jutbina, though not in flight, but on foot like human beings. Their feet were battered by the stones and roots of trees on the way. Thorns scratched their hands. And so they arrived at Muja's door. "Muja, have you taken our goats prisoner?" "Yes, I have captured them and locked them up in my pen. They receive fresh grass and spring water."

With tears in her eyes, the eldest Zana then begged him, "We are in your hands, Gjeto Basho Muja. Either kill us here at your house or give us back what is ours. Otherwise we must perish. We will throw ourselves from a mountain peak. But we are willing to give you back the attendants the way they were. We will return their horses and bring them to you. We will even bring your bride to your door in a golden carriage. You will have them all as they were before."

Muja answered calmly, "I do not want the attendants. I am not even interested in the bride. Leave them where they are, the attendants as stones and the bride in slavery. I can find a new wife in the Krahina or in the Kingdom of the Christians whenever I want. But I cannot let the three goats go for I have never caught anything like them before, although I have combed the mountain pastures many a time. When I remarry I will slaughter them and feed them to the guests. I will hang their golden horns on the wall to shine for me day and night."

When the three Zanas heard this they broke into tears, moaning and groaning so that the very rocks and trees took pity on them as if they had been women, not Zanas. But Muja was not to be moved. The youngest Zana advanced, wiped the tears from her eyes with her hair, clutched Muja's hand and swore, "Listen Gjeto Basho Muja, whenever you arrange for a marriage and have a bride to accompany over the mountain pastures, whenever you have a Baloz to kill, whenever you go hunting, whenever you need a place to rest and refresh yourself, come to our meadows, take your rest, refresh yourself or do battle. We give you our word of honour that we will do no harm to anyone, that we will say nothing harmful to anyone."

Muja hesitated. He reflected a moment and then said, "You are Zanas and Zanas you must remain! A word of honour is a word of honour and a promise is a promise. I shall give you back your wild goats." He then turned and called to Halil, "Halil, release the goats from the pen!" The moment the goats were out of the pen, the Zana's faces changed and they regained their vigour. They transformed themselves into light and flew off to the mountain pastures, leaving the Green Valleys behind them.

There they returned to the attendants of stone and their horses and brought them back to life as they had promised, saying, "Arise and depart! We wish you a safe journey. Return to Jutbina where Gjeto Basho Muja awaits you!" The attendants rubbed their eyes and said, "Oh, look how long we have been sleeping!" They did not remember having been turned to stone. They went to the spring, washed, refreshed themselves and mounted their steeds.

In the meantime, the Zanas had placed Muja's bride in a golden carriage and taken her back to Muja in Jutbina. When the attendants descended into the valley on their way to Jutbina, they began to sing and dance. Muja and Halil went out to welcome them. The mountain pastures echoed with the song of the Zanas:

"Zanas we are and Zanas we remain,

A word of honour is a word of honour,

And a promise is a promise."

The song of the good Zanas resounded from cliff to cliff in the mountains as a second and even bigger wedding was celebrated in Jutbina.

25.   Halil's Marriage

It was very cold that winter. The sun shone but gave little warmth. The wind raged like mad against the old plane tree in Jutbina. So much snow had fallen in the mountains that the beech trees had almost collapsed under the weight. Only the tips of the pines could be seen. The valley echoed from time to time with the sound of avalanches roaring down the mountainsides.

On such a winter's day, Muja was out hunting with his warriors when suddenly the weather changed. A dark wall of clouds approached, blotting out the sky and the surrounding mountain peaks and bringing with it new snow. The warriors could hardly see one another as they descended into the river valley because the new powder snow had covered them in a mantle of white. The biting wind took their very breath away, freezing everything in its path. But Muja's fortress was not far off on the riverbank and he invited them all in for dinner.

But how was Muja to warm up three hundred men with an oven alone? He brought out a jug of *raki* and a couple of barrels of wine. "Drink up, my friends, drink up!" he exclaimed. The warriors drank and could soon breathe freely again for the drink warmed their blood. Then a meal was brought in and they began to eat, converse and enjoy themselves as the snowstorm raged outside and the avalanches echoed through the valleys.

The warriors then turned to their host, saying: "Muja, we hope you will not take offense since we are sitting here as your guests, but we wish to ask you a question." "Speak up, men. I know that you are my friends so I won't be offended." "Why then has your brother Halil not yet married, Muja? All the other men of his age are married and have sons and daughters. It is not because of the money that you would have to give him, is it? Or is it too costly for you to hold a wedding? Your brother is often to be seen in New Kotor. We are afraid that someone will ambush him and take him prisoner to dishonour your family and outrage your clan."

Muja turned to his friends, saying, "I thank you, my companions, for having divulged your worries to me. I can assure you that it is by no means a question of money. I would not skimp if my brother were to marry. You yourselves have brothers and know what a joy it is for a younger brother to be able to make preparations for a wedding. He who has a brother has two hearts. You are well aware that Halil goes to New Kotor, but he does nothing wrong. He is a warrior and fights courageously like a man. If ever he should cause dishonour to our family, may he go blind. If ever he were to cause outrage to the clan, may he be struck by lightning and may Mother Earth cast him out of his grave the very first night."

Halil then rose and exclaimed, "By my brother and my sister I swear that I would rather die than marry! All the women in the Krahina and all the maidens of Jutbina are like sisters to me. I will perish if I don't have Tanusha, the daughter of the King of the Christians, for my wife. I saw her when we were allies. No maiden on earth is fairer than she. Her eyebrows are like the branches of the willow, her forehead is like the mountains in the moonlight, her eyes are like black cherries, her eyelashes are like a swallow's wings, her face is like a red apple shining among the branches, her nose is as slender as a blade of grass, her delicate mouth is like a blossom, her white teeth sparkle like pebbles in the sun after a rainfall. She has the neck of a dove, a body as slender as a fir tree. The skin of her hands is ..." Muja saw his enthusiasm and put his finger to his lips, but that only made Halil more excited.

Basho Jono, an old bachelor, then proclaimed, "We will all have our say here, Muja! I, too, did not marry, and not for want of money or friends, nor because I never found a maiden. I did not marry because I simply did not wish to!"

Then Aga Dizdar Osman jumped to his feet and addressed Halil indulgently, "Listen, my boy. Tomorrow a great day will dawn for you. We shall send thirty warriors out to find thirty fair maidens. You yourself can choose the best one. Then we will celebrate the wedding and marry you off properly..."

Halil interrupted him, "God forbid, warriors of Jutbina! Where in heaven or on earth has a brother ever married his sister? I have sworn to take the king's daughter, Tanusha, and marry only her. Listen therefore to my words, warriors of Jutbina! Up to now, I have lived a solitary life as quiet as the grave and have not married. What makes you possibly think that I would get married now?"

Halil then turned and cursed the mountain pastures: "You are at fault, oh, lofty mountain pastures! You are so weighted down in snow that I can find no path to reach the Kingdom of the Christians! Oh, if only a sea breeze would flow through the mountains and melt the snow to open the roads, our marriage could be celebrated!" The mountains heard Halil's cursing and rumbled in reply. The sea heard Halil's invitation to invade the mountains and sent forth a warm gale. A dark cloud approached bearing rain. Avalanches tumbled into the canyons, the mountains echoed their roar. In three days' time, the snow had melted away and gushed down into the rivers below.

The nightingale sang in the mountains and children frolicked once more in the meadows. The high mountain pastures were covered in green, the beech trees began to bud and flowers and grass grew in the valleys. Halil said to his brother, "Muja, give me your warhorse so that I can go and claim my Tanusha." But Muja refused. Halil was hurt by this refusal because his brother's steed was as swift as a bird in flight. But what could he do? He mounted his own horse and prepared to set off.

Muja's elderly mother scolded him, saying, "What made you do that, my son? Why didn't you give him your steed? If anything happens to him in the Kingdom of the Christians you will never forgive yourself." Muja suddenly regretted his decision and called his brother back. He bestowed upon Halil his warhorse and gave him a final piece of advice, "When you reach the border with the Kingdom, Halil, let the reins loose and the horse will take you directly to Vuk Harambash, my blood-brother. Tell him: 'Muja sends greetings and asks for money and arms to assist his brother in winning the king's daughter.' Have a safe trip, Halil!" Halil mounted the steed, said farewell to Muja and departed for the Kingdom.

The horse and its rider sped like an arrow, leaving the mountains and valleys behind them. Clusters of fir trees and groves of beeches flew past. They travelled for days on end, encountering no human beings. The sun proclaimed, "Halil shall be under my protection." The moon too bestowed its protection upon Halil. Even the mountain Oras declared, "Halil shall be under our protection." The mountain goats of the Zanas whispered, "Halil shall be under the protection of the sun as long as it shines. In the dark of night he shall be under the protection of the moon. May the Zanas protect his weapons."

Halil was startled and wondered, "What are these voices I hear among the pines? Can it be that the goats are talking?" The reply was immediate, "Make no mistake about it, Halil. We are not simple goats but three mountain goats who live with the Zanas." Halil listened attentively and said, "So this is the home of the Zanas! May your word never be broken, oh Zanas. May my eyes be under the protection of the sun, may my legs be under the protection of the moon and may my weapons be under the protection of the Zanas who hold watch and vigil."

When Halil had crossed the mountains, he saw a mighty river. On the other side of it was a broad plain. Halil descended from the mountain pastures to give his horse to drink, but when they arrived the horse shied away, backing off three steps. Halil then saw a human being leaning against a cliff. When he got closer, he recognized that it was no human being, but a mountain Ora herself. She asked Halil, "Where are you going, young man?" Halil replied courteously, "I am on my way to the Kingdom of the Christians to see Vuk Harambash." The mountain Ora laughed, confusing Halil until she explained, "Listen, young warrior, I know exactly why you have come. I caught sight of you in the Green Valleys and learned to cherish you like my own eyes. I have been watching over you for days now and followed you here to give you my protection. You will not find Vuk Harambash. He left the Kingdom many years ago. Come over here. Can you see yonder mighty river? They call it the Danube. Cast your eyes over to the other side, and look up there at that shadow. Can you see the white tents? And can you distinguish the red tent in their midst? Set off immediately holding the reins of your horse tightly and it will take you straight to the king's daughter."

Thereupon, the Ora vanished up into the mountains. Halil rode further down into the valley as the sun set and evening approached.

The nightingales up in the mountain pastures wondered, "What is wrong with the moon, for it is not rising." The mountain goats on the peaks responded, "Be patient, birds. You have nothing to do but sing. The moon has other tasks tonight. Someone is under its protection and it is accompanying him."

Halil spurred his steed on and reached the river. There he tied the horse to a young oak tree and approached the tents in the dark of night. When he got close to the red tent, he stopped and chose a spot to rest under a tree whose roots reached the river. There he sat down and waited for midnight.

At the stroke of midnight, Halil drew his sharp dagger, crawled on all fours up to the red tent and cut a hole in it. Putting his hand through the hole, he touched a forehead. It was that of Tanusha, the king's daughter. The maiden was startled and screamed. Three hundred other maidens rushed to her bedside, asking her, "Why did you scream? You've never screamed like that before." "Go back to bed, my good friends," replied Tanusha, "I simply dreamt that something touched me and I woke up screaming."

The maidens went back to bed, but Tanusha could not sleep. Suddenly, she noticed a ring rolling across the floor. Picking it up straight away, she saw on it the image of a young man. Tanusha wondered where she had seen the face before and recognized it as that of Halil. Just as she was about to speak, Halil said to her, "It is I, Halil. Do you believe me?" "How did you get here? You must think you have three hundred souls. But come in. Either we will escape for good or we will die here together." Halil waited no longer, saying, "Stay where you are for a moment!" Crouching in front of the tent, he drew his sword from its sheath and looked around, but could see no one. Then he entered the tent. The maiden took Halil by the hand and led him into another room containing her trousseau. There she took out some women's clothes embroidered in gold and gave them to him, saying, "Put these on, Halil. If they see you like that tomorrow, the king will behead the both of us." Halil changed his clothes and looked just like a maiden.

The next day dawned, dispersing the darkness of night. The sun, which was protecting Halil, rose but shone only faintly. The maidens had risen early to take their woollens down to the river to wash. There they sang songs as did their work. Tanusha, too, went down to the river with another maiden. The two held hands and sat down on the rocks on the bank of the river.

"Listen, Earthly Beauty," the other maidens said to Tanusha, "where did that girl come from who surpasses us all in beauty? Her eyes are like those of a Zana, her forehead is like the moon, her body is as slender as a pine tree in the mountain pastures. No one under the sun is as fair as she." "Be ashamed of yourselves, all three hundred of you!" replied Tanusha, "There is nothing on earth without compare.

She is a poor maiden and has been promised to the Pasha of Dumlik. But the poor thing has no dowry. Her father is dead and her mother gone. That is why she has come to the king to ask him for money. But leave me alone now. Wash your woollens and don't ask any more questions." Not another word was said. The maidens washed their woollens in silence among the rocks at the riverbank. Some of them even wept out of pity for the poor girl.

But what was the queen doing in Kotor? She had had a nightmare in which she saw a herd of three hundred white sheep with a black wolf in their midst. A black wolf in sheeps' clothing. On waking, she got up and went to the king. "Arise, king! You have but one daughter whom you haven't seen in a long time. Mount your best steed and go to see her. I have had a bad dream." "May it not come true," replied the king. "In my dream," she said, "I saw a wolf from Jutbina come and scatter the three hundred maidens who are protecting our daughter."

When the king heard this he rose, put on his boots and spurs, had his warhorse saddled and covered with a coat of mail, and set off for the banks of the Danube. When he arrived, he counted the maidens, one by one. There was one maiden too many, the prettiest one, so he asked his daughter, "Tanusha, your father is so happy to see you! But where did this maiden whose fairness surpasses that of all the others come from?" "She is a poor girl whose father is dead. Her mother is gone. She has been promised to the Pasha of Dumlik but has no dowry. That is why she came to me to ask you for something." The king was deeply moved on hearing this. "We will set off for New Kotor immediately," he said, "and take the maiden with us." The king ordered his courtiers to mount the three hundred maidens on horseback and set off with the whole caravan for New Kotor.

And so they departed. Tanusha rode at the end of the caravan hand in hand with Halil. They were surrounded by soldiers so they had no chance to escape. Three days later they arrived in Kotor. The three hundred maidens were given quarters in the houses of the town. Tanusha chose the strongest fortress on a cliff overlooking the sea. The fortress was built of polished marble, twelve stories high and three hundred feet long. There were verdant gardens with fresh water from which they could see the sailboats out at sea. Whenever anyone entered that fortress, it was as if his whole life was transformed.

Tanusha and Halil spent three days and three nights there eating, drinking and amusing themselves. "What shall we do to get back to Jutbina?" asked Halil. "Let your horse go," said Tanusha, "so that it crosses the sea. Then we will find a boat with oars and a sail. You row and I'll manage the sailand we'll get back to the Krahina as soon as a strong wind rises. Your horse will be waiting for us when we get there so that we can ride back to Jutbina. I am afraid to tell my mother, though, because I know her well."

When the queen saw Halil's steed galloping over the waves of the sea, she was sure that her dream had come true and that something had happened. She set off immediately to see the king. "May God smite you, husband. Our daughter has been in Kotor for three days now and neither you nor I have seen her." "Well, go and see her then," replied the king, "for I have no time. I have important affairs of state to tend to."

The queen readied herself and set off to visit the fortress overlooking the sea. She found the door locked and called gently, "Tanusha, your mother is so proud of you! Open the door so that I can see you, for I've missed you so." The maiden trembled and whispered to Halil, asking him what she should do. Halil replied, "Open the door and leave everything to fate." But the poor maiden did not have the courage to open the door and called to her mother, "I can't open, mother, for I am ill in bed and am so exhausted..." "I too was young once, my daughter. I often suffered what you are suffering now. I give you my word of honour that I will take care of you. But you must open the door first." The naive maiden descended the staircase and opened the door.

But the queen was now more like a ferocious monster than a gentle mother. When she saw Halil, she quivered like a snake and let out a scream. "May God take your life, daughter! You've filled the fortress with thugs from Jutbina!" She slammed the door behind her and fled to the king, screaming at him, "You're done for now, husband! The thugs of Jutbina have taken over, seized your fortress and blemished your daughter's reputation!" "Calm down, woman! What are you talking about?" shouted the king of Kotor, his cheeks ablaze. He set off, gathered his soldiers, ordered them to guard the shoreline and took the fortress on the cliffs by storm.

Halil offered no resistance. He was taken prisoner and tied up. The king seized the two of them, Halil and Tanusha. "So this is how you've dishonoured me, Tanusha? How could you dare let this thug from Jutbina into the fortress?" he asked his daughter. Tanusha was speechless. She threw her arms around Halil and refused to let him go. "This is the man I loved and still love today!"

But the king with his mighty army was unyielding. He cast Halil into a deep dungeon and threw Tanusha out into the streets. "So, daughter, may you perish in the streets. That's what you wanted. My door is sealed to you. You need never return!"

The maiden began to weep and lament, and wandered off down the first road she saw. People came out of their houses and felt sorry for her, but no one dared approach her because the king had dispatched his sentries to follow her. When Tanusha got to the edge of Kotor, she came upon a man called Jovan who asked her, "Why are you weeping, my poor Tanusha? I've never heard anyone lament the way you do. Come into my house!" "Your invitation is in vain, Jovan. I cannot enter for they have taken Halil prisoner. My father has expelled me from his house and cast me out into the streets." "My poor sister, who has caused you such pain?" "My own mother! Have pity on me, Jovan. Send a message to Muja telling him to come to Halil's assistance at once. Otherwise Halil will rot in prison." "I don't know any Muja," Jovan replied, "but there is a woman near here from the Krahina who will know where he is to be found. Her fortress is at the end of Kotor. The one with the new gate." Jovan then accompanied Tanusha up to the gate. There they met the woman from the Krahina who had just returned from a waterfall. "What has happened, poor Tanusha?" asked the woman. "I wish my fate on no one else," the maiden replied. "My father has thrown me out. I can never return. And they have taken Halil prisoner. If Muja doesn't come to save him, I'm afraid he will perish. My father will have him executed."

The woman, who was of good breeding, consoled Tanusha, saying, "Take courage, Tanusha. If Muja is alive he will be here within three days and marry you to Halil." She found a messenger whom she could trust and sent him straight away to Muja. The following day, the messenger, gasping from exhaustion, knocked at Muja's door and explained all that had happened. Muja listened and laughed aloud, saying as if Halil were standing in front of him, "You stupid ox of Kotor, did I not tell you that they would get you there? If the honour of Jutbina were not at stake, I swear I would not move an inch. But I must act to save you, if only for the sake of Jutbina."

Having said this, he climbed out onto the parapet of his fortress and proclaimed so that all of Jutbina and the Krahina could hear him, "To arms, warriors! Gjeto Basho Muja summons you! Come with me to do battle!" The warriors heard his call and were at his side immediately. When they asked what had happened, Muja declared that Halil had dishonoured them and had been taken prisoner in New Kotor. The honour of Jutbina and the whole Krahina was at stake. The three hundred warriors prepared for battle. The forests resounded and the rivers grew murky as their horses sped onwards to New Kotor. Dismounting at the seashore, Muja positioned his companions in the bushes and among the rocks, ordering them not to move or attack until he gave the signal.

Oh, what a multitude arrived that day in New Kotor! The king had summoned all his subjects to show them something they had never seen before. A thug from Jutbina was to be beheaded. Everyone assembled on a large square. It was a Sunday. In the middle of the square was a handsome young man, It was poor Halil with his hands and feet in chains. All of Kotor had come to laugh and make fun of him. Halil stared at them indifferently and suffered the humiliation in silence.

Finally the king rose to his feet, twirled the tips of his long moustache, opened his mouth and said to Halil, "Can you see death already, Halil? It is right beside you. Have you ever been in such dire straits before? Can anything be worse than death?" Halil responded bravely, "Listen to my words, king. A man is never in a real predicament until his final hour comes. But many things are worse than death. For an Albanian, death is less bitter than betraying a friend after giving one's word of honour or not having a crust of bread to offer to a guest. And know, king, that no matter what predicaments I was in before, I was all the freer afterwards. It will be no different this time!"

The king looked at his subjects assembled on the square and at his warriors surrounding Halil. He gave a forced smile and said, "If you have a final word to speak, speak it now, for your life is about to end at the post you see beside you. We are going to behead you. And the same treatment will be given to the other thugs of Jutbina."

"May God smite you, king, for only God knows who this post is really for. You must know that we Albanians are not afraid of death. Our ancestors taught us never to fear death or die in our beds, but to look death in the eye with a song on our lips and sword in hand. Such is the sweetest of deaths for a man. Will you allow me to sing one last song?" "Sing as much as you want, Halil. I would enjoy hearing a song from Jutbina - hearing it and laughing at it," said the king.

They untied Halil's hands and brought him a *lahuta*. He picked it up and began in a mighty voice to intone a mountain song in his mother tongue, a language the king did not understand. The people listened with great interest. The king, too, was intrigued by the song and asked an old man, "What is the song about? It sounds more like a war cry." The old man, who understood Albanian, told the king, "He is chastising the sun and moon and calling upon the Zanas to come to his assistance. And he is sending a final greeting to the oldest of the Zanas as is the custom of the Albanians." The king exploded with laughter, exclaiming, "Hey! There are no more Zanas left. The sun is ours, and the rivers too. Everything belongs to us!"

At that moment, a bird flew down from the mountains and perched on the branch of a beech tree nearby. Halil sang to the bird, telling it to send Muja greetings from his brother.

Gjeto Basho Muja heard the song and, thundering down into the valley, let out a strident war cry causing the very foundations of the fortresses to tremble and a tidal wave to swell in the sea. The mountains echoed as if a storm had broken. Muja's warriors rushed into battle letting no one escape. The carnage began. The warriors tore at each other with their teeth. The horses, too, bit into one another. The sea was covered with bodies floating in blood. Gjeto Basho Muja, untiring, fought on in the enemy's midst. Halil called out to him, "Take care not to slay the king, Muja! Free me from my chains first for I have sworn that he will breathe his last at this post." Muja freed his brother who rushed forth to take the king alive. And the king was indeed to perish with his back to the post.

The warriors of Jutbina put New Kotor to the torch and within minutes the whole town was ablaze. Muja went berserk at the sight of the blood and showed no mercy, neither with the fortresses collapsing around him nor with the burning bodies. Three times the sun set and three time the moon rose before the fires went out. Not a single stone in the town was still in place.

As the warriors set off to return to Jutbina, they turned to look back at New Kotor, proclaiming, "Hear our words, city of destruction. We have razed you to the ground! Should anyone ask you why, tell them it was because a mother betrayed her daughter."

Thus Muja saved his brother and Halil married the maiden he loved, though she was now an orphan.

26.   Muja and Halil Visit the Sultan

Muja and Halil were the greatest of heroes. Their spectacular deeds were known throughout the Krahina and the Kingdom of the Christians. They had never let a Baloz escape alive, they had never allowed a Christian king to invade Jutbina, or any warriors, guerrilla fighters or pandours to cross over the mountains from the Kingdom of the Christians. The two had invaded New Kotor with their band of thirty warriors, had done battle with the king, torn down his fortresses and set fire to his palaces. They had carried off maidens and always returned to Jutbina victorious with a song on their lips. When Muja's son Omer was treacherously slain, the two invaded Zahar with their friends and put everything to the torch. Naturally their companions often fell on the battlefield or were wounded in sword fights. Such is the nature of war. Gjeto Basho Muja had lost seven sons up in the mountains, all seven of them as young men. His beloved sons now lay under the grass among the beech trees and were mourned for by their mother Ajkunja, by the birds and by the Zanas of the mountain pastures. They mourned for them, and all Jutbina sang of their heroic deeds, for Muja's sons had fought as heroes and died as heroes.

And what happened thereafter? Messengers had been sent to Istanbul to seek the support of the Sultan. They had taken gifts with them and had fallen on their knees before the Sultan, adoring and praising him. "Sultan," they said slyly, "you are mighty and reign over land and sea. Why do you not reign over Jutbina? Muja and Halil hold sway there and do whatever they wish. They block the roads and highways, rob travellers and even murder little children. We beg of you, Sultan, vanquish Muja and Halil as you have vanquished the whole world. Seize the two of them, behead them and hang them from the walls so that all of Istanbul can see that they are common thieves."

The Sultan accepted the gifts which the messengers had brought and listened to what they had to say. He pondered a while and then clapped his hands. "What are your orders, oh Sultan?" his attendants asked, ready to fulfil his wishes. "Give me paper and a quill so that I can write a letter to Gjeto Basho Muja of Jutbina." They brought him some fine white paper, black ink and a sharpened quill. The Sultan sat on a pillow on the floor and began to write his letter. When he had finished, he folded the letter, sealed it with black sealing wax and handed it to a Tatar. "Take this letter to Muja of Jutbina in the Krahina. He is to appear before me immediately, otherwise I will send my army there and dismantle his fortress stone by stone. I will pursue him up into the mountains and hang him with a rope." The Tatar took the letter, mounted his steed and rode like the wind to Jutbina where he arrived sweating and covered in dust. There, he went straight to the fortress of Muja, knocked on the door, gave Muja the letter and returned immediately whence he had come.

Gjeto Basho Muja opened the letter and read it. He knit his brow and scowled. Halil, on seeing him, exclaimed, "Muja, I've seen you read many a letter but I've never seen you look so grim. Has a good friend or blood-brother died? Has another Baloz arisen from the sea and challenged you to battle? Or has the King of the Christians set off with all his warriors, commanders and pandours to invade Jutbina? Don't worry, Muja! Jutbina and the whole Krahina are behind us." "Be quiet or be damned, Halil. No one has died, no Baloz has arisen, no foreign king with his warriors, commanders and pandours has invaded Jutbina. But someone has made accusations about us to the Sultan, saying that we are blocking the roads, robbing travellers and even murdering little children. I don't know what to do, Halil! The Sultan has written that I should appear before him, otherwise he will invade us. It is a dreadful situation indeed. We cannot fight the King of the Christians and the Sultan at the same time. Should we barricade ourselves in our fortress and fight until we fall? Or should we take to the mountains and fight there until the Sultan and the King encircle us together. We could fight as long as we are able and then throw ourselves from the cliffs so that we don't fall into their hands alive." "Do you know what we should do, Muja?" said Halil. "Let us ask our mother. She will give us her advice." "Good, Halil, let's ask her."

They went to their mother and told her what the Sultan had written, saying they did not know what to do. The mother laughed, saying, "You will neither barricade yourselves in the fortress nor take to the mountains, but ready yourselves, saddle your steeds and ride directly to the Sultan who is waiting for you. Tell him that what others have told him is not true, that you do not block the roads, rob travellers and murder little children. You are true warriors and only fight with men on the battlefield." "The Sultan won't ask any questions, mother. He will simply execute us. He will call his moor and have him behead us right away." "No he won't, because you haven't done the things he has accused you of. You are not common thieves, but warriors. The Sultan ought to know this, and if he doesn't, you must tell him so. Saddle your steeds my sons and be off!"

At the crack of dawn Muja and Halil shoed and saddled their steeds, dressed and put on their armour. They covered their heads in cloaks and let the tips of their moustaches droop so that no one would recognize them as they passed through the Kingdom of the Christians. They bandaged the legs of their steeds so that they would limp. Everyone who saw them pass was surprised. "Who are those Gypsies as big as oak trees, with cloaks covering their heads and drooping moustaches?" "Never seen them before," said the people. Everyone watched them at a distance, but no one dared to approach. "Muja," Halil asked, "why are we putting ourselves to such shame? This is worse than death. Have we reached the battlefield yet?" "Yes, we have, Halil." They dismounted, unbandaged their legs of their steeds, threw off the cloaks and twirled their moustaches. The people standing nearby suddenly recognized who they were and fled, screaming, "It's Muja and Halil, Muja and Halil!" They locked themselves in their cellars. Now the two could continue their journey unhindered. They were off in a flash of lightning, leaving a cloud of dust and smoke behind them. The mouths of their steeds frothed and emitted a yellowish smoke from which the mountain oaks caught fire. The flames spread and masked the mountain pastures in their smoke.

Thus the brothers sped through the Kingdom of the Christians and through the Sultan's empire on to Istanbul. The Sultan's sons were awestruck at the sound of their approach, saying, "What is that roar? Is it thunder or cannon fire from the Kingdom of the Christians?" The Sultan replied, "It is neither the heavens nor cannon fire. Muja and Halil are on their way. I have summoned them."

The two brothers rode straight into the palace and dismounted. The guards were startled to see them and wondered if they were human beings or oak trees, but let them pass. Muja said to Halil, "Wait here, brother, and keep watch. If the Sultan calls the moor, you slay him first and call me. The blood in Istanbul and in the Sultan's palace will then be knee-deep, for I am armed." As Muja climbed the steps, the whole staircase creaked and sagged under his weight. The carpenters had to be called to repair and reinforce it. When Muja tried entering the hall, he found the door too small. Again the carpenters had to be called to enlarge it.

Finally Muja entered. The Sultan was sitting on a pillow on the floor and looking at him in awe. "Is it a human being or a mountain?" he wondered. Muja's head touched the ceiling, his thighs were as thick as the Sultan himself. He greeted the Sultan courteously: "Greetings, oh Sultan! I am Gjeto Basho Muja of Jutbina. You have summoned me and I have come. How are you faring, Sultan? How are your sons?" The Sultan offered him a seat and asked him about Jutbina and the Krahina, about his battles in the Kingdom of the Christians and about the Sea Baloz. Muja answered his questions, then grinned and asked, "Sultan, are you going to call your moor now to have me beheaded?" The Sultan stroked his beard and looked quite surprised. "No, Muja," he said, "why should I call the moor? I had heard much about you and wanted to meet you." Muja sat a little while longer and chatted with the Sultan. Then he said, "Allow me now to take my leave, Sultan, for my brother Halil is waiting for me downstairs."

A hook on Muja's trousers, however, caught on the pillow on which the mighty Sultan was sitting. When Muja rose to leave, he dragged the pillow and the Sultan after him right to the top of the stairs, without noticing a thing. At the staircase he extricated the hook, left the Sultan sitting there and descended. When he reached the bottom of the stairs, he and Halil mounted their steeds and rode back to Jutbina.

27.   Muja Avenges Halil's Death

Halil was dead. The warrior who made all of New Kotor and Zahar tremble and who was dreaded throughout the Kingdom of the Christians as far as the Danube, had been slain. His friends had buried him up in the mountain pastures. Muja was alone, bereft of his companion. The lofty mountains too were lonesome, for the warriors' cry was no longer to be heard. Only the cuckoo remained in a dried-up stream bed, its chant echoing plaintively over the meadows.

One day, a voice arose from the depths of the earth and addressed the bird: "Cuckoo, oh cuckoo, listen to my words! I am sending you a message." The cuckoo replied, "I am indeed surprised to hear a human voice on these solitary mountain peaks and yet see no humans. I am used to being here alone, and to tell the truth, have never heard a voice up in these mountains here. Where are you speaking from?" The same voice spoke again, saying, "I am of the dead, cuckoo, that is why you cannot see me. I lie under the earth." "But who are you?" "I am Halil, brother of Gjeto Basho Muja. Listen to my message, cuckoo, and take it to my brother. Say to him: Oh, Muja of Kladusha, I, your brother Halil, send you greetings from the mountain pasture where I lie. I fear neither wind nor rain, neither snow nor cold, neither thunder nor lightning.

But God has caused me to suffer great hardship. It is Captain Kreshto of the Kingdom of the Christians. Every Sunday, he comes here to hunt. Nor does he come alone. He brings three hundred companions with him. They all stand in front of my grave and vilify me, shouting: 'Halil, get up and rise from the grave so that we can fight man to man! You used to block the roads, do battle with us and frighten our friends out of their wits. The whole Kingdom right up to the Danube trembled at the very mention of your name. You slew many a warrior with your sword, razed many a fortress and carried off many a maiden. I have now come to avenge myself. I will never leave you in peace, even in death!' So speaks Kreshto over and over. He stomps on my grave with his feet and pounds it with his cudgel, never letting my bones rest. Then he summons his three hundred companions and they all stomp on my grave. I have told him, Muja, that a dead man is dead and cannot rise to do battle. I would like to rise, Muja, but I cannot. I lie six yards under the earth covered by a heavy tombstone. If you wish to do battle, Kreshto, I told him, then call on my brother Muja and he will face you. If you are still my brother, Muja, rid me of this pest so that my bones can finally come to rest. Have you understood, cuckoo?" "I understand," it replied from the bed of the dried-up stream. "Bear my message to Muja. In our courtyard we have a withered mulberry tree. Perch there and wait until my brother hears your call. It may be that they curse you, but do not take offense. Will you give him my message anyway?" "I will, Halil," replied the cuckoo. "I am off to Jutbina. Farewell Halil!"

The cuckoo spread its wings and set off, flying straight to Jutbina. On arrival, it landed on the mulberry tree and sang its "cuckoo". Muja's wife heard the bird, opened her window and shouted angrily, "Be off, bird of ill tidings! A cuckoo landed on the mulberry tree at the same time last year and brought us the news of Halil's death. Go away or Muja will come out and pluck your feathers." The cuckoo replied in an injured air, "I have never been to this area, nor did I bring you news of Halil's death. But listen to me now. I come from Halil's grave in the mountains. Halil heard me there and asked me to bear greetings to Muja. He also gave me a message and I shall not depart without having given it to him even if you try to kill me."

Muja heard the cuckoo and rushed out into the courtyard addressing the bird gently, "Speak, cuckoo! If you wish to enter our home, if you want anything to eat or drink, please come in and stay as long as you like." The cuckoo replied from its perch on the withered mulberry tree, "No, Muja, that is not why I am here. I have come because Halil gave me a message for you." The cuckoo then repeated word for word what Halil had told it. Muja listened and said to the bird, "Farewell, cuckoo! Greet Halil for me and tell him that I will be there next Sunday." The cuckoo then took to the air and flew back to the mountain pastures.

On Friday, Muja went out onto the parapet of his fortress and summoned his warriors to battle. All of Jutbina and the whole Krahina heard his call, seized their weapons and gathered immediately in front of Muja's home. They asked why he had summoned them and he informed them that they were to leave Saturday to do battle in the mountains. He invited all the warriors to stay with him and showed them great hospitality. They spent the night at his home until Saturday came.

In the dark of night they set off, led by Muja, and rode up into the mountains, arriving on Sunday morning at Halil's grave. There Muja said to them, "My friends, conceal yourselves on both sides of the road. That is the direction Captain Kreshto and his band of three hundred companions will take when they come to defile Halil's grave. Promise me that you will not talk or fight until I give the word." The warriors promised and lay in ambush, waiting silently. The only noises to be heard were the wind rustling in the beech trees and the murmur of the spring.

At daybreak, the call of hunters could be heard in the distance. Then came a deafening roar as Captain Kreshto appeared with his three hundred companions. He walked up to Halil's grave, stood on the tombstone and stomped on it three times, calling loudly, "Rise from your grave, Halil, and let us do battle!" But he could speak and defile the grave with his feet and cudgel no longer, for at that very moment Muja's deep voice resounded in the mountain. "I will give you satisfaction, Captain Kreshto!" Kreshto froze and said, "Holy God! What was that voice thundering in the mountains? Has the dead man actually risen from his grave?" Kreshto's three hundred companions froze too. Muja delayed no longer. Drawing his sword, he sprang forth. Kreshto tried to retreat but Muja slew him with one fell stroke. Once again, Muja's voice thundered: "Such is the vengeance for defiling Halil's grave!"

28.   Gjergj Elez Alia

Gjergj Elez Alia had always been the greatest of heroes. For years he had been the strongest in the land of our forefathers and had always defended its honour. With cudgel and sword in hand he fought enemies who came from land and sea to ravage and enslave our country. Gjergj Elez Alia brought all enemies to their knees.

In the course of his many battles, however, he had received nine wounds and now lay nine years in his tower wasting away. Everyone had forgotten him and abandoned him to his fate, except his sister. She sat day and night at his bedside, cleansed his wounds for nine years with spring water, rinsed them with her tears and dried his blood with her hair. She bound his wounds with their mother's shawl. Their father's old clothes provided shade. His weapons hung at the foot of the bed. Whenever he looked at them, he felt his heart beating fervently and was filled with a ray of hope.

When his sister bound his wounds, he endured the pain like a man. There was but one pain Gjergj could not endure, that of seeing his beloved sister with him in the high tower, shut in as if buried alive, looking after him and caring for his wounds. This pain caused Gjergj to rage. His sister had never had any pleasure in life. Her friends had enjoyed the fruits of their youth, had fallen in love, married and had children. She lived alone in the tower with her sick brother Gjergj.

As the ninth year passed, the word spread that a swarthy Baloz had risen from of the sea, a mighty and cunning giant, worse than anything that had ever befallen the land before. This evil Baloz had demanded a heavy tribute from the country: every family was to give it one young maiden and a roast of mutton. Day after day, it continued its murderous course. Week after week it devastated whole regions. It had slain so many warriors that no one had the courage to oppose it, for its cudgel was huge, its sword razor-sharp and its lance able to transfix all bodies in its path. The whole country suffered from the evil deeds of the Baloz.

Gjergj Elez Alia knew nothing of these evil deeds. He wasted away in bed like an unburied corpse. No friends came to tell him their woes or to ask his help since they all knew well that he could not even get up and walk to the door.

When the turn came for Gjergj's house to pay tribute to the Baloz, the sister began to weep, curse and lament, "Why, oh why has death forgotten us, brother? Our parents are already resting in peace under the linden tree, the brother is at death's door in his own house and the sister is now to fall prey to the Baloz. Why doesn't the tower simply collapse and bury us. Death would be sweeter than a life without honour."

At that moment, Gjergj awoke and looked around, unaware of what was happening. He could feel moisture on his face and thought that the tower was decaying and letting the rain in. With a heavy heart he looked up at his sister and saw the traces of tears on her pallid cheeks. In his rage he cursed the tower. "May you turn black, oh tower! May you rot from top to bottom and be inhabited by snakes! How can you let raindrops fall on my bed?" His sister wiped the tears from her eyes and said, "No, brother, it is not raining nor is the roof leaking. Your wounds and the solitude have weakened you so much that you don't know what you're saying. I have just been weeping, brother!" Gjergj stroked her arm with his emaciated hand, stroked her face, looked into her tender eyes and spoke, this time more lucidly, "Why are you weeping, sister? I have been wasting away for nine years now, and in all these nine years your brother Gjergj has found no peace, he has trembled like the leaves of the beech tree in the sunlight. Have you not had food and drink over these nine years? Has your brother not left you clothes? Has he offended you or bored you so that you now want to leave him and marry?"

The sister took his hand, placed it on her forehead and replied, "Oh, brother! It is your suffering that has confused you and made you talk this way. I would rather be buried alive than think of marriage. I have enough to eat and drink, and enough clothes. Nor have you ever offended me. You have been a brother and a father to me. But now, Gjergj, the time has come for me to tell you of the calamity which has befallen us. You have not risen and gone out the door once in all these nine years and your sister has never complained. But why should I now have to suffer the disgrace of being offered to the Baloz?"

When Gjergj heard this, he suddenly forgot his wounds and sprang to his feet as if he had never been ill. A hero, slim and slender as he had always been, he stood there and said to her, "Sister, take the warhorse into town at once and bring it to the smith who is my blood brother. Bring him greetings from Gjergj and tell him to fit the steed with shoes of iron and nails of bronze, for I am going to challenge the Baloz. If my blood brother will not shoe the steed, take it to the other smith who is my friend." The maiden mounted the steed and rode as swiftly as she could into town to see the blood brother. When she greeted the smith and asked him on behalf of her brother to shoe the steed, he began making excuses. In the nine years Gjergj had been shut up in the tower, the smith had forgotten they were blood brothers. He proposed slyly, "If you were to be kind to me, young maiden, and do me a favour, I'd save your brother Gjergj and shoe his steed so well that he could fly with it like the wind."

The maiden was shocked and turned away from him. "How can you say a thing like that, oh smith? May your tongue wither! I thought I had knocked on the door of a blood brother, but find instead that I have knocked on the door of some wandering minstrel. I've done enough favours to my parents whose bodies now rot under the earth and to my brother Gjergj who has been wasting away for nine years now."

Breaking off her indignant reply to the devious smith, she mounted her steed and rode to the other smith, greeting him on behalf of her brother and conveying his request. The second smith lost no time and shoed the steed as if it were his own. Then he replied, "Greet Gjergj for me. May he be victorious in his battle with the Baloz!"

The maiden set off, expressing her gratitude to the smith, and returned home that evening where Gjergj was waiting for her under the linden tree. He was already dressed and bearing his weapons. Gjergj had heroically overcome the pain in his body to defend the reputation of his house and homeland and to seek vengeance. Gjergj Elez Alia then sent his greetings to the Baloz, telling it, "I have no maiden for you, Baloz! The sheep of my land have not been fed for you. I have but one sister but cannot offer her to you, because otherwise I would have no one to tend my wounds. I therefore challenge you to combat on the battlefield."

When the next day dawned, Gjergj and the Baloz arrived at the battlefield and began exchanging insults. The Baloz was dressed in a heavy coat of armour with a steel helmet on its head and armed with a huge cudgel and a long sword. Even its steed was covered in armour and the earth itself trembled as they advanced. When the Baloz caught a glimpse of the emaciated Gjergj on his steed, it began to laugh and called out, "Have you come back from the grave, Gjergj? Why have you called me to the battlefield in vain? Do you not know that I am the Sea Baloz? I have toppled many a hero from their steeds and sent them to the underworld. I can topple you with my little finger." Gjergj replied, "You have spoken well, Baloz! I have indeed been at death's door for these nine years. But you have brought me back to life. You have demanded my sister before doing battle with me. You have demanded sheep before asking the shepherds. Now I have come to teach you the ancient customs of our people. For we never give up anything without a fight. We will never give our sisters to the Baloz without doing battle with it first. Get ready, Baloz, your final hour has come!" Thus spoke Gjergj Elez Alia!

Then they spurred their steeds and galloped onto the battlefield. The cunning Baloz seized the first opportunity and hurled its cudgel. Gjergj's steed dropped down on its front legs and ducked, and the heavy cudgel flew over Gjergj's head twenty-four yards down into the valley. When it hit the ground, a cloud of dust rose twenty-four yards in the air. Now it was Gjergj's turn. He hurled his cudgel so expertly that it struck the Baloz right on the head. The Baloz collapsed and fell over dead. As it hit the ground, the earth gave a shudder, and its steed took flight. Gjergj swiftly drew his sword and chopped the monster's head off. He hung the head from his saddle, dragged the rest of the body by the feet through the bushes and thickets and threw it into a well where the blood of the swarthy Baloz blackened the whole river.

Then the victorious hero returned home, gathered his friends around him and said: "Lend me your ears, my friends! I am leaving you my tower and giving you all my money, my animals and my possessions! Take good care of the sister of Gjergj Elez Alia!" The hero then embraced his sorrowful sister who was waiting for him.

And at that very moment, the two hearts ceased beating and the brother and sister passed away. No one had ever seen a simpler and sweeter death. Their friends grieved for them and buried them in a grave wide enough for both brother and sister in their embrace. Around the grave they constructed a thick wall so that no one might forget how much the brother loved his sister and how much the sister had loved him.

29.   Aga Ymer of Ulcinj

Aga Ymer of Ulcinj was in the prime of his life when he married. The day after his wedding the young man received an order from the Sultan saying, "Aga Ymer of Ulcinj, you must depart immediately for war. The enemy has invaded..." The order was terrible, for it separated the young man from his young wife, but as Aga Ymer was a true warrior, he lost no words. He rose, saddled his steed, gathered his weapons and bid farewell to his parents. Then he returned to his young bride and said, "My beloved wife, the Sultan has called me up. I must go to war immediately." "Take me with you, Aga Ymer," she begged him. "No, I cannot take you with me," replied Aga Ymer. "I am going to war and war is for men only. I want you to promise me not to marry again, but to wait until I return. Tell me how long you will wait for me, my love." "I will wait nine days." "Nine days is not very long. I have a great distance to travel and the war can last a long time. If you love me as I love you, you will wait nine years and nine days. When nine years and nine days have passed and I have not returned, you may marry and live happily, for that will mean that I am dead." The young wife sighed, "All right, Aga Ymer, I will wait for you for nine years and nine days." They both gave their word of honour. Aga Ymer bid farewell to his wife, mounted his steed and set off content for war. The steed galloped so swiftly that it left a cloud of dust behind them, for the rider was in great haste to do battle.

Aga Ymer of Ulcinj was heroic but there were many enemies. In his first battle, a multitude of cavalrymen dressed in coats of armour attacked, encircling him and setting upon him with their swords. Aga Ymer fought bravely, slew many an enemy and wounded others until they killed his steed. Aga Ymer continued fighting on foot until his sword was shattered. The enemy took him prisoner and tossed him into the dungeon of a castle surrounded by high walls. They treated him with respect, for Aga Ymer was a hero and heroes are always treated with respect.

Days in the dungeon turned to weeks, weeks turned to months and months to years. But Aga Ymer never lost hope, for his wife had promised to wait for nine years and nine days. He ate, drank, cheered his friends and played the lute. The daughter of the foreign king was quite astonished. "Who is that man," she wondered, "who doesn't seem to mind being prisoner in a foreign land?" "He is called Aga Ymer of Ulcinj," they told her. "He must be a strong man." "Yes, he is strong and merry and cheers the other prisoners with his words and songs."

Aga Ymer was indeed full of hope because he was waiting for the Sultan to pay the ransom for his release. "I have fought many years in his service," said Aga Ymer to himself, "I have always obeyed his orders and gone whenever he summoned me." But Sultans have the habit of forgetting the people who have helped them, and Aga Ymer had been forgotten by this Sultan, who had never even considered paying the ransom. And so nine years passed. The fatal day approached, the ninth day which his wife had promised to wait for before she remarried. Aga Ymer fell into a state of profound dejection. His eyes lost their colour, he could no longer eat, drink or make merry. His friends were surprised and asked him what the matter was, but he gave no reply, crouched instead in silence with his head bowed. The king's daughter heard no more music and asked, "What is wrong with Aga Ymer? His voice is no longer to be heard." "He has not eaten or drunk anything for days," they told her, "he no longer sleeps or plays his lute." "Call Aga Ymer to me," said the king's daughter. On being brought to her and asked what the matter was, Aga Ymer replied that he could no longer eat or drink because of a bad dream. "What kind of bad dream?" asked the king's daughter. He then told her his dream: "I dreamt I saw my home, blackened and in ruins. My father was dead and forgotten, my mother blind. I saw my wife, too. She was about to remarry. I have only spent one night with her. The next day I received orders to go to war. I fought and was taken prisoner. We had sworn to be faithful to one another and my wife promised to wait nine years and nine days for my return. The nine years have since passed and now the nine days are running their course. I beg of you, daughter of the king, ask you father's permission to release me for a few days. I will return home, talk to my wife and come back to the dungeon." "I can ask him, Aga Ymer, but as you know, my father the king demands nine sacks of silver for your release." "But where, oh where, can I get the nine sacks, daughter of the king? I have been a prisoner for nine years now." "If I release you, Aga Ymer, what will you give me as a pledge that you will return?" "I give you my word of honour, daughter of the king."

Since the king's daughter knew that Aga Ymer was an Albanian and would rather die than break his word of honour, she said to him, "Rise, Aga Ymer, saddle the bay horse and you'll be in Ulcinj in three days." Aga Ymer's companions lamented, "How unfortunate we are! Aga Ymer is being released and leaving us behind." But he replied, "What is wrong with you, my friends? As long as I survive, I will return and we will wait out the time together. Farewell!" They wished him luck on his journey. Aga Ymer saddled and mounted the bay horse and set off towards Ulcinj.

The horse sped like an arrow over mountains and valleys. "Swiftly, horse, swiftly so that we may reach my beauty before she remarries." The horse galloped day and night until it was exhausted. Aga Ymer, too, was fatigued, but they continued their course. In three days and three nights they arrived, catching sight of the fair town of Ulcinj shimmering before them on the water. "Oh, Ulcinj, Ulcinj, I have carried your image in my heart my whole life long!" sighted Aga Ymer. "Night after night for nine years I dreamt of you! For nine years now I have been longing to kiss your earth." The waves were breaking on the beach, a fresh breeze was blowing, the sea-gulls circled in the sky above.

And there glimmered the house of Aga Ymer, too, as if in a dream. "Am I really here?" he asked himself. As he was dying of thirst, he stopped as a fountain to drink. There he saw his aged mother who did not recognize him. "Greetings, old woman." "Good day, prisoner!" "How do you know I am a prisoner?" inquired Aga Ymer. His mother replied, "By your long shoulder-length hair. Where have you come from, prisoner?" "I have just arrived from Spain." The mother then asked, "Have you ever seen my Aga Ymer or heard anything about him?" "Yes, I saw him three weeks ago," he replied, "Aga Ymer was killed. I myself washed his corpse, mourned him and paid my last respects." The aged woman began to weep and, although it caused him great pain, he did not reveal the truth to her. Instead he inquired, "Who are those people over there passing in such a hurry, old woman? What are the volleys of fire echoing in the hills?" "They are the companions of Pasha Veli, that son of a dog, who have come

157

to collect the bride and take her back to his home. The cannon fire is for the wedding." "Which bride are they collecting?" "It is the wife of my son Aga Ymer."

Aga Ymer sprang to his horse and rode off towards the wedding party. "Greetings, wedding attendants." "Greetings prisoner. Which land have you come from?" "From Spain." "Have you ever seen Aga Ymer or heard anything of him?" they asked. Aga Ymer told them, as he had his mother, that Aga Ymer had been killed three weeks before. The wedding attendants were relieved to hear this, but the bride began to weep under her veil.

Aga Ymer became angry and said, "Aga Ymer gave me a message. May I speak to the bride for a moment?" "Yes, as long as you wish, prisoner." Aga Ymer approached the bridal coach and asked the bride, "Would you recognize Aga Ymer?" She replied, "How could I possibly recognize him? I only slept with him one night and then waited nine years for him. His poor mother, however, told me that he has a scar on his right arm where a horse bit him." Aga Ymer rolled up his sleeve and showed her the scar. The bride recognized him instantly, rejoiced, got out of the coach, threw off her veil and said to the attendants, "Have a pleasant journey, companions of mine. I am accompanying my true husband. This is Aga Ymer whom I married and who will be my husband forever and ever." Aga Ymer made room for his bride on the horse and they went home.

The next morning he mounted his bay horse again to set off for Spain as he had promised. "Swiftly, horse, swiftly, for I gave the king's daughter my word of honour!" They left fair Ulcinj behind them and the horse galloped day and night.

But what was going on in Spain in the meanwhile? The king had not seen or heard of Aga Ymer for some time. He asked for news of him and was told that his daughter had released him, but that he would return. The king summoned his daughter immediately and asked right away, "What happened to the prisoner Aga Ymer?" "I let him go, father," she replied, "he had to see his wife because she was going to marry someone else. He gave me his word of honour that he would return in three days. Today is the last day and he will return."

The king was furious, crying, "No, he has deceived you. He won't return!" and ordered his daughter to be beheaded. "Wait until dark, father," the daughter implored him, "Aga Ymer will return. He won't break his word." "He'll never come back," countered the king.

"Once they escape from prison, they never return. They are like birds in a cage. Once you open the door, they're gone." "He will return. He gave me his word of honour," insisted the king's daughter. "A word of honour is but a word, my daughter, and words are soon gone with the wind. Even kings break their word."

At that moment, a horseman appeared on the horizon, approaching swiftly. Soon he was at the gates of the fortress, dismounted from his sweating horse and greeted the king's daughter! "I gave you my word and have returned. I was your prisoner and now I am your prisoner again." The king looked down at him in amazement and said, "Aga Ymer, you are indeed an honest man and have kept your word. You shall be released!" He then turned to his guards and gave orders, "Release Aga Ymer and his nine companions and let them go wherever they wish."

30.   Scanderbeg and Ballaban

Albania was faced with a mighty Turkish invasion, but managed to defend itself. A second, even greater invasion then took place and was again repulsed. A third, fourth and fifth invasion followed. Under the leadership of Gjergj Kastrioti Scanderbeg, however, the Albanians were able to counter each of these invasions for they fought with courage for their country, their honour, their lives and their children. Over long years and in the course of the many battles, the little province of Albania had become a graveyard for the armies of the Ottoman Empire. Armies attacked and never returned home, as if they had vanished from the very face of the earth.

Finally Sultan Murad himself came, with soldiers as numerous as the sands of the seashore, and he, too, was defeated. He returned home and this time took with him another army even greater and headed by his Janissaries, and yet it, too, was vanquished. On his deathbed, the mighty Sultan Murad lamented: "What shame! I have lived in vain! I have conquered the whole world, I forced Bulgaria and Serbia into submission, I claimed victory over Greece and reached the very Danube, conquering the wide plains of Romania and Hungary beyond that river, but I was never able to defeat little Albania. I almost had it in the palm of my hand when Scanderbeg drove me out."

The son of Sultan Murad, Mehmed the Great, followed in his father's footsteps, except that he was much crueler. He besieged and waged war against Constantinople the magnificent surrounded by its three walls. When Mehmed defeated the city, the most beautiful and wealthiest on earth, he set up his golden throne there and called himself the Victorious. Following this great deed, which caused all of Europe to tremble, Mehmed resolved to force Albania into submission as his dying father had begged him to do. Thus Sultan Mehmed assembled a huge army with both infantry and cavalry, and headed it himself to march against Albania. The very earth quaked as the iron-girded army marched by. The rivers were left without water after it had passed, for its horses and soldiers had drunk them dry. No grass grew where it had marched.

Accompanying the Turkish Sultan was Ballaban Badheri, an Albanian who had betrayed his country and was now leading the Turks. Ballaban had been a great hero, but he betrayed both his lineage and his people, and fought for the Turks to gain high office, fame and fortune. He had taken part in many wars and had been first to plant the crescent flag on the walls of Constantinople. Sultan Mehmed had therefore made Ballaban a pasha and conferred upon him gifts and honours. But honour for the Turks had a bitter aftertaste to the Albanians, for Ballaban had no compassion with their sufferings, neither with the land he trampled upon, nor with the homes he razed to the ground, nor with Albanian blood he spilled. Sultan Mehmed set out with this great army to force Albania into submission, but Albania had Scanderbeg!

When Scanderbeg received word that the Turks were again to invade Albania, he assembled his troops and set forth to do battle with them. But how few they were, compared to the Turkish hordes! The Albanians made their camp on the bank of a sparkling river, setting up their tents in the shade. They ate, drank and made merry as if celebrating a wedding instead of going to war.

After some time, they caught sight of a Turk riding towards them, carrying a white flag in his hand. They rode out to meet him and block his path. "Who are you and what do you want here?" "I am a messenger of the mighty Sultan of the Turks and wish to speak to your lord, Scanderbeg." "Get off your horse then and come with us." And so, they took him to Scanderbeg. The messenger greeted Scanderbeg politely, saying, "Lord of the Albanians, the mighty Turkish Sultan has sent me to ask you where you wish to do battle with him." Scanderbeg answered curtly, "Go and tell your lord to come and see for himself." When the messenger returned, Sultan Mehmed asked him, "Did you see Scanderbeg?" "Yes, Sultan, I saw him." "Did you also see his warriors?" "Yes, I did." "Does Scanderbeg have a large army?" "He has but a small army though his soldiers all have shining, courageous eyes. They were singing and dancing a sword dance and waiting impatiently for the order to attack." "What is this sword dance, messenger?" asked the Sultan. "It is an Albanian dance, oh ruler over land and sea. It would send a shiver down your spine to see how those men, as huge as oak trees, were leaping and dancing with their naked swords and crossing their blades as if in battle. They forced me to stand in their midst and crossed swords over my head, but without touching me at all." "What happened then?" "The Albanians are not afraid of death, mighty Sultan, especially death in battle. They say that death in battle by the sword is sweeter than honey."

The mighty Sultan Mehmed sighed and said to himself, "If only I had these people under my sway, if only they would do battle for me!" He turned to the messenger again and asked, "Why is it they say that death in battle is sweeter than honey?" "Because they say they are fighting for their freedom, for their country. They also swear by the sword, mighty Sultan." "Only by the sword?" "No, by the earth, by water and stones, too. And by bread and salt. They say that honour is paradise and disgrace is hell." "And this Scanderbeg, what was he like? Was he afraid?" "No, mighty Sultan, he showed no fear. When I arrived, he was eating with his warriors. He rose and received me standing, with both hands resting on the hilt of his sword, like a god of war. He said only, 'Go and tell your lord to come and see for himself.'" Mighty Sultan Mehmed was infuriated and exclaimed, "I'll show these Albanians what death is. I'll dispatch my army and mow them down like grass. Then we will see if they still rise and dance their sword dance"! "As you wish, mighty Sultan!"

Sultan Mehmed jumped to his feet and gave orders for the drums to be sounded. Immediately the drums began to beat. The noise filled the whole valley and echoed through the canyons. "Send me my shield bearers!" proclaimed the Sultan. The shield bearers appeared at once chanting in unison, "Long live the mighty Sultan! Our lives belong to you! We await your command!" Sultan Mehmed, son of Murad the Great, said to them, "Tell me, shield bearers, which one of you is brave enough to bring me Scanderbeg, dead or alive?" They all heard his words, yet none of them replied. They trembled at the very name of the Albanian hero.

In the ensuing silence, Ballaban Badheri, who had betrayed his own people to fight under the Ottoman flag, stepped forth, "What will you give me, mighty Sultan, if I bring you Scanderbeg?" "I will give you nine hundred thousand ducats of gold and all Albanian lands that you may reign as Pasha as long as you live. You shall be free to execute whomever you please and as many as you please." "You will have him this evening, either dead or in chains," Ballaban promised.

The Sultan was overjoyed for he knew that one could only fight fire with fire and that it would take an Albanian to beat an Albanian. He raised his arm and gave the signal for battle. Nine trumpeters of the Janissaries blew their horns, followed by ninety-nine trumpeters of the other troops. The drums pounded. The Turks drew their sabres, let out a savage war cry and, under the eyes of the Sultan, victor of Constantinople, rushed heroically into battle. The Sultan sat and observed the battle from in front of his silken tent on a hilltop overlooking the river. He could hardly wait for Ballaban Badheri to bring him Scanderbeg, either dead or in chains.

The Tatar archers strung their bows with three arrows each and all fired at the same time, causing the very sky to go black. The Turkish army resembled a swelling sea about to engulf Scanderbeg's small band of warriors. And the battle began. The sparkling river at which the Albanians had camped turned crimson with blood. The Turks attempted to cross the river, but were unable to do so for the Albanians held it firmly. As the battle raged, Scanderbeg waited for his warriors from the mountains who were still to arrive.

Meanwhile, Ballaban had found a spot at which to cross the river with his men. Scanderbeg rushed to block his path and shouted in Albanian, "Come on, come on, Ballaban Badheri! You betrayed your people for a spoonful of Turkish soup! Bravo, what a hero!" Ballaban trembled and turned pale, but stood his ground. Scanderbeg called to him a second time, "You'd love to make a hundred thousand ducats of gold and have Albania as your pashalic, wouldn't you? You shall feel the blade of my sword. Come nearer." Ballaban froze. Scanderbeg called to him a third time, "Attack, traitor, or I will attack first!" Treacherous Ballaban, advancing with his warriors, hurled his lance. Scanderbeg tried to back off but lost control of the reins of his steed and was wounded in the shoulder. The steed too was struck. Scanderbeg fell from the animal and dropped to his knees, but managed to rise to his feet in no time. The Turks cheered and encircled him without delay. Ballaban was now confident of his nine hundred thousand ducats of gold. Scanderbeg supported himself against a mighty oak tree and drew his sword. All those who approached too closely were cut to pieces. The others backed off, but then lunged with Ballaban for the final attack.

As Scanderbeg, completely encircled by the enemy, fought on by himself, two thousand warriors, led by Dukagjin and Livet, rode down from the mountains to his assistance. Clasping their naked swords, they swooped down like a snowy avalanche sweeping away everything in their path. When Scanderbeg saw the warriors coming, he laughed and rejoiced, shouting "Welcome, Dukagjin! Over here, come and help me for I am doing battle with the traitor, holding a sword in one hand and our glorious flag in the other." He then set upon the enemy again like a fire raging in the brush. Headless bodies and severed heads filled the ditches. The Turks either fell or retreated. Only one of them resisted: Ballaban Badheri. They fought on man to man. Scanderbeg did not want to slay Ballaban, but to take him prisoner. At last, he shattered Ballaban's sabre and left him standing unarmed with his head bowed. Scanderbeg wounded him slightly in his right ear, saying, "Now return to your master, dog!"

The Turkish army fled. The Albanians pursued it through the canyons and over streams until it was crushed. The drums were smashed and rolled aimlessly along the ground, the crescent flags were caught up in the bushes. Ballaban, covered in blood and with his head bowed, returned to his master's tent. The Turkish Sultan asked him, "My, my, Ballaban, you are wounded in the head. What of your bragging now? I thought you wanted to bring me Scanderbeg's head this evening?" Ballaban fell to his knees to beg forgiveness of the Sultan, answering, "Mighty Sultan, ruler over land and sea! Hear my words! I was not able to bring you Scanderbeg dead or alive because not only his own strength helped him, but the entire country was behind him. I fought in many battles under your father, I have challenged many a warrior and returned victorious, but I have never met anything like Scanderbeg." The Sultan replied in fury, "Ballaban, cover your head, sign of your infidelity, for I am going to have it removed to appease my wrath at the annihilation of my army. You gave me your word that I would bring the Albanians under my sway this time and you have broken it." The Sultan then gave his Janissaries a sign. They seized the traitor Ballaban, tied him to a tree and beheaded him.

The avalanche of sabre-bearing Albanians was still approaching. When Sultan Mehmed saw them coming, he mounted his steed and fled in haste, leaving his silken tent and his dead warriors behind. The Albanians pursued him but he continued to flee in panic. Once again, Scanderbeg had overcome the superior strength of the Turks.

31.   Shega and Vllastar

It was spring and the sun was shining with renewed strength. No Turks were to be seen outside the walls of Koroni on that festive day during which, according to an ancient custom, the doors and thresholds of the houses were decorated with flowers and greenery.

A pretty young maiden strolled out of the town to pick flowers on the Plain of Koroni. Singing a song of sorrow in her faint and delicate voice, she stooped to gather the flowers.

The Turks had destroyed everything when they passed through her native village. They had put the whole village to the flames and carried off her little brother. No one knew what had become of him. Her father had not been in the village at the time for he was off fighting in Scanderbeg's army. Shega's uncle had taken her and seven other children up to the mountains to escape the war. But when the Turks arrived there, too, he returned down into the valley with his companions to do battle. Shega continued alone from peak to peak trying to escape the carnage. In the end, she arrived back in Koroni where she had relatives. This town had been attacked by the Turks many times. They had left many dead in their path, had disappeared, attacked other towns and then suddenly turned up again outside the walls. What would happen tomorrow? Would she ever see the land of her birth again?

Climbing slowly up into the hills, the maiden sang her song of sorrow and picked the flowers. As the sun set, she tied them into a bouquet. When she noticed that it was getting dark, she turned, and with the bouquet of flowers in her arms, hurried back down to Koroni. All of a sudden, a Turkish horseman appeared before her, seized her by the hair and forced her onto his horse. The flowers fell from her grasp to be trampled by the horse as it sped off. Nature took pity on the screaming maiden, but the Turk did not.

He took her to his commander, a handsome, not as rough-looking young man who wore a knife in his belt and a sword at his

165

side. He forced the maiden into his tent and stared at her with eager eyes. He watched her for a long time and then made his approach. She stepped back into the corner, glaring at him fiercely.

There was a bright moon shining that night. Circling the tent above was a black bird which spoke in a human voice, "What a bird of misfortune I am. A brother is about to kiss his sister!" This the black bird repeated two or three times.

Coming even closer to the maiden, the Turk went pale. "Keep away from me, you bastard!" she shouted in Albanian. The Janissary froze and asked, "Are you Albanian?" "Yes," she replied, "how do you know our language?" He gave no reply, but after a while inquired again, "What family do you come from?" "I am from the clan of the Mirditas, a clan of horsemen and warriors." "Did you have a brother?" "Yes, I had a brother, but the Turks captured him when he was little and made him a Janissary. And now misfortune has placed me in your hands." "What was your brother's name?" "He was called Vllastar," she replied. The Janissary clapped his hands and exclaimed, "Then you are my sister Shega! I am Vllastar, your brother!" The two then embraced and wiped away the tears of joy which were streaming down their cheeks.

Vllastar asked his sister, "Where is our mother now, Shega?" "Mother died in the flames when the Turks burnt down our house." "And what became of our father?" "Father was fighting in Scanderbeg's army when the Turks attacked and razed everything to the ground. He is still with them to avenge us. If you were to come to Albania, you might stand eye to eye with him. You would do battle and kill one another. You are no Albanian. You have become a foreigner." "No," exclaimed Vllaster, "I was an Albanian and still am! We will never do battle with one another but fight shoulder to shoulder to free our native land." He whistled and five other Janissaries entered the tent, all as huge as oak trees, girded with daggers and bearing sword in hand. "You summoned us, my lord?" they asked. "Yes, brothers," said Vllastar, "come over here. Do you recognize this maiden?" "No, my lord, we don't." "This is my sister Shega." The Janissaries bowed their heads and greeted her respectfully. Vllastar continued, "Blood is flowing in our homeland. Our country's leader, Scanderbeg, is doing battle and resisting the Turks. My father is fighting them, too, and so are your fathers. Let us return, brothers, and fight for our native land!" "You have spoken our very thoughts," they replied.

And so the seven of them set off for Albania to fight the Turks there. Shega and Vllastar led the group and returned joyfully to the land of their ancestors.

32. Rozafat Castle

Ancient Rozafat Castle rises proudly over the wide Buna River and over the city of Shkodra. Who knows when the first foundations of the castle were laid? Its history is lost in the mists of the Illyrian age.

There is a legend about the construction of Rozafat Castle which has been transmitted to us from antiquity. Fog lay over the Buna for three days and three nights blanketing the river completely. When three days and three nights had passed, a strong wind began to blow, dissipating the mists and making Mount Valdanuz visible once again. Up on the mountain there were three brothers at work building a castle. The foundations they built during the daytime always collapsed at night, so that they could never finish the castle.

One day, an old man came by and greeted the three brothers, saying, "I wish you success in your work!" "We wish you success, too, old man, though we ourselves are not doing very well. Day after day we work and build and at night the foundations collapse. Do you know what we can do to make the walls stay put?" "Yes, I do," replied the old man, "but it would be a sin if I told you." "Let the sin be ours, because we are the ones who want to build the castle." The old man reflected for a while and then asked, "Are you married? Do you all have wives?" "Yes, we are married," they replied, "Each of us has a wife. But tell us what to do to build the castle." "If you really want to finish the castle, you must swear never to tell your wives what I am going to tell you now. The wife who brings you your food tomorrow you must bury alive in the wall of the castle. Only then will the foundations stay put and last forever."

Thus spoke the old man and departed. But alas, the eldest brother broke his promise and revealed to his wife at home everything that had happened and told her not to go to the place where the castle was being built the next day. The second oldest brother broke his promise, too, and told his wife everything. Only the youngest brother

168

kept his word and said nothing to his wife at home. The next morning the brothers rose early and went to work. Their axes resounded, rocks were crushed, the walls rose and their hearts beat faster and faster...

At home the mother of the three brothers knew nothing of their agreement. She said to the wife of the eldest brother. "The workers need bread, water and their wine flask, daughter-in-law." But she replied, "I'm sorry, dear mother, but I really cannot go today. I am ill." The mother then asked the second wife who answered, "My word, dear mother, I cannot go either, for I must visit my parents today." The mother then turned to the youngest wife, saying, "My dear daughter-in-law, the workers need bread, water and their wine flask." She got up and said, "I would willingly go, mother, but I have my young son here and am afraid he will need weaning and cry." "You go ahead," said the other two daughters-in-law, "we shall look after the boy. He won't cry." So the youngest and best wife stood up, fetched the bread, water and the wine flask, kissed her son good-bye on both cheeks and set off.

She climbed up Mount Valdanuz and approached the place where the three workers were busy. "I wish you success in your work, gentlemen!" But what was wrong? The axes stopped resounding, their hearts beat faster and faster, and their faces turned pale. When the youngest brother saw his wife coming, he hurled his axe away and cursed the rocks and walls. "What is the matter, my lord," his wife asked, "why are you cursing the rocks and walls?" Her older brothers-in-law smiled grimly and the oldest one declared, "You were born under an unlucky star, sister-in-law, for we have sworn to bury you alive in the wall of the castle." "Then may it be so, brothers-in-law," replied the young woman, "I have but one request to make. When you wall me in, leave a hole for my right eye, for my right hand, for my right foot and for my right breast. I have a small son. When he starts to cry, I will cheer him up with my right eye, I will comfort him with my right hand, I will rock him with my right foot and wean him with my right breast. Let my breast turn to stone and the castle flourish. May my son become a great hero, ruler of the world!"

They then took the young woman and walled her into the foundations of the castle. This time the walls did not collapse, but stayed put to rise higher and higher.

Even today, at the foot of the castle, the stones are still damp and mildewed from the tears of the mother weeping for her son.

Notes

1. The Boy and the Earthly Beauty
    Source: Mitko (1878), reprinted in *Folklor shqiptar 1, Proza popullore* (1963), ed. Z. Sako et al.
    Earthly Beauty (Alb. *e bukura e dheut*): a supernatural being in Albanian mythology, the quintessence of beauty, embodying either good or evil, though usually the latter. She can do magic, is crafty and demanding of the hero. She can indeed be won by the hero if he succeeds in performing the labours required of him. The Earthly Beauty figure exists in the folklore of many other cultures: cf. Mod. Greek *Pentámorfi* and *i kalí tou tópou*, Italian, Aromunian, Turkish, Kurdish, and Syrian, but is especially popular in the Balkans. The name 'Earthly Beauty' is most likely a taboo term for some deity of the underworld in antiquity. Tinglimaimun: a fictive distant and uninhabited desert region. Its etymology is uncertain, though the second half of the word is no doubt related to Turkish *maimun* 'monkey'.

2. The Scurfhead
    Source: Mitko (1878), reprinted in *Folklor shqiptar 1, Proza popullore* (1963), ed. Z. Sako et al.
    Scurfhead (Alb. *qeroz*): this popular figure in Albanian folktales is intelligent and artful. His fate is 'marked' either by his scurfy appearance or by an animal hide he wears as a disguise. In Albanian folklore he usually appears as the youngest of three brothers who triumphs in the end. The dragon (Alb. *llamje*) is a monster which guards waterholes and springs. It is related to the Modern Greek *lamia*. Earthly Beauty: see No. 1.

3.   The Three Friends and the Earthly Beauty
      Source: Mitko (1878), reprinted in *Folklor shqiptar 1, Proza populllore* (1963), ed. Z. Sako et al.
      Earthly Beauty: see No. 1. *Kordha* is the Albanian word for the sabre, *ylli* for the star and *deti* for the sea. The act of declaring someone as one's brother (Alb. *vëllamëri*) is a tradition in the Balkans, cf. Serbo-Croatian *probratimstvo*. Kulshedra: a fire-spewing snake-like female dragon usually with seven heads, comparable to the Greek hydra. She is evil and often guards the Earthly Beauty. The word kulshedra derives from Latin *chersydrus* and Greek *khersydros*, an amphibious monster.

4.   The Three Brothers and the Three Sister
      Source: Dozon (1879), reprinted in *Folklor shqiptar 1, Proza populllore* (1963), ed. Z. Sako et al.
      Kulshedra: see No. 3. Oka: Turkish unit of weight equalling 1.24 kilos or 2.75 pounds.

5.   The Youth and the Maiden with Stars on their Foreheads and Crescents on their Breasts
      Source: Dozon (1879), reprinted in *Folklor shqiptar 1, Proza populllore* (1963), ed. Z. Sako et al.
      Earthly Beauty: see No. 1. Kulshedra: see No. 3. A Muslim king could have up to four wives.

6.   The Shoes
      Source: Dozon (1879), reprinted in *Folklor shqiptar 1, Proza populllore* (1963), ed. Z. Sako et al.
      The prince refuses to marry the second king's daughter not because he is already married but because of the king's behaviour. Being a Muslim he could have up to four wives.

7.   The Girl Who Became a Boy
      Source: Dozon (1879), reprinted in *Folklor shqiptar 1, Proza populllore* (1963), ed. Z. Sako et al.
      Kulshedra: see No. 3.

8.   The Maiden in the Box
       Source: Meyer (1896-1897), reprinted in *Folklor shqiptar 1,
       Proza popullore* (1963), ed. Z. Sako et al.
       Smyrna: former name of Izmir, city on the west coast of
       Turkey. Piastre: old coin in Turkey and the Middle East.

9.   The Tale of the Youth Who Understood the Language of the
       Animals
       Source: Pedersen (1895), reprinted in *Folklor shqiptar 1,
       Proza popullore* (1963), ed. Z. Sako et al.

10.   The Stirrup Moor
       Source: Pedersen (1895), reprinted in *Folklor shqiptar 1,
       Proza popullore* (1963), ed. Z. Sako et al.
       The Moor, Alb. *Arap*, a figure to be encountered in Turkish
       folklore too. He is black or dark-skinned and usually evil,
       though also capable of doing good. The word comes no doubt
       from the Turkish word for Arab. Vjosa: river in southern
       Albania flowing into the Adriatic north of Vlora. Jinn: a
       supernatural spirit in Arabic and oriental folklore, which can
       assume either human or animal form. The jinns can live on
       earth or in the underworld. They marry and have their own
       royalty. Earthly Beauty: see No. 1.

11.   The King's Daughter and the Skull
       Source: Frashëri (1936), reprinted in *Folklor shqiptar 1, Proza
       popullore* (1963), ed. Z. Sako et al.
       Arap: see No. 10. Earthly Beauty: see No. 1.

12.   The Bear and the Dervish
       Source: Dozon (1879), reprinted in *Folklor shqiptar 1, Proza
       popullore* (1963), ed. Z. Sako et al.
       Dervish: Muslim monk, in Albania usually of the Bektashi
       order.

13.   The Snake and the King's Daughter
       Source: *Folklor shqiptar 1, Proza popullore* (1963), ed.
       Z. Sako et al.

Kulshedra: see No. 3.

14.   Gjizar the Nightingale
Source: Pedersen (1895), reprinted in *Folklor shqiptar 1, Proza popullore* (1963), ed. Z. Sako et al.
Dervish: see No. 12. Earthly Beauty: see. No. 1.

15.   Half Rooster
Source: *Pralla popullore shqiptare* (1954).
The half rooster (Alb. *gjysmagjeli*) or half chicken motif in folklore exists in many cultures: '*kutsópettos*' in Greece, '*moitié de coq*' recorded in French in 1759, '*mitat de gal*' in Languedoc, '*de halve haan*' in Flemish, '*il galluccio*' in Italian and '*el medio pollo*' in Chile.

16.   The Boy With No Name
Source: *Folklor shqiptar 1, Proza popullore* (1963), ed. Z. Sako et al.
Dervish: see No. 12. Ramadan: 30 days in the ninth month of the Islamic calendar during which Muslims fast from sunrise to sunset. Jinn: see No. 10. Scurfhead: see No. 2.

17.   The Barefaced Man and the Pasha's Brother
Source: Jarnik (1883), reprinted in *Folklor shqiptar 1, Proza popullore* (1963), ed. Z. Sako et al.
A barefaced man (Alb. *qose* or *spano*), i.e. without a moustache, was someone to be avoided, a portent of evil, not only in Albania but also in Muslim Bosnia, cf. the Albanian saying "May God protect you from bearded women and barefaced men." Although full beards were rare, virtually all Albanian men used to wear a moustache. In communist Albania the taboo was reversed; the moustache became a rarity and was viewed as a sign of conservatism and reaction. Kulshedra: see No. 3.

18.   The Foolish Youth and the Ring
Source: Dozon (1881), reprinted in *Folklor shqiptar 1, Proza popullore* (1963), ed. Z. Sako et al.
Piastre: see No. 8.

19. The Princess of China
    Source: Dozon (1879), reprinted in *Folklor shqiptar 1, Proza popullore* (1963), ed. Z. Sako et al.
    Turkish girls' school: During the centuries of Ottoman rule in Albania, Albanian-language schools and books were illegal, most Albanian children being educated at Turkish-language schools. It is therefore understandable for our hero to ask where the local Turkish girls' school is to be found.

20. The Jealous Sisters
    Source: Dozon (1879), reprinted in *Folklor shqiptar 1, Proza popullore* (1963), ed. Z. Sako et al.

21. The Grateful Snake and the Magic Case
    Source: Dozon (1879), reprinted in *Folklor shqiptar 1, Proza popullore* (1963), ed. Z. Sako et al.

22. The Maiden Who Was Promised to the Sun
    Source: Dozon (1879), reprinted in *Folklor shqiptar 1, Proza popullore* (1963), ed. Z. Sako et al.
    Kulshedra: see No. 3.

23. Muja's Strength
    Source: *Tregime të moçme shqiptare* (1987), ed. M. Kuteli.
    The 'Cycle of Muja and Halil' forms the core of the so-called *Këngë Kreshnikësh* (Frontier Warrior Songs), oral epic verse of the northern Albanians. The *Këngë Kreshnikësh*, still sung by old men accompanied by their (one-stringed) *lahutas* and (two-stringed) *çiftelis* not only in Albania but also in southern Bosnia, Montenegro and Kosovo, are the literary reflections of legends portraying and glorifying the heroic feats of warriors. The 'Cycle of Muja and Halil' indeed preserves much of the flavour of heroic cultures of the past such as those in Homer's Iliad in Greek, El Cid in Spanish, the Chanson de Roland in French, the Nibelungenlied in German and the Russian Byliny. The leaders of this band of 30 Albanian 'agas' or warriors are Gjeto Basho Muja (or Muji or Mujo) and his brother Halil. The name Muja (pronounced mooyoh) derives no doubt from

Mustafa though it is believed in folk etymology to be related to the Albanian verbal root *muj* 'to overcome, be able'. Gjeto Basho is adapted from the Serbian and Turkish title *četobaša* (head of a band). The warriors inhabit the frontier region between the Ottoman Empire and Austria-Hungary. The Albanians, being Muslims, live in the *krahina* (province), referring to Muslim territories in general (cf. Serbo-Croatian *krajina*), as opposed to the 'Kingdom' (Alb. *kralia*) of the Christians, or lands to the north under the sway of the Emperor of Austria and other Christian rulers. Our warriors make their home in Jutbina, which can be identified either as the town of Udbina on the Lika river in western Croatian about 50 km northeast of Zadar or as the village of Udbina on the Drinjača river in eastern Bosnia. Kladusha, the birthplace of Muja and Halil, is somewhere near Jutbina (Udbina), possibly the town of Kladanj in eastern Bosnia. According to Maximilian Lambertz (1917), Kotor and New Kotor refer not to the Bay of Kotor which is on the coast of Montenegro but to a region between the Lika and Krbava rivers. Zana: see No. 24. Drangue: semi-human figure of Albanian mythology. Drangues are born with wings under their arms and have supernatural power, especially in their wings and arms. Their primary aim in life is to combat and slay Kulshedras.

24. Muja and the Zanas
Source: *Tregime të moçme shqiptare* (1987), ed. M. Kuteli.
'Cycle of Muja and Halil': see No. 23. Zana: figure in Albanian mythology. Zanas are mountain spirits who dwell near springs and torrents in the northern Albanian Alps. They are courageous and often bestow their protection on Albanian warriors, but can also do evil. Originally a pre-Roman deity, the term Zana is related etymologically to the Latin Diana, Roman goddess of the hunt and moon. Lahuta: Albanian stringed instrument. Baloz: see No. 26.

25. Halil's Marriage
Source: *Tregime të moçme shqiptare* (1987), ed. M. Kuteli.
'Cycle of Muja and Halil': see No. 23. Zana: see No. 24. Ora: protective female spirit in northern Albanian mythology

whose name is often taboo. Everyone has a protecting Ora from birth onwards. Lahuta: see No. 24.

26. Muja and Halil Visit the Sultan
Source: *Tregime të moçme shqiptare* (1987), ed. M. Kuteli.
'Cycle of Muja and Halil': see No. 23. Baloz: a huge monster in Albanian mythology. It usually arises from the sea and exacts tribute in the form of food and young maidens. Pandour: force of Croatian soldiers. Zahar: probably the present-day port of Zadar (Zara) on the Adriatic coast 70 km. from Udbina (Jutbina).

27. Muja Avenges Halil's Death
Source: *Tregime të moçme shqiptare* (1987), ed. M. Kuteli.
'Cycle of Muja and Halil': see No. 23. Zahar: see No. 26.

28. Gjergj Elez Alia
Source: *Tregime të moçme shqiptare* (1987), ed. M. Kuteli.
Gjergj Elez Alia: legendary figure in Albanian oral literature, symbol of fraternal fidelity. Baloz: see No. 26.

29. Aga Ymer of Ulcinj
Source: *Tregime të moçme shqiptare* (1987), ed. M. Kuteli.
Aga Ymer: legendary character in Albanian oral literature, figuring in the motif of reunification of brother and sister or of husband and wife. Aga is a Turkish title for a landowner. Ulcinj: (Alb. *Ulqin*, Italian *Dulcigno*) town on the Montenegrin coast near the Albanian border. Ulcinj and the surrounding area are even today largely Albanian-speaking.

30. Scanderbeg and Ballaban
Source: *Tregime të moçme shqiptare* (1987), ed. M. Kuteli.
Scanderbeg or Skanderbeg (Alb. *Skënderbeu*): Albanian prince and national hero (1405-1468). His real name was George Castrioti (Alb. *Gjergj Kastrioti*). Sent by his father as a hostage to Sultan Murad II, he converted to Islam, and after education in Edirne, was given the name Iskander (Alexander) and the rank of bey (hence Scanderbeg). In 1443, after the Turkish defeat at Nish at the hands of John Hunyadi,

Scanderbeg abandoned the Ottoman army, returned to Albania and embraced Christianity. He took over the fortress of Kruja and was proclaimed commander-in-chief of an independent Albanian army. In the following years, he successfully repulsed thirteen Ottoman invasions and was widely admired in the Christian world for his resistance to the Turks, being titled 'Athleta Christi' by Pope Calixtus III. Albanian resistance held out until after Scanderbeg's death on January 17, 1468 at Lezha (Alessio). In 1478, however, his fortress at Kruja was taken and Albania was to return to over four centuries of Turkish rule. For Albanians, Scanderbeg is the symbol and quintessence of resistance to foreign domination and is a source of much inspiration in both oral and written literature. Janissaries: corps of Turkish infantrymen which existed from 1329 to 1826. The ranks of the Janissaries were filled primarily with abducted Christian children, many of whom Albanians. Under Murad I they grew into an elite and powerful troop, forming the Sultan's personal guard.

31. Shega and Vllastar
     Source: *Tregime të moçme shqiptare* (1987), ed. M. Kuteli.
     The motif of reunification of brother and sister occurs in many folktales. Shega is the Albanian word for pomegranate, Vllastar for sprout or scion. Koroni: (Mod. Greek: *Koróni*) settlement on the Peloponnese or Morea, inhabited largely by Albanians in the Middle Ages. Mirdita: Albanian tribe from the mountainous region of northern central Albania of the same name. Janissaries: see No. 30.

32. Rozafat Castle
     Source: *Tregime të moçme shqiptare* (1987), ed. M. Kuteli.
     Rozafat Castle: ruins of a no doubt originally Illyrian fortification on the outskirts of Shkodra in northern Albania. The motif of a woman being walled in during the construction of a castle or bridge is widespread in Albania and based no doubt on a reality. At the beginning of the twentieth century animals (sheep, goats, chickens) were still sacrificed on such occasion and their remains immured to 'stabilize' the foundations of bridges.

Bibliography

BELLIZZI, Mario

> *Vallja e zaravet. La danza delle fate. Fiabe e leggende delle comunità italo-albanesi del Parco Nazionale del Pollino, Calabria e Basilicata.* A cura di Mario Bellizzi (Edizioni Prometeo, Castrovillari 2000) 315 pp. Bilingual (Italian-Albanian) edition of fables and legends of the Italo-Albanians of Calabria.

BERISHA, Anton

> *E Bukura e Dheut bahet nuse. Përralla shqiptare.* Zgjodhi dhe përgatiti Anton Berisha (Flaka e vëllazërimit, Skopje 1992) 159 pp.

BERISHA, Anton & MUSTAFA, Myzafere (ed.)

> *Anthologji e përrallës shqipe* (Rilindja, Prishtina 1982) 419 pp. Anthology of sixty Albanian folktales.

ÇABEJ, Eqrem

> Albanische Volkskunde. in: *Südost-Forschungen,* Munich, 25 (1966), p. 333-387.

CAMAJ, Martin

> *Racconti popolari di Greci (Katundi) in provincia di Avellina e de Barile (Barili) in provincia di Potenza.* Studi Albanesi 3 (Istituto di Lingua e Letteratura Albanese dell'Università di Roma, Rome 1972). Collection of Arberesh tales with an Italian translation.

CAMAJ, Martin & SCHIER-OBERDORFER, Uta (ed.)

> *Albanische Märchen* (Diederichs, Düsseldorf 1974) 275 pp. Albanian folktales in German translation.

ÇETTA, Anton

> *Tregime popullore, I. Drenicë* (Rilindja, Prishtina 1963) 330 pp. Volume devoted primarily to Albanian folktales from the Drenica valley in Kosovo.
> - *Prozë popullore nga Drenica.* 2 vol. (Enti i teksteve, Prishtina 1970, reprint 1990) 331 & 347 pp. A collection of seventy-two folktales from the Drenica valley (Kosovo).
> - *Balada dhe legjenda* (Instituti Albanologjik, Prishtina 1974) 349 pp.
> - *Këngë kreshnike 1. Letërsia popullore. Vëllim II* (Instituti Albanologjik, Prishtina 1974) 395 pp.
> - *Albanske narodne balade.* Prev. Esad Mekuli. Predg. Vladimir Bovan. Biblioteka Jedinstvo, 85 (Jedinstvo, Prishtina 1976) 167 pp.
> - *Përralla 1* (Instituti Albanologjik, Prishtina 1979). Ninety Albanian folktales.

- *Përralla 2* (Instituti Albanologjik, Prishtina 1982). One hundred forty-four Albanian folktales.
- *Nga folklori ynë. Bleni II. Kallëzime dhe përrallëza* (Rilindja, Prishtina 1989) 410 pp.

ÇETTA, Anton, SYLA, Fazli, MUSTAFA, Myzafere & BERISHA, Anton (ed.)
    Këngë kreshnike III (Instituti Albanologjik, Prishtina 1993) 441 pp.

CINQUEMANI MARTORAMA, Micaela
    Fiabe e leggende albanesi. Illustrazione di Giuseppe Ferrara (Pompei, Rome 1971) 131 pp. Falbes and legends in Italian translation.

COOPER, Paul Fenimore
    Tricks of Women and Other Albanian Tales. Intro. by Burton Rascoe. (Morrow, New York 1928) 220 pp. English translation of Dozon (1881) and Pedersen (1895, 1898).

DINE, Spiro Risto
    Valët e detit prej Spiro Risto Dine (Mbrothësia, Sofia 1908) 856 pp. Important collection of Albanian folklore from the Rilindja period, including folktales and songs.

DOZON, Auguste
    Manuel de la langue chkipe ou albanaise par Auguste Dozon, consul de France. Grammaire, vocabulaire, chrestomathie (Ernest Leroux, Paris 1879) 348 pp. Including twenty-four folktales in Albanian.
- *Contes albanais, recueillis et traduits par Auguste Dozon, auteur du Manuel de la Langue Chkipe* (Ernest Leroux, Paris 1881, reprint New York 1980) 264 pp. French translation of tales in Dozon (1879).

ELSIE, Robert
    Dictionary of Albanian Literature (Greenwood, Westport & New York 1986) 171 pp.
- Albanian Literature in English Translation: a Short Survey. in: *The Slavonic and East European Review*, London, 70. 2 (April 1992), p. 249-257.
- *Anthology of Modern Albanian Poetry. An Elusive Eagle Soars*. Edited and translated with an introduction by Robert Elsie. UNESCO Collection of Representative Works (Forest Books, London & Boston 1993) 213 pp.
- *History of Albanian literature.* East European Monographs 379. ISBN 0-88033-276-X. 2 volumes (Social Science Monographs, Boulder. Distributed by Columbia University Press, New York 1995) xv + 1,054 pp.
- *Dictionary of Albanian Religion, Mythology and Folk Culture* (C. Hurst & Co., London / New York University Press, New York 2000) 357 pp.
- *Albanian Folktales and Legends.* Selected and translated from the Albanian by Robert Elsie. Dukagjini Balkan Books. (Dukagjini, Peja 2001) 240 pp.
- *Handbuch zur albanischen Volkskultur. Mythologie, Religion, Volksglaube, Sitten, Gebräuche und kulturelle Besonderheiten.* Balkanologische Veröffentlichungen, Bd. 36. Fachbereich Philosophie und Geisteswissenschaften der Freien Universität Berlin. (Harrassowitz, Wiesbaden, 2002) xi + 308 pp.

- Zihni Sako. in: *Enzyklopädie des Märchens: Handwörterbuch zur historischen und vergleichenden Erzählforschung.* Herausgegeben von Rolf Wilhelm Brednich, Band 11. Berlin & New York: Walter de Gruyter, 2004., p. 1053-1055.
- *Albanian Literature: a Short History.* (I. B. Tauris, London 2005) 291 pp.
- *Leksiku i kulturës popullore shqiptare: besime, mitologji, fe, doke, rite, festa dhe veçori kulturore.* Përktheu nga anglishtja Abdurrahim Myftiu (Skanderbeg Books, Tirana 2005) 282 pp.
- The Rediscovery of Folk Literature in Albania. in: *History of the Literary Cultures of East-Central Europe: Junctures and Disjunctures in the 19th and 20th Centuries.* Volume III. Edited by Marcel Cornis-Pope and John Neubauer (John Benjamins, Amsterdam & Philadelphia 2007) p. 335-338.
- Albanian Tales. in: *The Greenwood Encyclopedia of Folktales and Fairy Tales.* Donald Haase (ed.). Vol. 1, (Greenwood Press, Westport CT 2008) p. 23-25.
- *Historical Dictionary of Albania.* Second edition. Historical Dictionaries of Europe, no. 75. (Scarecrow Press, Lanham, Maryland, Toronto & Oxford 2010) lxxiii + 587 pp.
- *Historical Dictionary of Kosovo.* Second edition. Historical Dictionaries of Europe, no. 79. (Scarecrow Press, Lanham, Maryland, Toronto & Oxford 2011) lvi + 395 pp.

ELSIE, Robert & MATHIE-HECK, Janice
Songs of the Frontier Warriors: Këngë Kreshnikësh. Albanian Epic Verse in a Bilingual English-Albanian Edition. Edited introduced and translated from the Albanian by Robert Elsie and Janice Mathie-Heck (Bolchazy-Carducci Publ., Wauconda, Illinois 2004) xviii + 414 pp.

GIAMPIETRO, Giuseppina
Mala vila, 'piccola fata'. Fiabe, racconti e leggende italo-albanesi e serbo-croate (Federico Motta Editore, Milan 1992). Includes Italo-Albanian fables and legends.

GURAKUQI, Karl & FISHTA, Filip
Visaret e kombit. Vëllimi 1. Kângë trimnije dhe kreshnikësh. Pjesë të folklorës së botueme. Botimet e Komisjonit të kremtimevet të 25 vjetorit të vet-qeverimit 1912-1937 (Nikaj, Tirana 1937, reprint Rilindja, Prishtina 1996) 323 pp. A masterful collection of heroic and epic songs.

FRASHERI, Stavro
Folklor shqipëtar (Durrës 1936) 387 pp. Collection of eleven folktales.

HAHN, Johann Georg von
Albanesische Studien. 3 vol. (Fr. Mauke, Jena 1854, reprint Karavias, Athens 1981) 347, 169, 244 pp. One of the first publications to include Albanian folktales.
- *Griechische und albanesische Märchen.* Gesammelt, übersetzt und erläutert von J. G. v. Hahn, k. k. Consul für das östliche Griechenland. 2 vol. (Engelmann, Leipzig 1864, reprint Georg Müller, Munich & Berlin 1918) 319 & 339 pp.

HASLUCK, Margaret Masson Hardie

    Këndime Englisht-Shqip or Albanian-English reader. Sixteen Albanian *folk-stories, collected and translated, with two grammars and vocabularies* (Cambridge University Press, Cambridge 1931) xl + 145 pp. Sixteen tales in Albanian and English collected by Hasluck in Elbasan and appendixed to her (now outdated) grammar.

HAXHIHASANI, Qemal (ed.)

    Këngë popullore legjendare. Zgjedhur e pajisur me shënime nga Q. Haxhihasani (Instituti i Shkencave, Tirana 1955) 331 pp.

-   *Këngë popullore historike.* Zgjedhur e pajisur me shënime nga Qemal Haxhihasani nën kujdesin e Zihni Sakos (Instituti i Shkencave, Tirana 1956) 408 pp.

-   *Epika legjendare (Cikli i kreshnikëve).* Vëllimi i parë. Folklor shqiptar II (Instituti i Folklorit, Tirana 1966) 592 pp.

-   *Balada popullore shqiptare* (Naim Frashëri, Tirana 1982) 184 pp.

-   *Epika legjendare.* Vëllimi i dytë. Folklor shqiptar. Seria II (Akademia e Shkencave, Tirana 1983) 376 pp.

-   *Epika historike.* Vëllimi i parë. Folklor shqiptar. Seria III (Akademia e Shkencave, Tirana 1983) 496 pp.

HAXHIHASANI, Qemal & DULE, Miranda (ed.)

    Epika historike. Vëllimi i dytë. Folklor shqiptar. Seria III (Akademia e Shkencave, Tirana 1981) 764 pp.

-   *Epika historike.* Vëllimi III. Folklor shqiptar. Seria III (Akademia e Shkencave, Tirana 1990) 774 pp.

HAXHIHASANI, Qemal, LUKA, Kolë, UÇI, Afred & TRESKA, Misto (ed.)

    Chansonnier epique albanais. Version française Kolë Luka. Avant-propos Ismail Kadare (Akademia e Shkencave, Tirana 1983) 456 pp.

HAXHIHASANI, Qemal & SAKO, Zihni (ed.)

    Tregime dhe këngë popullore për Skënderbeun (Instituti i Folklorit, Tirana 1967) 288 pp.

JARNIK, Jan Urban

    Zur albanischen Sprachenkunde von Dr. Johann Urban Jarník. Programm der Realschule in Wien (Brockhaus, Leipzig 1881) 51 pp.

-   *Příspěvky ku poznání nářečí albánských uveřejňuje Jan Urban Jarník.* Pojednání král. české společnosti nauk. Řada VI, díl 12. Abhandlungen der Königlich-Böhmischen Gesellschaft der Wissenschaften zu Prag, 12 (Tiskem Dra. Edvarda Grégra, Prague 1883) 65 pp. Folktales and anecdotes, mostly from Shkodra.

-   Albanesische Märchen und Schwänke. in: *Veckenstedts Zeitschrift für Volkskunde* 1884.

JOCHALAS, Titos P. [= GIOCHALAS, Titos P.]

    Arbanitika paramythia kai doxasies. Neraides, daimones, xorkia, psychiasmata. ISBN 960-90735-0-6. (s.e., Athens 1997) 256 pp. Collection of folktales and beliefs of the Albanians (Arvanites) of Greece.

KAJTAZI, Halil
  Proza popullore e Drenicës. 3 vol. (Enti i teksteve, Prishtina 1985) 319, 341, 81 pp.
KOMNINO, Gjergj
  Këngë popullore lirike (Instituti i Shkencave, Tirana 1955)
KRETSCHMER, Paul
  Neugriechische Märchen (E. Diederichs, Jena 1919) xii + 340 pp. Includes a number of tales common to Greece, Albania and Turkey.
KULLURIOTI, Anastas [= KULURIÔTÊS, Anastas]
  Albanikon alfabêtarion kata to en Helladi homilumenon albanikon idiôma ekkatharisthen kai epidiorthôthen boêthêma tôn goneôn kai egcheiridion tôn albanikôn teknôn. Avabatar arbëror pas përgluhës arbërore si flitetë nd' Ejadë e përqëruar' edh' e përndrequrë ndihmës printvet edhe dorëmbaitôrë dielmvet arbërorvet (Hê fônê tês Albanias, Athens 1882) 164 pp. Contains folktales, poetry and proverbs in Albanian and Greek.
KURTI, Donat
  Prralla kombtare mbledhë prej gojës së popullit. 2 vol. (Shkodra 1940, 2nd edition Shkodra 1942)
KUTELI, Mitrush (ed.)
  Tregime të moçme shqiptare (Naim Frashëri, Tirana 1965, 1987, 1998) 254 pp. A collection of thirty-five legends.
-   *Fiabe e leggende albanesi.* Tr. E. Scalambrino (Rusconi, Milan 1993) 185 pp.
LAMBERTZ, Maximilian
  Volkspoesie der Albaner, eine einführende Studie. Zur Kunde der Balkanhalbinsel. II. Quellen und Forschungen 6 (Sarajevo 1917)
-   *Albanische Märchen und andere Texte zur albanischen Volkskunde.* Schriften der Balkankommission. Linguistische Abteilung 12 (Wiener Akademie der Sprachwissenschaft, Vienna 1922) 256 pp. A collection of 61 tales and legends in Albanian and German.
-   *Zwischen Drin und Vojusa. Märchen aus Albanien.* Märchen aus allen Ländern, Bd. 10 (Leipzig 1922) Twenty-four Albanian folktales in German translation.
-   *Die geflügelte Schwester und die Dunklen der Erde.* Albanische Volksmärchen. Übersetzt und herausgegeben von Professor Dr. Maximilian Lambertz (Erich Röth Verlag, Eisenach 1952) 225 pp. Includes twenty-seven Albanian folktales in German translation.
-   *Albanien erzählt. Ein Einblick in die albanische Literatur* (Volk & Wissen, Berlin 1956) 191 pp.
LESKIEN, August
  Balkanmärchen aus Albanien, Bulgarien, Serbien und Kroatien (Eugen Diederichs, Jena 1915, 1919) 332 pp. Includes Albanian folktales.
LUTFIU, Mojsi
  Prozë popullore dibrane (Flaka e vëllazërimit, Skopje 1988) 179 pp.

MEYER, Gustav
Albanische Märchen, übersetzt von Gustav Meyer, mit Anmerkungen von Reinhold Köhler. in: *Archiv für Litteraturgeschichte*, Leipzig, 12 (1884), p. 92-148. Reprint: Cleveland ca. 1965. Fourteen Albanian folktales in German translation.

- *Kurzgefaßte albanesische Grammatik, mit Lesestücken und Glossar* von Gustav Meyer (Breitkopf & Härtel, Leipzig 1888) 105 pp. Includes southern Albanian (Tosk) folktales.
- Albanesische Studien. 5: Beiträge zur Kenntnis der in Griechenland gesprochenen albanesischen Mundarten. in: *Sitzungsberichte der philosophischen-historischen Classe der kaiserlichen Akademie der Wissenschaften*, Vienna, 1895, 134, Teil 7.
- Albanesische Studien. 6: Beiträge zur Kenntnis verschiedener albanesischer Mundarten.
  in: *Sitzungsberichte der philosophischen-historischen Classe der kaiserlichen Akademie der Wissenschaften*, Vienna, 1896, 136, Teil 12.

MIRACCO, Elio
Favole, fiabe, racconti di S. Nicola dell'Alto, Carfizzi, Pallagorio, Marcedusa, Andali, Caraffa, Vena di Maida, Zangarona. A cura dell'Istituto di Studi Albanesi dell'Università di Roma (Bulzoni, Rome 1985) xvi + 368 pp. Fables and folktales of the Italo-Albanians of Calabria.

MITKO, Thimi [= MITKO, Euthymios]
Albanikê melissa (Bêlietta sskiypêtare). Syggramma albano-hellênikon periechon meros historias 'Dôra Istrias - hê Albanikê fylê', Albano-Hellênikas Paroimias kai Ainigmata, Albanika kyria onomata, Asmata kai Paramythia Albanika, kai Albano-Hellênikon leksilogion meta parabolês Albanikôn lekseôn pros archaias hellênikas. Syntachthen hypo E. Mêtku (Typ. Xenofôntos N. Saltê, Alexandria 1878) 257 pp. The 'Albanian Bee', including twelve Albanian folktales and legends.

- *Bleta shqypëtare.* E përshkroj me shkrojla shqype e përktheu shqyp dhe e radhiti Dr. Gjergj Pekmezi, Konsulli i Shqypërisë (Rabeck, Vienna 1924, reprint Harper Woods, MI, 1988) 304 pp.
- *Vepra* (Akademia e Shkencave, Tirana 1981) 756 pp.

MUÇI, Virgjil
Përralla shqiptare për 100 + 1 natë. 2 vol. (Çabej, Tirana 1996) 259 + 254 pp.

- *Përralla shqiptare.* Bleu i tretë (Korbi, Tirana 2003) 272 pp.
- *Përralla shqiptare.* Bleu i katërt (Korbi, Tirana 2005) 272 pp.

OMARI, Donika (ed.)
Përralla shqiptare. I zgjodhi dhe i përgatiti për botim Donika Omari (Naim Frashëri, Tirana 1990) 320 pp.

PALAJ, Bernardin & KURTI, Donat
Visaret e kombit. Vëllimi II. Kângë kreshnikësh dhe legenda. Mbledhë e redaktuem nga At Bernardin Palaj dhe At Donat Kurti (Nikaj, Tirana 1937; reprint Rilindja, Prishtina 1996) 286 pp.

PEDERSEN, Holger
Albanesische Texte mit Glossar. Abhandlungen der philologisch-historischen Classe der Königl. Sächsischen Gesellschaft der Wissenschaften. Vol. 15 (Hirzel, Leipzig 1895) 207 pp. Thirty-five Albanian folktales collected in Corfu and Albania.

- *Zur albanesischen Volkskunde von Dr. Holger Pedersen,* Privatdozent der vergleichenden Sprachwissenschaft an der Universität Kopenhagen. Übersetzung der in den Abhandl. d. königl. Sächs. Ges. d. Wiss. phil.-hist. Cl. XV vom Verf. veröffentlichten alb. Texte (Einar Moller, Copenhagen 1898) 125 pp.

PERRONE, Luca
Novellistica italo-albanese. Testi orali raccolti dal Prof. Luca Perrone ordinati e tradotti in italiano a cura dell'Istituto di Studi Albanesi della Università di Roma. Studi Albanesi, vol. 1 (Olschki, Florence 1967) 602 pp. Collection of one hundred seventy-nine Arbëresh folktales, fables and anecdotes from Calabria, in Albanian and Italian.

PHURIKIS, Petros A. [= PHOURIKÊS, Petros A.]
Hê en Attikê hellênalbanikê dialektos. in: *Athêna,* Athens, 44 (1932) p. 28-76; 45 (1933) p. 49-181. Folktales of the Albanian minority in Attika.

PITRÈ, Giuseppe
Fiabe, novelle e racconti popolari siciliani raccolti ed illustrati da Giuseppe Pitrè. 4 vol. (L. P. Lauriel, Palermo 1875). First collection of Albanian folktales from the Arbëresh settlements of Piana dei Albanesi (Piana dei Greci) and Palazzo Adriano in Sicily.

REINHOLD, Karl Heinrich Theodor
Noctes pelasgicae vel symbolae ad cognoscendas dialectos Graeciae Pelasgicas. Collatae cura Dr. Caroli Henrici Theodori Reinhold, Hanovero-Goettingensis, classis Regiae medici primarii (Sophoclis Garbola, Athens 1855) 163 pp. One of the earliest publications of Albanian folktales.

RUCHES, Pyrrhus J.
Albanian historical folksongs 1716-1943 (Argonaut, Chicago 1967) 126 pp.

SAKO, Zihni et al. (ed.)
Pralla popullore shqiptare (Instituti i Shkencave, Tirana 1954) 223 pp.

- *Mbledhës të hershëm të folklorit shqiptar (1635-1912)* (Instituti i Folklorit, Tirana 1961) 563 pp.

- *Proza Popullore.* Folklor Shqiptar I. (Akademia e Shkencave, Instituti i Folklorit, Tirana 1963, 1966, 1966, 1966) 462, 579, 580, 616 pp.

- *Chansonnier des preux albanais.* Introduction de Zihni Sako. Collection UNESCO d'Oeuvres Représentatives. Série Européenne (Maisonneuve & Larose, Paris 1967) 143 pp.

SAKO, Zihni, HAXHIHASANI, Qemal, LUKA, Kolë (ed.)
Trésor du chansonnier populaire albanais (Académie des Sciences, Tirana 1975) 332 pp.

SAMOJLOV, David (ed.)
  Starinnye albanskie skazanija. Perevod s albanskogo (Izdat. Khudozhestvennaja Literatura, Moscow 1971) 223 pp.
SHALA, Demush
  Këngë popullore legjendare (Enti i teksteve, Prishtina 1972) 448 pp.
- *Këngë popullore historike* (Enti i teksteve, Prishtina 1973)
- *Letërsia popullore* (Enti i teksteve, Prishtina 1986, 1988) 352 pp.
SKENDI, Stavro
  Albanian and South Slavic Oral Epic Poetry (American Folklore Society, Philadelphia 1954, reprint Kraus, New York 1969) 221 pp.
SOTIRIOS, K. D. [= SOTERIOU, K. D.]
  Albanika asmatia kai paramythia. in: *Laographia,* Athens, 1 (1909), p. 28-106; 2 (1910), p. 89-120. Includes Albanian folktales from Greece.
STANI, Lazër (ed.)
  Me dymbëdhjetë çelësa. Përralla popullore. Përgatitur nga Lazër Stani (Lidhja e Shkrimtarëve, Tirana 1994) 47 pp.
TREIMER, Karl
  Von Meer zu Meer. Albanische Volksmärchen (Akademia e Shkencave, Tirana s.a. [1976]) 195 pp. Thirty-five Albanian folktales in German translation.
TRUHELKA, Ciro
  Arnautske price. Albanische Märchen. Proben albanischer Volkspoesien. Bd. 1-2. (Sarajevo 1905)
TUKAJ, Mustafa
  Faith and Fairies. Tales Based on Albanian Legends and Ballads. Edited by Joanne M. Ayers. (Skodrinon, Shkodra 2002) 154 pp.
UHLISCH, Gerda
  Die Schöne der Erde. Albanische Märchen und Sagen (Reklam, Leipzig 1987, reprint Röderberg, Cologne 1988) 308 pp. Forty-eight Albanian tales and legends in German translation.
VLORA, Ekrem bey
  Aus Berat und vom Tomor. Tagebuchblätter. Zur Kunde der Balkanhalbinsel I. Reisen und Beobachtungen 13 (D. A. Kajon, Sarajevo 1911) 168 pp.
WEIGAND, Gustav Ludwig
  Albanesische Grammatik im südgegischen Dialekt (Durazzo, Elbassan, Tirana). Mit zwei Tafeln (Johann Ambrosius Barth, Leipzig 1913) xiv + 189 pp. Includes folktales from Tirana and Elbasan.
WHEELER, Post
  Albanian Wonder Tales. With illustrations by Maud and Miska Petersham (Garden City 1936 / Lovat Dickenson, London 1936) 255 pp.

Recent Books Published in the Series "Albanian Studies," Edited by Robert Elsie

Volume 1
Tajar Zavalani, *History of Albania*. Albanian Studies, Vol. 1. London: Centre for Albanian Studies, 2015. ISBN 978-1507595671. 356 pp.

Volume 2
Robert Elsie, *Albanian Folktales and Legends*. Albanian Studies, Vol. 2. London: Centre for Albanian Studies, 2015. ISBN 978-1507631300. 188 pp.

Volume 3
Robert Elsie, *The Albanian Treason Trial (1945)*. Albanian Studies, Vol. 3. London: Centre for Albanian Studies, 2015. ISBN 978-1507709511. 348 pp.

Volume 4
Robert Elsie, *Gathering Clouds: The Roots of Ethnic Cleansing in Kosovo and Macedonia – Early Twentieth-Century Documents*. Second expanded edition. Albanian Studies, Vol. 4. London: Centre for Albanian Studies, 2015. ISBN 978-1507882085. 244 pp.

Volume 5
Robert Elsie, *Tales from Old Shkodra: Early Albanian Short Stories*. Second edition. Albanian Studies, Vol. 5. London: Centre for Albanian Studies, 2015. ISBN 978-1508417224. 177 pp.

Volume 6
Robert Elsie, *Kosovo in a Nutshell: A Brief History and Chronology of Events*. Albanian Studies, Vol. 6. London: Centre for Albanian Studies, 2015. ISBN 978-1508496748. 119 pp.

Volume 7
Robert Elsie, *Albania in a Nutshell: A Brief History and Chronology of Events*. Albanian Studies, Vol. 7. London: Centre for Albanian Studies, 2015. ISBN 978-1508511946. 93 pp.

Volume 8
Migjeni, *Under the Banners of Melancholy. Collected Literary Works*. Translated from the Albanian by Robert Elsie. Albanian Studies, Vol. 8. London: Centre for Albanian Studies, 2015. ISBN 978-1508675990. 159 pp.

Volume 9
Robert Elsie and Bejtullah Destani (ed.). *The Macedonian Question in the Eyes of British Journalists (1899-1919)*. Albanian Studies, Vol. 9. London: Centre for Albanian Studies, 2015. ISBN 978-1508696827. 311 pp.

Volume 10
Berit Backer. *Behind Stone Walls: Changing Household Organisation among the Albanians of Kosovo*. Edited by Robert Elsie and Antonia Young, with an introduction and photographs by Ann Christine Eek. Albanian Studies, Vol. 10. London: Centre for Albanian Studies, 2015. ISBN 978-1508747949. 328 pp.

Volume 11
Franz Baron Nopcsa, *Reisen in den Balkan. Die Lebenserinnerungen des Franz Baron Nopcsa*. Eingeleitet, herausgegeben und mit Anhang versehen von Robert Elsie. Albanian Studies, Vol. 11. London: Centre for Albanian Studies, 2015. ISBN 978-1508953050. 638 S.

Volume 12
Robert Elsie, *Handbuch zur albanischen Volkskultur: Mythologie, Religion, Volksglauben, Sitten, Gebräuche und kulturelle Besonderheiten*. Albanian Studies, Vol. 12. London: Centre for Albanian Studies, 2015. ISBN 978-1508986300. 484 S.

Volume 13
Jean-Claude Faveyrial. *Histoire de l'Albanie*. Edition établie et présentée par Robert Elsie. Albanian Studies, Vol. 13. Londres: Centre for Albanian Studies, 2015. ISBN 978-1511411301. xxiv + 530 pp.

Volume 14
Margaret Hasluck. *The Hasluck Collection of Albanian Folktales*. Edited by Robert Elsie. Albanian Studies, Vol. 14. London: Centre for Albanian Studies, 2015. ISBN 978-1512002287. 474 pp.

Volume 15
Ali Podrimja. *Who Will Slay the Wolf. Poetry from Kosovo*, edited and translated by Robert Elsie. Albanian Studies, Vol. 15. London: Centre for Albanian Studies, 2015. ISBN 978-1514100301. 163 pp.

Volume 16
Robert Elsie. *Keeping an Eye on the Albanians. Selected Writings in Albanian Studies*. Albanian Studies, Vol. 16. London: Centre for Albanian Studies, 2015. ISBN 978-1514157268. 556 pp.

Volume 17
Michael Schmidt-Neke. *Über das Land der Skipetaren: Buchbesprechungen aus 25 Jahren*. Herausgegeben von Robert Elsie. Albanian Studies. Vol. 17. London: Centre for Albanian Studies, 2015. ISBN 978-1514737705. 413 pp.

Volume 18
Robert Elsie. *Classical Albanian Literature: A Reader*. Albanian Studies, Vol. 18. London: Centre for Albanian Studies, 2015. ISBN 978-1515132769. 248 pp.

Volume 19
Edith Durham. *Twenty Years of Balkan Tangle*. Second Edition. Edited and introduced by Robert Elsie. Albanian Studies, Vol. 19. London: Centre for Albanian Studies, 2015. ISBN 978-1515310440. 253 pp.

Volume 20
Edith Durham. *High Albania*. New Edition. Edited by Robert Elsie. Albanian Studies, Vol. 20. London: Centre for Albanian Studies, 2015. ISBN 978-1516996766. forthcoming.

Volume 21
Edith Durham. *The Burden of the Balkans*. Second Edition. Edited by Robert Elsie. Albanian Studies, Vol. 21. London: Centre for Albanian Studies, 2015. ISBN. forthcoming.

Made in the USA
Las Vegas, NV
28 May 2023

72660010R00105